The Return

of the

SPANISH LADY

Also by
VAL DAVIS

Track of the Scorpion

Wake of the Hornet

Flight of the Serpent

The Return
of the
SPANISH LADY

VAL DAVIS

THOMAS DUNNE BOOKS/ST. MARTIN'S MINOTAUR ✠ NEW YORK

M
DAVIS

THOMAS DUNNE BOOKS.
An imprint of St. Martin's Press.

www.minotaurbooks.com

Designed by Lorelle Graffeo

ISBN 0-312-26224-8

First Edition: March 2001

10 9 8 7 6 5 4 3 2 1

To Ruth Cavin

Acknowledgments

The author is indebted to the staff of the Harrison Memorial Library for all their help over the years. Their dogged pursuit of reference material has saved many a blunder. If technical gremlins persist, they are strictly the author's and not theirs.

Historical Note

The great subway train wreck on the Brighton Beach line actually occurred in November of 1918, not at the end of August as depicted in this novel. The causes remain the same. Ninety-three people lost their lives. Memories of the accident were so terrible that the city fathers changed the name of the street where it happened, Malbone Street, to Empire Boulevard. The accident eventually resulted in the Brooklyn Rapid Transit company falling into receivership.

The Return

of the

SPANISH LADY

PROLOGUE

The snowflakes were so beautiful. Round and round they swirled, in and out of his head. He took a deep breath and thousands of crystalline daggers stabbed at his lungs. He shook himself and the world steadied. His exhaled breath hung in front of his face like ejected ectoplasm.

He laughed and swatted the ghostly cloud away. My better self, he thought. No, Mary is my better self. He fumbled inside the fur-lined jacket and withdrew the diary. With shaking hands he gripped the stub of a pencil and began to write.

It's no good, Mary. I know that now. We made it out of Point Bristol okay, but it was too late. Jack was singing at the top of his lungs and the rest of us thought it was funny. All I could think of was getting back to camp. Then halfway back, Mike threw up all over the plane and it quit being funny.

I kept hoping it was just bad booze, but when I heard the death rattle in Jack's throat I knew it was all over. I've heard that sound too many times before. Somehow I managed to get the plane back, though not in one piece, and I buried them. I did the Christian thing and gave them a permanent testament, but there'll be nobody to do the same for me. I hope you get this, Mary, because my last thoughts were of you.

Almost as an afterthought he added, *tell Ned Duffy he was right.*

The pencil fell from his hand and sank into the snow. All this snow is burning me, he thought. It's burning me alive. He forced himself to move forward, staggering to the wreckage of the plane. Not a bad landing, he thought, considering the undercarriage was ripped away. He rummaged inside the cockpit and retrieved a tin box. Thrusting the diary inside took all his strength and he fell heavily against the side of the plane. That's when he saw her.

She was standing at the edge of the clearing they used as a makeshift runway. At first she was hard to see in the shadows. Then she stepped forward and smiled. He couldn't take his eyes off her. Her dress was long and flowing like a ball gown. The matte black fabric set off the sparkling jet of her luxuriant hair that cascaded almost to her knees.

You're so beautiful, he thought, and found himself irresistibly drawn forward. He felt on fire with a heat indistinguishable from lust. He floated toward her and just as he reached her outstretched arms he hesitantly looked down. How had he managed to cross the clearing without making a single mark in the snow?

1

Early each morning Nicolette Scott handed her ID card to the guard on the Jefferson Drive entrance. Each morning he tipped his hat and opened the door for her. And each morning she stepped inside the National Air and Space Museum and felt like a tourist.

This morning was no different. Gazing up at the Wright Brothers' Flyer suspended from the ceiling, Nick caught her breath just as she had done on her first day on the job. That had been two months ago, a stroke of luck she still found hard to believe. The job offer had been totally unexpected. One moment she was out of work, fired during one of Berkeley's tenure wars, and in the next the museum's director was on the phone, asking if she'd be interested in interviewing for an assistant curator's position.

He'd read about her work in the *National Geographic*, he said, and had been impressed by her recovery of a lost World War II bomber and the remains of its crew. Her find had finally ended the crew's official status, missing in action. What the article hadn't said was that most archaeologists considered her a maverick. Worse yet, many viewed her field of historical archaeology, the study of the near past, as little better than trash picking. As for her specialty, historic aircraft, even her father thought it more of an obsession than a proper line of work.

She felt a momentary pang of doubt. She had to admit to herself that she'd made a mess of things at Berkeley. Her father had studied there under the great John Buettner-Janusch and she'd always dreamed that someday people would speak her name with the same respect that they mentioned Buettner-Janusch's or even her father's. It all seemed out of reach now. She just hadn't learned to play the political games so necessary to survive in academia.

She laughed. You'll just have to be satisfied with all this, she told herself.

Nick shifted her gaze to the Spirit of St. Louis. As always she felt awestruck, imagining Lindbergh alone in that small, vulnerable plane trying to cross the vast Atlantic.

And you, Nick reminded herself, got airsick the last time you flew one of those twenty-passenger, short-hop commuter jets.

She took a deep breath, savoring the smell of the museum. Floor wax and history, she decided. There was no other way to describe it. History was all around her, the Bell X-1 in which Chuck Yeager broke the sound barrier, the rocket-powered X-15, and the Apollo 11 Command Module. But the feeling of silent reverence would end the moment the doors opened and the tourists flooded in. Then the smell would dissipate, and the noise would drive off the spirits of so many great pilots.

For the moment, not a soul was in sight, though she suspected there were people waiting for her upstairs. She'd been called in early to attend a special session of the museum's collections committee. Her summons had come from Curator Donald Alcott, the museum's number-two man.

"Nick," he'd said on the phone last night, startling her because she thought he was only vaguely aware of her existence, "I need your help and your expertise on a special project."

She'd broken out in a Cheshire grin, she remembered, delighted that he'd called on her, the museum's junior staff member.

"As you know, Nick, I chair the Collections Committee, which oversees all new museum acquisitions. I've called a special meeting for seven A.M. tomorrow morning, and I'd like you to be there."

Why so early? she'd wanted to ask but kept the question to herself. All she managed was, "I'm looking forward to it, sir."

"Splendid. By the way, we'll be meeting in Gallery 203. I thought it would be much more appropriate than one of our stodgy conference rooms."

The comment caught her by surprise, since she'd always thought of him as stodgy, with his dark suits, dark ties, and rimless bifocals.

"Will I need to bring anything?"

"Just yourself," he'd said. "And your brains," he added after a pause.

Just thinking about the compliment made her grin. She took another wistful look at the Spirit and checked her lapel watch. She had ten minutes to spare. Not enough time to sightsee, so she headed for the stairs.

Gallery 203 was devoted to Sea-Air operations and featured a simulated aircraft carrier, aptly named the USS Smithsonian. A cluster of metal folding chairs had been set up on the replica hangar deck. The chairs faced a small, portable podium, behind which stood a World War II Douglas Dauntless dive bomber.

Margaret, Alcott's matronly administrative assistant, intercepted Nick beneath the suspended Boeing F 4B-4, a carrier-based fighter from the 1930s.

"You're the first one to arrive," Margaret announced, eyeing Nick critically.

For a moment, Nick had the feeling that Margaret was about to send her home to change. But instead she got a nod of approval for her calf-length tailored skirt, silk blouse, and Navajo-patterned vest. The coolness in Margaret's eyes made it plain, however, that approval stopped at Nick's red hair, which she'd recently cut short rather than go through a daily fight with her unruly curls.

Behind her Nick heard footsteps on the stairs, and she turned to see Dr. Alcott and Paul Evans, the museum's director, stepping onto the landing. Behind them straggled half a dozen members of the committee, both civil service and political appointees.

Evans greeted her with an outstretched hand. "Nick, it's good to see you again. This ought to be right up your alley."

Nick felt tongue-tied. She'd spoken to the man just twice, once on the phone months ago and once during her job interview. After that, she'd been turned over to Alcott.

"Thank you, sir," was all she could manage.

"This will be your first collections meeting, won't it?"

She nodded.

"Well, I'm depending on you, and so is Alcott here. I know he looks like a fusty old professor, but don't let him intimidate you."

Nick smiled despite herself. Evans, whose dress and demeanor was as regal as British royalty, was far more intimidating.

"That's the spirit," Evans said, nodding toward the elevator, whose lights indicated it was on the way up. "I believe our guests have arrived, so I'll leave you in Alcott's hands. The committee's his bailiwick."

Without another word, Evans turned and wandered off in the direction of the Einstein Planetarium.

"Don't let him fool you," Alcott whispered. "He'll probably be watching our every move on closed-circuit. Now have a seat while I fetch our guests."

The guests, two men, stepped out of the elevator looking as awestruck as Nick had on her first trip to Sea-Air Ops. All that was needed was the thundering crash of a catapult and the roar of high-performance engines to make the aircraft carrier illusion complete.

Alcott guided the men, one elderly, the other young enough to be his grandson, to their chairs.

"Oh, dear," Alcott said, patting one of the hard metal seats, "we should have thought to provide cushions."

"I'll fetch some," Margaret said.

"Give Nick the agendas, then," Alcott said. "She can hand them out while you're doing that."

One glance told Nick there was only a single item printed on the page beneath the Museum's letterhead. She didn't read it until everyone had a copy and she was sitting down beside the older man, whose hands trembled slightly as he studied the page.

The agenda item read: Aichi D3A1, proposed recovery.

Nick caught her breath. An Aichi D3A1 was a Japanese dive bomber. Squadrons of them had led the sneak attack against Pearl Harbor. To have one on display at the museum would be a living symbol of that "day of infamy," as President Roosevelt had called it.

Alcott stepped to the podium and gestured expansively. "Look around you, gentlemen"—he paused to acknowledge Nick—"and lady. I can think of no place more fitting for our discussion today. December seventh, 1941, was a turning point in history for our country. Until then we had been a sleeping giant. Then planes like the Aichi, or the Val as our forces nicknamed them, awoke that giant. Until now"—he held up the agenda sheet—"we thought no Vals had survived the war. It wasn't so much good shooting on our part, as Japanese policy. They didn't rotate their pilots and planes. They flew them to death. And that brings us to our guests. First, Mr. Wes Erickson.

The elderly man stood.

"Mister Erickson shot down the plane we're here to talk about."

For a moment Nick saw only a stoop-shouldered, white-haired man. Then he turned to recognize the committee and she caught sight of his clear blue, fighter pilot's eyes. Nick caught her breath. She'd known another man with piercing blue eyes, pilot's eyes, but that had been a long time ago.

"Some of you will recognize the man with him," Alcott went on. "Fred Ivins."

As soon as Ivins stood beside Erickson, Alcott continued. "Fred and his firm have been good friends to the museum for years. I dare say our present collection would be a good deal smaller without his dedication to our cause on behalf of the Ellsworth Group. Or E-Group as we call them affectionately."

Nick had never heard of E-group, though any company with the resources Alcott implied had to be rich and powerful. As for Ivins, he looked too young to head such an operation. His age, she guessed, couldn't have been more than forty, ten years her senior.

"Fred, how would you like to do this?" Alcott asked, the deference in his voice confirming that E-Group had to be very important indeed.

Ivins laid a hand on Erickson's arm. "Wes, why don't you relax for a moment, while I start the ball rolling."

With a nod, Alcott left the podium to Ivins and sat beside Nick.

"Thank you, Donald, and my thanks to the committee," Ivins began. "I know you've been called here on short notice, but if you'll be patient with us, I think you'll find it worthwhile. First let me say that E-Group feels honored to be able to help the museum. In fact, the museum was foremost in our chairman's mind when he heard Wes Erickson's story. I remember how excited Jon McKenna was when he called me into his office to show me the Army Air Corps newsletter that reported it. 'This is something for the museum,' Jon McKenna told me. 'And, for the American people.' "

Beside Nick, Alcott nodded appreciatively.

"You see, our Mister Erickson fought in one of America's forgotten battles, the Aleutian campaign in World War Two."

It was Nick's turn to nod. The war in the Aleutians had been spin-doctoring at its worst, though it was called propaganda in those days. Soon after this country had been struck a near-fatal blow at Pearl Harbor, the Japanese invaded the Aleutian Islands. Pearl Harbor was one thing, the politicians thought—an ocean separated America from Hawaii. But the Aleutians were part of continental America, and that meant Americans weren't as safe behind their oceans as they thought. So the government played the Aleutian campaign as nothing more than a skirmish. The West Coast bombings were hushed up altogether.

"Men like Wes stopped the Japanese before they could come any closer to home," Ivins went on as if reading Nick's thoughts. "He shot down enough enemy planes to make him an ace. One of those planes has brought us here today. The Val. With that said, I'll turn you over to our fighter pilot, Wes Erickson."

While the two men exchanged places at the podium, Nick leaned close to Alcott and ventured a whispered question. "Who's E-Group?"

"Pharmaceuticals," he whispered back. "Very big."

Erickson leaned on the podium to steady himself. "I was with the Fifty-fourth Fighter Squadron, flying P-38 Lightnings out of Umnak. The Lightning was a damn good plane for its time, with enough armor and speed to give its pilot an edge in a dogfight. It might not have been as nimble as a Zero, but it was hell against anything as slow as a dive bomber like the Val. No contest at all. The Lightning was well over a hundred miles an hour faster, with tremendous firepower, four machine guns and a cannon."

He paused to take a deep breath. "I was on patrol just off the Alaskan coast when I spotted the Val. When I saw that it was alone, I remember saying to myself, 'This is your lucky day.' One on one, it was like shooting fish in a barrel. I was whooping like an Indian as I dove after him."

Erickson's face flushed as he gestured with his hands, the way pilots do when explaining their maneuvers. "The Val was a two-man job, pilot and rear gunner. So when he turned tail and headed for land, I figured the gunner must have spotted me right off. Why the pilot headed for land, I don't know, since he was carrier-based and had to have come from somewhere out at sea."

He shrugged, a self-deprecating gesture that Nick had often seen her father use when Nick's mother was in one of her moods.

"Thinking back on it," Erickson continued, "the pilot had to know it was all over but the shooting. Maybe that's why he decided to get some land under him. You don't bail out over water cold enough to kill you in minutes if you don't have to.

"Whatever his reasons, that pilot was good. He hopscotched that plane all over the sky, playing tag with me. But like I said, it was only a matter of time. When I got my shot, I didn't miss. My first burst blew away part of the rear canopy. Probably his gunner was killed outright. A second later, the Val started to go down. He wasn't burning or anything. Maybe I hit an oil line, or maybe the engine seized up. Who knows?"

He smiled wanly. "Maybe I should have gone in again for the kill, but I didn't. Instead, I circled, watching him try to land that crippled bird. He was one hell of a pilot, I'll say that for him. He set her down in the snow nice and easy. You know what he did then?"

Erickson grabbed hold of the podium and closed his eyes, swaying slightly. "I can see him now. I've been seeing him for years, like a ghost haunting me. He slides back the canopy, climbs out of the cockpit, and comes to attention. Then he looks up at me flying over, and snaps me a salute. A regular highball. It was like something out of that old movie, *Beau Geste*. There he was, in the middle of all that snow, knowing he was going to freeze to death within hours. It was the bravest damn thing I ever saw."

When the old man opened his eyes, they glistened with tears. "There was nothing I could do for him. Chances were he'd be dead by the time I landed back at base. Besides, there was a war on. We couldn't waste gas and equipment rescuing Japs."

He shook his head. "I was young then. I didn't give it much thought. Now, I know better. Now, I want to see his remains properly buried and his memory honored."

"And what better way to do that," Ivins interjected, "than to restore the Val and put it on display here at the Smithsonian. That's where E-Group comes in. Our chairman, Jon McKenna, is offering to fund the entire expedition, including recovery and all restoration costs."

Alcott leapt to his feet. "Certainly, an Aichi would be a wonderful addition to our museum, but recovery after so many years might not be possible."

"You're the one with the expert." Ivins nodded at Nick.

"Yes, of course," Alcott agreed. "Ms. Scott, do you think the Aichi could be salvageable?"

Nick had once tracked down a B-24 in the jungles of New Guinea. But there was nothing left to salvage but pieces of metal, bone fragments, and the dog tags from the crew. Heat and rain did that. Snow could be just as bad, depending on the situation.

She stood. "Mr. Erickson, are you sure there was no fire after the Val landed?"

"Not a hint of it."

"What was the landscape like?"

Erickson closed his eyes once again. "A flat snowfield at the base of a mountain peak." His eyes popped open. "I think I'd know it if I saw it again. The trouble is, in those days we didn't have any good maps of the area. If you can believe it, we were flying using Rand McNally road maps. I've been checking maps ever since and I think I've narrowed it to a five-mile section of the Hammersmith Mountain range. It's at the base of one of five or six peaks."

Nick thought about avalanches. They could be helpful in providing a permanent covering for the artifact in question. But they could also tear an airplane to pieces.

"And there was no other damage that you could see, is that correct?"

"His landing gear buckled when he landed," Erickson answered. "But that was it, apart from the rear canopy I shot away."

That meant the interior would have been immediately exposed to the elements, Nick thought.

"Well, Nick?" Alcott prompted.

"There are no easy answers in archaeology."

"I seem to remember scientists finding a mammoth perfectly preserved in the ice," Ivins put in.

"It's melting ice I'm worried about, Mister Ivins," Nick told him. "Water can be very corrosive. But several World War Two aircraft have been successfully recovered from arctic sites. Have you thought of doing a flyover to check the condition of the site in question?"

"That's a problem. The Hammersmith Mountains are right in the center of the Szczesiak National Wildlife Refuge. All entry is strictly prohibited, including low-level flights. It's the last known habitat of Hammersmith's bear, a nearly extinct variant of *Ursus arcto horribilis*. A kind of grizzly," Ivins added.

"I'm sure an exception could be made for the Smithsonian," Alcott said eagerly. "What about it, Nick? Would you like to have a go at recovering that airplane?"

"If Ms. Scott's willing," Ivins said, "I'll arrange for an aerial reconnaissance of the area the moment we have permission to overfly the refuge."

Erickson asked, "Do you think we might actually see the plane after all this time?"

"It's late summer," Nick said. "By now whatever snow is going to melt will have done so. Something could be exposed. But then if that's been happening year after year, the corrosion problem could be catastrophic to a metal artifact. The best we can hope for, is a benign site, one that's geologically stable and on the shady side of the mountain where there's likely to be less melting and runoff."

"Good enough," Ivins said. "Say the word and I'll start things moving."

Alcott nodded zealously. "For something this important, I'll go along on the expedition as well."

Ivins coughed discreetly. "E-Group's chairman does have a couple of favors to ask. First, he'd like me to accompany Mister Erickson on the expedition."

"Mister Erickson!" Alcott exclaimed.

The stunned look on the curator's face prompted Erickson to say, "I may look as old as Methuselah, but I still walk three miles every day. So don't worry about me. I'll hold my own. Besides, I'm the only one who knows where to look."

"There are other considerations," Alcott said, shaking his head.

"Just hear us out," Ivins responded. "E-Group will assume full responsibility for Mister Erickson's well-being. We'll put that in writing too, and provide full insurance coverage. If you'd like, we'll even hire a doctor to accompany us on the expedition. We'll also provide a documentary camera crew to film the recovery. When it's done, E-Group will sponsor it on PBS as a Smithsonian special."

Alcott, rubbing his hands together eagerly, turned to Nick and said, "Unless you see any other problems we haven't covered, I say we give it a try."

Nick was about to mention the possibility of bad weather in Alaska late in September, then thought better of it. A fully funded, well-equipped expedition ought to be in and out quickly enough.

"I'm ready," she said. "It's a chance of a lifetime."

"That's the spirit. I can see the Aichi now." He peered toward the gallery's high ceiling. "We can suspend her in midair as if she were attacking Pearl Harbor all over again."

His voice dropped to a whisper intended for Nick's ears only. "Wait for me in my office, while I escort the committee members to their cars."

Outside the museum, Ivins held Erickson's arm as they walked toward Independence Avenue. When they'd arrived at the museum, the old man had seemed vibrant and full of life. Now he moved listlessly and his bony arm felt fragile as Ivins clutched it.

"That took a lot out of me," Erickson admitted. "I didn't sleep much last night, thinking about this meeting."

"I know how you feel. I was up half the night myself."

Erickson nodded at him. "I know you're just being kind, Mister Ivins, but don't worry. I'll be fine once we get going. It's just that I've been dreaming about this day for so long, and now you and E-Group have made an old man's last wish come true."

Ivins smiled. "Let me put you in a cab. The sooner you get back to the hotel, the sooner you can start resting up for the trip."

"You're a kind man."

The moment Erickson's cab drew away from the curb, Ivins fished a slim cell phone from his pocket and pushed the redial button. He let it ring once, alerting his limousine driver, then disconnected.

Damn, it was good to be rid of the old fart. What a pain in the ass he was, constantly telling those war stories of his. Worse yet was pretending to enjoy them. He snorted. What the hell! Let the old fart enjoy himself for a while. After all, he was going to make Ivins rich, and E-Group even richer.

It could have been so damn easy if it weren't for those bears. Without them and their goddamned wildlife refuge, E-Group could have walked right in and taken what it wanted. There'd have been no need to play games with Erickson or the museum.

Ivins clenched his teeth. He'd have to go along with the charade. Erickson and his maudlin war stories were needed for the moment, as was the Scott woman and the museum's backing. Once they weren't needed though . . .

Ivins smiled to himself as his limo pulled up to the curb. Once inside, he used the car's encrypted phone to contact E-Group's chairman.

"Well?" McKenna demanded without preamble. "Did they buy it?"

"Hook, line, and sinker."

2

Ned Duffy braked to a stop, dismounted, and wheeled his bicycle onto the sidewalk in front of police headquarters. As always the building's dirty white granite looked in need of a scrubbing, though God knew how many people it would take to scour an entire square block of stone. He glanced up and down Center Street and didn't see a soul. The only vehicle in sight was a brand-new screen-sided Model T police wagon parked out front, ready for quick use in case the socialist war protesters got up to their shenanigans again.

Duffy smiled. The new mayor, John Hylan, always found money for those who could deliver the votes. He certainly wasn't called "Red Mike" for his political sympathies, having won on the

Tammany Hall ticket. Duffy almost turned away to head over to City Hall. Perhaps he'd get lucky and run into a demonstration. He could use a good story, since nothing worth reporting had come his way in weeks. And there was nothing his editor at the *World* hated more than paying reporters who didn't produce. But even socialists knew better than to congregate during times like these.

"God save us," he murmured. For a moment he was tempted to leave his bicycle outside, then he shook his head. This was Chinatown after all.

Puffing, he carried the contraption up the steps and between the two massive stone lions that guarded the front entrance.

Inside, O'Malley, the desk sergeant, glowered at him and said, "This ain't no garage."

To soften him up, Duffy handed over a cigar, which all but disappeared inside O'Malley's beefy fist. His fist, like the rest of him, was on a scale so massive that even the toughest hoodlums mended their ways in his presence.

O'Malley ran the cigar under his nose, grunted once, and nodded his approval. "All right, Duffy, you can park it against the wall in the corner there. Just make sure nobody falls over it."

Duffy complied without a word. A cigar went only so far, and a reporter needed his sources friendly.

Back at O'Malley's desk, Duffy dug into his pocket for a light, and lit the sergeant's cigar. It was a rite they went through each time Duffy arrived to check the crime blotter. And each time Duffy felt intimidated by the giant policeman.

As always O'Malley blew smoke rings and said, "There's Irish, Black Irish, and you, Duffy, runt Irish."

One day, Duffy promised himself, he'd write a story about the goings on in the bowels of police headquarters. When that day came, of course, he'd have to be high enough in the hierarchy of the *New York World* to be untouchable. His lowly reporter's status wouldn't deter even a rookie cop from beating the hell out of him.

Forcing a smile, Duffy shoved a cigar into his own mouth. "For the love of God, Sergeant, tell me you've got something.

The afternoon edition's wide open and I haven't written a word all day."

"Not a thing," O'Malley said.

"I'll take a Chinatown bar fight. A maiming. Anything."

"Lord save us, I never thought I'd see the day when you'd be desperate enough to write about chinks."

"It's the criminal classes I blame," Duffy said. "I don't know what the hell they are coming to."

O'Malley retreated behind his desk. "And it's a good thing too, since we seem to be a mite shorthanded about now. On the other hand if it keeps up like this, we'll both be out of work."

Duffy shuddered. If he lost his job at the *World* he wasn't sure what he'd do. If only things weren't so darned slow. Since late August less and less seemed to have been happening. It was so hot maybe the criminal classes had decided to up and leave New York for the summer.

"Have you got anybody in the cells?" Duffy asked.

"Drunks. That's it."

Duffy pulled a flask from his coat pocket and offered it to the sergeant.

O'Malley shook his head. "I'll drink with you, but I prefer · my own if you don't mind."

Duffy had never known the sergeant to turn down a free drink before but he was in no mood to question even small favors. He gulped enough rotgut to nearly empty his flask and set fire to his stomach.

The phone on the desk rang.

"This may be your lucky morning," O'Malley said. He wiped the mouthpiece with his hand before speaking into it. "Police headquarters, Sergeant O'Malley speaking." He listened for a moment, then nodded at Duffy. "Yeah, he's here. Hold on." He shoved the phone at Duffy. "It's your editor, Greenberg."

"My city editor's name is Green."

"Sure."

Duffy reached for the phone. They were checking up on him now. He hadn't thought that the drinking was noticeable.

Hell, everybody drank. And just because he hadn't brought in any stories lately didn't mean that he was lying down on the job.

"This is Duffy," he answered tentatively.

"Dammit, Duffy, I can barely hear you."

Duffy shouted, "How's that?"

"Get off your ass. I need a leader for the inside front page."

"The crime beat's dead unless you want me to start committing my own crimes."

For a moment there was silence on the line, as if Green were actually considering the idea. "Get yourself in here," he said finally. "I've got another assignment for you."

"What?" Duffy asked, suspecting the worst.

"Visiting the dead."

"For Christ's sake, that's a copy boy's job."

"We haven't got enough of them left."

"What about Conner? I'm senior to him."

"He called in sick," the editor replied. "Some damn thing must be going around. If I find that they've all spending the day at Brighton Beach, they're through, just like you'll be if you don't get up here."

"Jesus," Duffy breathed. "What about Newmark?"

"I'm looking at him right now. The dead are burying him. He needs help. It's down to you, Duffy. How soon can you get here?"

Duffy shook his flask. The hollow sloshing told him he'd have to stop somewhere on the way for a refill. "Fifteen minutes."

"Make it ten," Green said and slammed down the receiver.

Duffy dropped the phone into its cradle and banged his head against the front of the desk.

"What's wrong with you?" O'Malley asked. "You look like someone died."

"Me. I'm as good as dead. I can't believe it, they're calling me in to compile Death Notices."

3

Nick was bursting with the news about her new assignment. Just a few weeks ago she had made the acquaintance of Gordon Hurst, a military historian who frequented the museum. He was one of the few people that she had met who shared her love of airplanes and seemed to understand the excitement she felt about discovering a long-abandoned warbird in some remote corner of the earth. Even her father did not fully understand her passion. Although he never discouraged her in her chosen field, he often tried to get her interested in what he considered to be a more respectable specialty. The study of the Anasazi of a thousand years ago was as recent as he thought any archaeologist should get to modern history.

Gordon was different. She remembered the first time she had laid eyes on him at the museum. He had been lying on the floor, hands laced behind his back, gazing up at an Albatros, a German biplane from World War I. The single-seat fighter had been restored to full glory. Its paint was factory-fresh, its tail striped with vibrant green-and-yellow squadron markings.

"Are you all right?" Nick had exclaimed, fearing that he'd slipped.

"Von Richtofen, the Red Baron, flew a plane like this," Hurst said without looking up to see who was disturbing him. "Most people think he made all his kills in a red Fokker Triplane, but he won fifty-nine of his eighty-odd fights in one of these beauties."

Show off, Nick thought to herself as she responded, "I see it's a D Va type. Unless I'm mistaken, the tail stripes are those of its squadron, Jagdstaffel 46."

Hurst craned his neck to get a look at her. At that moment, he'd reminded her of a startled teenager caught doing something off-limits.

"I'm Nick Scott," she'd said, offering him a hand. "I work here."

Gordon Hurst shook her hand but got to his feet on his own power.

She recognized the name immediately and had read his books. "Thank God," he laughed, "I thought the tourists were upon me. A knowledgeable tourist at that, the worst kind."

In a crew-neck sweater, jeans, and sneakers he could have passed for a grad student. Only the wrinkles around his eyes betrayed him. Thirty-five, Nick had guessed, which gave her four years to write something the equal of *German Air Power*.

Forget it. She was lucky to be working, let alone have time to write and research anything on such a grand scale.

His smile grew wider. "I've read about you. You're the archaeologist who finds airplanes."

She smiled back. "Usually it's my father people remember."

"Oh, I've heard of him, too. Who hasn't? The guru of the great Southwest. The cannibal Anasazi and all that. Bows and arrows bore me. I like my warfare a bit more modern and up to date."

"And German, I'd say." Nick nodded at the Albatros and the nearby Fokker D.VII.

"I don't discriminate. Take that Spad, for instance, a fine plane. So is the Sopwith Snipe. If your father's Anasazi had airplanes like those, he'd have a competitor."

Hurst took a deep breath as if savoring the atmosphere around him. "There's nothing like the planes of this era. No armor plate, no protection for the pilot. Nothing fancy. When you flew one, the wind was in your face like the breath of God."

Like the breath of God, Nick said to herself, remembering that conversation now. There were few men of her acquaintance who could say something like that and not sound like a fool. She smiled to herself as she strode down the hallway to the small office that Hurst had wrangled out of Alcott while he did research at the museum.

She knocked and called out, "Gordon, are you working?"

He opened the door. "More like communing with the gods of war."

"And what great wisdom are they imparting today, oh Great Historian?"

He laughed and replied, "Damn all, to tell the truth. Let's go get a cup of coffee. My brain cells are screaming for caffeine."

"I have something to tell you that might wake you up," Nick replied, barely able to contain herself.

"Coffee first," Hurst insisted. "I have been cooped up in this airless broom closet, which your boss laughingly calls an office, and you expect me to be alert. I need air, light, and the company of a beautiful, intelligent woman. Then I will be able to properly appreciate the importance of what you have to say to me."

"Very well, if it takes the cafeteria's coffee to properly appreciate me, so be it."

As soon as they had filled their cups Nick said, "The Aleutians, what do you know about them?"

"Woman, have you no mercy? Let's see . . . the Aleutians,

they're cold, wet, and the weather is a bitch. Now how's that for a snappy comeback?"

"I can see I've come to the right man," Nick quipped.

"Seriously, what's your interest in the Aluetians?"

"Gordon, swear that you won't tell a soul until it's made public."

"I swear," he replied with a smile, "on Von Richtofen's grave."

There were times when Nick felt that Hurst didn't take her seriously and she hesitated. She knew that he was very professional in his approach to his work. She thought she could trust him and was dying to share her excitement with someone who could understand what it meant to her. She took a deep breath. "We're after an airplane that went down in 1942. An Aichi dive bomber."

"As far as I know, those islands have been pretty well picked over. I seem to remember that we recovered a Zero from one of the Aleutian Islands early in the war. At the time, the Zero was the top fighter in the Pacific, so we used it to design a better one of our own. Other than that, I've never heard of anything collectable except the usual flotsam of war, rifles, ordinance, food cans, and that kind of litter."

She felt disappointed at his reaction. "You sound like my father."

He laughed. "Is that good or bad?"

"Our plane went down on the Alaskan mainland."

"Considering the climate in the Aleutians, that's a stroke of luck."

"The museum is mounting an expedition. I'll be accompanying Doctor Alcott."

"Nick, that's wonderful. Where are you going to be looking?" he asked.

"We only know its general location, but the pilot who saw it go down is coming with us."

"I envy you. It's a chance of a lifetime. If you were selling tickets, I'd pay a month's salary to go along." He smiled wistfully. "So how can I help you?"

Nick felt an inner glow. Perhaps Hurst could use her field notes when she returned. More exciting yet, perhaps they could work on something together. She wouldn't let her thoughts get ahead of reality. "I'm an archaeologist, remember?" Nick answered, "not a historian. I could use some general background on the campaign."

"Buy me a second cup of coffee and you've got yourself a deal."

"You come cheap," Nick laughed.

"Be warned," Hurst smiled. "Free advice is worth the price you pay for it."

Over his second cup, Hurst said, "It was a terrible mistake you know. The Japanese invasion of the Aleutians was a massive blunder of their military intelligence. We snookered them, though we didn't know it at the time. And we have Jimmy Doolittle to thank for it.

"What happened," he continued, "was pure luck. When Colonel Doolittle launched his B-25 bombers from the deck of the carrier Hornet on April eighteenth, 1942, the Japanese assumed the attack had come from the Aleutian Islands. It never occurred to them that a heavy, twin-engine bomber could be launched from the deck of an aircraft carrier. So they went after the Aleutians to prevent a second attack, and perhaps even an invasion of the Japanese mainland.

"For our part, military planners saw the Doolittle raid as little more than a propaganda ploy, a way of bucking up America's morale after Pearl Harbor."

Hurst paused to stare pointedly at his empty coffee cup. Nick obliged by fetching him a refill.

"In any case," Hurst went on once he'd added cream, "Admiral Yamamoto, the man who'd masterminded the attack against Pearl Harbor, made a terrible mistake. He split his forces and dispatched two carriers and a task force to the Aleutians. Had those ships been at the battle of Midway in June of forty-two, the course of history might have changed. If we'd lost at Midway, Yamamoto's forces would have been free to invade Hawaii."

Hurst pushed his third cup of coffee aside untouched. "The Japanese got suckered. It's as simple as that. Sure, their Aleutian task force did manage to bomb Dutch Harbor and land troops on Kiska and Attu. They even held onto those islands for more than a year. But the weather was a constant battle. Resupply was damn near impossible."

Nick said, "I seem to remember reading about Japanese strikes against the mainland."

Hurst snorted. "If you can call them that. A few small, collapsible seaplanes were launched from submarines to bomb the Oregon coast. The Japanese thought they'd start forest fires, but they failed to take Oregon's rainfall into account."

"And Alaska?" Nick probed.

"Nothing to speak of. That's why your Val surprises me."

"Our pilot says he thought it might have been off course and lost."

Hurst nodded. "The Aleutian weather was our best weapon. Half the time the Japanese fleet didn't know where it was because of the fog. So maybe your Val couldn't find his carrier. What kind of condition is the plane in?"

"We're keeping our fingers crossed," Nick said, "but our pilot says it made a soft crash landing. Of course, we're hoping it might be one of the planes that actually bombed Pearl Harbor."

Hurst whistled appreciatively. "I'll say one thing, if you actually find one of the raiders from Pearl Harbor, you'll be as famous as your father."

"I doubt that. He's been working at it a long time."

"This will do it. Trust me. The media will love you."

"I'm not after notoriety, Gordon, you must know that."

Hurst nodded. "You're after more than an airplane. You're after a piece of history. Just to touch it is . . . Well, it's better than anything I can think of."

"My father says the same thing. It used to drive my mother crazy."

"And what do you say?"

"I still have high hopes," she said, remembering what Elliot's actual words had been: touching an artifact that's been lost for a thousand years is better than sex. Her thoughts veered away from the possibilities, but she realized that she was blushing.

Hurst started to smile, then laughed out loud. "You're like me. You live in the past. If I could command a genie, my first wish would be to be back in 1918 flying that Albatros. Back then it was as close to being a bird as man had ever been."

"You make war sound romantic, but what about the soldiers in the trenches?"

Before Hurst could respond, Margaret, Alcott's assistant, entered the cafeteria.

"Excuse the interruption, Mister Hurst, but Doctor Alcott would like to see you before you leave the museum today."

"More brain picking, no doubt," Hurst said. "Well, now's as good a time as any. Lead the way, Margaret."

As he was leaving the gallery, he glanced back at Nick, grinned, and said, "I didn't get a chance to tell you what my second and third wishes would be."

"May all your wishes come true," she called.

4

Gordon Hurst couldn't believe his ears. Moments ago he'd been envying Nick Scott. Now he felt sorry for her as he listened to her boss, Donald Alcott, calmly stab her in the back.

He thought about how happy she'd been. In fact, it had seemed to have been the first time he had seen her truly happy since he'd met her. If he refused they would probably ask someone else. However, he felt obliged to offer token resistance. "I've just spoken with Ms. Scott. My understanding is that she's to be your expert on this expedition."

Alcott smiled indulgently. "Let's just say she's very young and new to the museum."

"Have you told her about this, that you're inviting me to come along as your expert?" He of course knew that

Alcott had done no such thing, but he hoped to at least make the man squirm a little.

The curator folded his hands on his desk. "It will probably be best if we call you our adviser. How does that suit you?" Alcott drummed his elegantly manicured fingers on what looked to be a pristine blotter.

Hurst, his mind racing, rose from the chair in front of Alcott's desk and pretended to be examining one of the curator's framed college degrees. Certainly, Hurst wanted to go. His last book hadn't done as well as he'd hoped although it had been well received by the critics. He felt stalled on the sequel and he was bored with museum research. This was a chance to make a bit of history instead of recording it after the fact.

He enjoyed Nick's company. She was easy to talk to and he'd had the feeling that their friendship could deepen into something more. The trouble was, academic jealousies had been known to turn into lifelong vendettas. And Nick Scott didn't look like the type who'd roll over without a fight. She was too much like him, possessive and obsessive.

"I don't like poaching on someone's else turf," he said, knowing full well that Alcott wouldn't take the protest seriously.

"There's no question of that," Alcott said. "After all, she's new and untested. I wouldn't be doing my job if I didn't protect the museum's interests."

Though Hurst had been expecting just such a response, he couldn't help sighing with relief. The lure of laying hands on a Japanese dive bomber was like a Siren song inside him, growing louder by the moment.

Before it deafened him completely, he paid token homage to his scruples. "I've read her work. She's made some important finds." In deference to Alcott he added, "Hiring her was a wise choice."

"That wasn't my decision," Alcott said.

"And this is?"

Alcott swiveled his desk chair until he was facing his Ivy League laurels. "Did Ms. Scott tell you about our financing?"

"We didn't get around to that."

"There you have it, then." Alcott faced Hurst again, a knowing look on his face. "She left out the crucial point of the expedition."

Hurst would have thought the Aichi itself took precedence over everything else, but kept the notion to himself.

"The Ellsworth Group is defraying all expenses," Alcott went on. "As you know, much of our work here at the museum depends on grants, corporate and otherwise. Which is exactly why I want you to be with us on this expedition. We can't afford any kind of mistake that might alienate one of our most important sponsors. Accordingly, I've arranged a handsome honorarium for you, Doctor Hurst. Gordon, if I may? What would you say to fifty thousand dollars?"

Hurst's jaw dropped open. Jesus. That was one hell of an honorarium. And for what? Two weeks' work at the most, maybe less.

"Of course," Alcott added, lowering his voice, "we won't mention your stipend to any of the others. After all, you'll be earning more in a few days than Ms. Scott will be making in the next year. Now, what do you say? May we count on you?"

The Siren song, fueled by fifty thousand voices, overwhelmed his conscience.

"I'm your man," Hurst said, reminding himself that if he didn't take the job, someone else would. Perhaps Nick would see the wisdom of having his expertise on hand. Hadn't she already come to him for help? It was the most natural thing in the world that he would want to come. He felt a small resentment against Nick for not fighting to keep the excitement and, yes, he admitted to himself, the glory all to herself.

5

Nick spent what was left of the morning in the museum's library, poring over books on Japanese aircraft. By lunchtime the Aichi D3A1 seemed like an old friend, as did its look-alike cousins, the Nakajima B5N2 torpedo bomber and the Mitsubishi Ki-51 attack bomber. As a precaution, she committed all three to memory, though it seemed unlikely that a pilot like Erickson would have incorrectly identified his target. But mistakes happened, especially in the excitement of combat.

Pilot error, she reminded herself, could be as much a career killer as an archaeologist's improper identification of an artifact.

Under the librarian's watchful eye, Nick copied photographs, blueprints, and specifications of all three planes, enough for half a dozen spiral-bound sets to be used as handy reference guides for those on the expedition.

By the time she finished, it was midafternoon. Rather than break for a late lunch, she bought a sandwich from a vending machine and took it back to her office, such as it was. She laughed to herself thinking about Gordon complaining about the office assigned to him. As far as she was concerned, a cubicle would have been preferable to the cell-sized enclosures the museum reserved for junior staff. All were monastic, anti-septic white, and equipped with government-issue gray metal furniture.

She'd yet to provide any decoration of her own. A colorful poster would help, she thought as she tore open the tuna salad sandwich. Or better yet, photographs of airplanes, which she could get from the museum shop. Or maybe she could requisition them.

She shook her head at the thought of the government paperwork required, and bit into her sandwich. The taste rivaled her mother's forays into food poisoning.

Tempting fate, Nick swallowed. For an instant, her esophagus threatened rebellion before the mouthful shimmied on its way.

"Thanks for the memories, Elaine," Nick murmured, then realized she was being unfair. Her mother's cooking hadn't killed them after all, though Elliot did have his stomach pumped one Thanksgiving, but Elaine had blamed that on the flu.

Nick peeled open the bread and eyed the fish filling. It looked benign enough, but then so had Elaine's turkey dressing. With a sigh, Nick clapped her sandwich back together and dropped it into her gray wastebasket.

"Nothing personal, Elaine."

What she needed more than food was company. She hadn't been in Washington long enough to make any friends except for Gordon Hurst. The other assistant curators, all of whom had more seniority, were unlikely candidates, considering the choice assignment she'd just been handed.

She hadn't yet told her father. He'd spent much of their recent visit arguing about her chosen specialty. "The last time you went after an airplane, you damn near got us killed. And that plane got you fired, unless I'm mistaken," he'd complained.

"Funny, I seem to remember that it was all your idea," she'd shot back.

"Perhaps I thought you needed a little break from school. However, I hadn't anything permanent in mind."

"Besides, I'm suing the university, aren't I?"

"And if you win?" he'd replied sarcastically.

He was quite right, of course. She didn't want her job back at Berkeley. In fact, she'd burned her bridges there, selling both her condo and her car before heading east, with one stopover in Albuquerque to see Elliot.

Of course she'd struck the match knowing full well that Elliot was her safety net. Time and again, he'd urged her to work for him at the University of New Mexico. His offer had been renewed during her recent visit. They'd been sitting in his office in the Scott wing of the university's museum at the time, surrounded by his most recent Anasazi finds, when he'd made his pitch. "Nick, it's time you came to your senses. Join my museum staff and I can offer you instant tenure."

"And my airplanes?" she'd responded.

"Maybe you could fit them in on your sabbaticals."

"I'll be living with them full-time at the Smithsonian," she countered.

"You mark my words. Those Washington bureaucrats hate anyone who's the least bit competent. It makes them look bad. They'll be back-stabbing you the moment you walk in the door."

"Have you ever heard of nepotism? My back wouldn't be any safer here."

"What's the point of being the grand old man of South-western archaeology if you can't abuse your power?" he replied.

"You're not that old, Elliot, and Elaine would never have let you get away with calling yourself grand."

"And you?"

"I thought you were grand when I was a little girl."

"And now?"

"Now I want to make a name for myself without you pulling the strings," she said.

"Suit yourself, but keep your back to the wall just the same."

His comment had flashed through her mind the first time she met Dr. Alcott, but in light of his endorsement by choosing her as their expedition expert she thought that Elliot's fears, and hers, had been unjustified.

She was tempted to phone and tell him so, but decided against tying up a government line. Regaling him with her Aichi could wait until she was back at her apartment and on her own time.

Instead, she logged onto the Internet and initiated a search for the Szczesiak National Wildlife Refuge. The museum's computer system, usually sluggish this time of day, responded promptly. On impulse, she decided against calling up geographical data and clicked on Hammersmith's bear. As the animal's photograph began downloading on her screen, the phone rang.

"Doctor Scott," she said.

"That's funny," her father answered. "I always thought I was Doctor Scott."

"Elliot, you must be a mind reader."

"I like my students to think so."

"And your daughter?"

"May I remind you that you were once my student."

Nick sighed. Thank God she hadn't gone to work for him.

"How does it feel now that you're surrounded by airplanes?" he continued. "Or do you still prefer digging them up rather than actually playing with them?"

"I'm fine, Elliot, how are you?"

"Don't change the subject," he said. "Just tell me you're sorry you didn't take my offer."

"Coming here was the luckiest thing that ever happened to me. The museum is sending me to Alaska to hunt down a very important airplane."

"How many times have I told you, airplanes aren't safe?"

"This one bombed Pearl Harbor," she said, stretching the point since this particular Val's history was yet to be determined.

"All right. I surrender. Tell me about it."

Briefly, Nick sketched in the background, including the old

pilot and the PBS special to be filmed around him. When she finished, Elliot whistled appreciatively. "It sounds promising. As your old teacher, maybe I ought to come along with you."

"That would be one Doctor Scott too many."

He snorted. "Perhaps it's just as well. I prefer my digs in a warm desert, not the icy tundra."

"Alaska isn't the north pole."

"It can be cold this time of the year."

"I've checked the weather, Elliot. It's as warm there as it is here. Besides, we'll be in and out before you know it."

"When your mother complained about my digs, I always said the same thing. 'I'll be back before you have time to miss me.' "

"You disappeared every summer, and you know it. Besides, I'm not you, Elliot. I'm not going to vanish for months at a time."

"It was my job."

As a child, Nick had wanted to disappear too, but settled for building model airplanes in her room and dreaming of flying away to join her father's dig.

She said, "Do you know what Elaine used to say about you and your Anasazi? She said you were nothing but a treasure hunter at heart."

"It takes one to know one."

Nick laughed. "Elliot, there's something you can do for me. I'm going to need a digger."

"Are you looking for a strong back, or someone who knows what he's doing?"

"I'd call you a sexist, but I need a strong back. It would be a plus if he were a pro."

"I do know a student working on his doctorate at the university in Fairbanks. A good man."

"Don't tell me he was one of your undergraduate students."

"How did you guess?"

"With you it's either your old boy network or your old-student network."

"His name is Mike Barlow. You'll like him. He's older than most students. He's your age. He did a stint in the service after he left me."

"Do you have his phone number?"

"Just his e-mail. Hold on. I'll call it up on my computer."

"Since when have you had a computer?"

"Okay, my secretary will call it up."

A moment later he gave her the e-mail address and one last parting shot. "Don't say I didn't warn you about airplanes." He hung up before she could respond.

Vintage Elliot, she thought, cradling the receiver. He loved having the last word.

She went back to her computer and was admiring the Hammersmith's bear, when the truth dawned. Elliot's timing was too good to be true, especially because it was early afternoon in Albuquerque, the time of day that Elliot guarded jealously, time for communing with his Anasazi relics. Calls to him at this time usually went unanswered, even when they were from Nick. So why had he changed his routine? He hadn't bothered to ask about her new apartment, or anything personal at all. And the last thing he'd said was a not-so-subtle reminder to be careful.

Had he known about the expedition when he phoned? she wondered. If so, he had to have had inside information. But from whom? Certainly, Elliot had acquaintances everywhere, and his worldwide reputation assured him access to just about anyone.

Nick took a deep breath, forcing herself to relax. The more she thought about it, the more convinced she became that Elliot had a spy in the museum. Only two candidates came to mind, the curator himself, Paul Evans, or Dr. Alcott, since he was the one who'd asked her to accompany him on the dig.

"Elliot," she said through clenched teeth, "I'm going to wring your neck if you pulled strings to get me this job."

Fuming, she logged off the refuge site and e-mailed Mike Barlow.

6

Fred Ivins hunched before he knocked on the chairman's door. He would have arrived barefoot if he dared, anything to make himself shorter. But his six-foot three-inch frame was impossible to camouflage.

"Come!" Jonathan McKenna's voice sliced through the oak panel as if it had been a Japanese Sojii screen.

Tucking his chin against his chest, Ivins opened the door and crossed the threshold into another world. Outside the chairman's office, E-Group headquarters was strictly utilitarian. But inside McKenna's realm Hearst's Castle had a true rival, though on a somewhat smaller scale. Furniture, carpets, lighting fixtures, all took Ivins's breath away each time he entered. He marveled at everything but the art. That he couldn't understand. McKenna could have afforded Rubens, Renoir, or even a Michangelo. Instead, he collected Eskimo sculpture. The world's greatest collection, or so Ivins had been told, though as far as he was concerned the sculpture didn't look much better than the lumps of clay slapped together by kids.

Two men and a woman were already in the office with McKenna, but it was easy to overlook their presence. It would take a commanding figure to dominate the office and that figure was McKenna. At the moment, he was sitting at his enormous desk, half hidden by a marble figure that represented a bear or a seal, Ivins couldn't remember which. The figure was squat and had a brutish power, just like McKenna, whose thick body and silver-gray hair made him look sixty, though he was much younger.

Ivins slumped so far his shoulder muscles protested.

"Sit," McKenna commanded, refusing to look up until Ivins was seated facing him, in a chair short-legged enough to diminish even an NBA center.

Ivins sagged with relief the moment McKenna came out from behind his sculpture, a sure sign that Ivins's height had been forgiven for the moment.

"Look at this piece," McKenna said, running a hand over the sculpture's highly polished surface. "It's one of a kind, the only one in the world. And the artist is dead, so there can't be any more." He smiled without showing teeth. "The thing is, no one else can touch it but me."

Ivins stifled the urge to reach out and rap the damned thing with his knuckles.

"Collecting is part of my genius," McKenna continued. "It's the reason we're here right now. My collecting brought us the diary. Without it, we wouldn't have the key to the Flying Dutchman, would we?"

Ivins bit his lip, knowing full well he wasn't expected to reply, only to listen until the great man deigned to ask a direct question. No one spoke up. The others seemed to know how the game was played.

"Report," McKenna barked.

Ivins summarized the meeting, keeping his eyes on McKenna. He wondered who the others were and how familiar they were with the situation.

"There's one thing more, sir. Doctor Alcott has asked for some supplemental funding. He wants to add an additional expert to the expedition. He's asked for one hundred thousand. Since it was within my signature authorization, I took the liberty of authorizing it."

"Real people?" McKenna snapped.

For a moment Ivins was caught off guard until he remembered that only a very wealthy or politically connected person was considered *real* by McKenna.

"No, I think not. He's certainly well known in his field and is the author of a couple of books, but beyond that he's a nobody."

Before Ivins could continue, McKenna held up his hand. He turned to the younger of the two men and asked, "Will this present a problem?"

The man, who appeared to be in his early thirties, managed to appear at ease and also somewhat bored. He was wearing jeans and a T-shirt, but his expensive hand-tooled boots and razor-cut hair screamed money. Ivins envied his nonchalance. He replied with a curt, "No." The answer seemed to satisfy McKenna.

"Why?" he asked, turning back to Ivins.

"Why?" Ivins echoed, his voice rising in panic.

"Do you have any idea why Alcott proposed an additional expert?" McKenna enunciated each word as if he were talking to an idiot.

"I don't think he likes the Scott broad," Ivins blurted out.

"Dear lady, I apologize for Mister Ivins's crude language," McKenna said to the woman sitting next to the young man. Ivins could tell that the head of E-group was enjoying himself at Ivins's expense. Let him, Ivins thought to himself. Let them all think I'm a fool. But not such a fool that I get fired, his weaker self added.

"Any idea why?" McKenna continued.

"The word is her father, who's some kind of muck-a-muck, made a call to the museum's head man, Evans. They're old friends it seems. That's how she got the job and our boy Alcott is pissed about it."

"For Christ's sake, I thought you said she was good."

McKenna's inquiring scowl had edges sharp enough to maim.

"The best, sir," Ivins rushed to say. "When it comes to lost airplanes, she's the one people talk about. She's been written up in *National Geographic*. As far as I can tell, she could have gotten the job on her own."

Ivins paused to see how his comments were going over. When he saw no sign of danger, he continued. "Men like Alcott are civil servants at heart. To them, job security is everything. They never hire anyone good enough to take their place."

"Are you giving me fact or opinion here?" McKenna said.

"My assessment."

McKenna smiled. "Let's see what Ms. Jarvis has to say." He nodded at the woman.

She opened a folder that she had been holding and commenced to read "Nicolette Scott, born Albuquerque, New Mexico, 1971. Parents Elliot Scott and Elaine Fastbinder. Mother deceased under, shall we say, unclear circumstances."

"Ah," McKenna said, "how unclear?"

"It's easy to read between the lines," Jarvis replied. "The daughter came home from junior high and found her mother face down in bed. The coroner ruled it accidental, but it was probably a covered-up suicide."

"The husband playing around?"

"No evidence of that, and we dug very hard."

McKenna looked disappointed.

"She does have a juvenile record of sorts," Jarvis continued. "She was picked up for joy riding after hot-wiring a car. The charges were later dropped."

"Go on," McKenna prompted.

"No other traces of a criminal record. There was some suspicion that she was involved in something very nasty out in the Sonoran desert last year, but I can't get an angle on what it was. The Bucket and Shovel Brigade were all over a rumored research installation out there but they did too good a job to leave any traces."

"Are you telling me that she's *real people?*"

"No, sir. There's no evidence of that at all."

McKenna shook his head. "I don't like surprises. You're supposed to be the best. Give me my money's worth."

Ivins noticed that the woman had the fortitude to bristle. "You got your money's worth," she answered. "You can be assured that she is not connected to any, shall we say, meaningful organization."

"You'd better be right. Time is of the essence and there's no way I'm putting back the expedition date to check any further. Doctor Posner?" he asked, turning to the only person in the room who had not yet spoken.

Posner nodded. "We are continuing to take temperature measurements from the drill holes in the Chena River floodplain. They have verified that much of the undisturbed discontinuous permafrost south of the Yukon River has warmed significantly and some of it is actually thawing. Average temperatures in Alaska have risen one degree per decade over the past thirty years. It has become as much as two degrees Celsius warmer in the winter, although summer temperatures have not been so greatly affected."

"The bottom line, Doctor," McKenna commanded.

"Our computer models indicate that this is probably the last year that we can reliably depend on the condition of the permafrost."

"Probably?" McKenna asked.

Posner cleared his throat. "There is some margin of error. However, that same uncertainty indicates that it may already be too late."

Ivins waited for the explosion that didn't come. Instead McKenna smiled the way a wolf smiles before attacking.

"Ivins, get that expedition cracking. Jarvis, remember I don't tolerate sloppy work. Doctor Posner, thank you for the weather report. The three of you can leave."

As they rose to leave Ivins noticed that the young man had

not been included in the dismissal. He was also the only one who had not been addressed by name.

"There you have it lady and gentlemen," McKenna called out after them. "McKenna proposes, and God disposes. But remember, McKenna disposes also."

7

Nick felt as if her head would split. She went over the list of special equipment that she thought might be needed for the expedition. She had to present it to Dr. Alcott by the end of the day. Despite his assurances that E-group would provide all the necessary equipment she had little faith in armchair archaeologists. Her research confirmed her fears that the location of the wreck might not be easy. There had been a similar expedition to the Arctic that had attempted to recover a squadron of B-17s and P-38s that had run out of gas and been forced to land on the ice eight hundred miles north of the Arctic circle.

Her Val hadn't landed so far north nor was the terrain as inhospitable. She laughed to herself. She was already referring to the plane as *her* Val. She'd better try to think of it as the museum's. It would be nobody's if they didn't bring the right equipment. Conventional subsurface radar had proved to be unreliable and Nick was agonizing over whether E-group's largesse would stretch to the experimental Icelandic equipment when a voice broke her concentration.

"You'll go blind trying to read those notes," Gordon Hurst said. "Let me take you away from all this and ply you with the cafeteria's best brew made from mountain-grown beans, each individually selected by a gentleman of the Latin persuasion."

"I'd love to, but I can't."

"Of course you can," Hurst persisted. "Besides, I've got something to tell you."

"Gordon, I really can't. I've got to get this list to Alcott. Right now it contains everything but the kitchen sink. If we took everything I have on it we'd need a C-5 for transport. I've got to get it down to size."

"What's on it?" Hurst asked.

"I've been doing some research. In 1942 two B-17s and six P-38s crash-landed in Greenland. They'd been caught in bad weather and ran out of fuel."

"You're talking about the Lost Squadron," Hurst replied.

"Right. Now when the first expedition tried to locate the planes they used magnetometers. They didn't come up with anything. Of course, they thought that the planes were only under forty feet of snow."

"And metal detectors don't work much beyond that depth."

"Exactly," Nick continued. "But the second expedition got the Navy to use antisubmarine equipment that's used to detect subs hundreds of feet under the water. And still nothing."

"So," Hurst asked, "what's your point."

"It wasn't until the expedition went to the University of Iceland and acquired an experimental subsurface radar device that they were successful. Most subsurface radar uses high-frequency signals in the hundred and twenty megahertz range. That frequency works well where there is no melting water. The experimental radar has a much lower frequency that works better in temperate ice that is a mixture of both ice and water."

"And the experimental radar found the planes under two hundred and fifty feet of ice," Hurst replied. "Nick, I am an aviation historian. I'm very familiar with that particular expedition."

"Yes, of course. I'm sorry. I got carried away, but the point is, we have no ice reports. There's no way of knowing the precise conditions under which our Val is buried. We're a small expedition. We can't possibly take in both types of equipment. I've assembled a list here that covers all possible contingencies and it's twice as long as it should be."

"That's easy," Hurst replied and picked it up and neatly tore it in half.

"Gordon," Nick protested, "sometimes, I really don't think you take me seriously."

"Funny," Hurst replied. "I was thinking the same about you." He turned around and walked out of the area.

Nick nearly got up to follow him, then changed her mind. She felt a mixture of disappointment and anger. She'd thought that he was different from most men in her field. Now she wasn't so sure. It was natural for him to feel left out of what could be a major event in aviation history. Still, she wished that he had behaved in a more adult manner. She sighed and returned to her list. She had to admit to herself that talking to Gordon had helped her to clarify her thoughts. There was someone who might be able to tell her about ice conditions. Mike Barlow had been eager to participate. Perhaps he could get the information she needed.

Mike Barlow was just leaving his small apartment when the e-mail notice came through. He wavered at the doorway, anxious to join the pizza and beer crowd at Murphy's. I should have turned the damn thing off, he said to himself, as he turned back to the computer. It was probably some undergrad wanting a head start on the class notes for the fall.

He clicked on the mail notice and was pleased to see that the message was from Dr. Scott. The young, beautiful, Dr. Scott, he reminded himself.

He looked around his bare room and was satisfied that he was ready for any emergency. His bag was already packed, a single duffel containing his field gear. The refrigerator was empty, its natural condition, except for the occasional moldy bread.

They can't be canceling at this stage, he told himself, so relax. This was the chance of a lifetime, working with Elliot Scott's daughter. Hell, he'd been wound up ever since the elder Scott had contacted him. Until that moment, Barlow wouldn't have bet money that his old professor even remembered his name. And now here he was, doing a favor for the grand old man of Southwestern archaeology, a favor that would be returned one day, Scott had promised. Jesus, that might be enough to guarantee him a job once he graduated. These days a Ph.D. was lucky to work the oil line, let alone teach.

He let out his breath in relief. It wasn't a cancellation. She wanted ice condition details from him. He could do that. Johnny-on-the-spot, that's me. He thought carefully about how to frame the reply. Can't make it sound too easy. He got up and paced the room.

He stopped to take another look the old *National Geographic* he scrounged from the library, the one with the article on Nick Scott. In all her photos, which had been taken in the jungles of New Guinea, she was wearing shorts, a sweat-stained work shirt, and a Chicago Cubs baseball cap. Even so, she was the best-looking archaeologist he'd ever seen.

He touched one of her photographs and sighed. Doing this kind of favor was going to be a pleasure.

Tomorrow he'd be meeting her at the airport in Anchorage. Then he'd know if her photographs lied.

The magazine, he noted, was only two years old, so she couldn't have changed that much.

"Keep your mind on business," he muttered. It would be better if she looked like a real loser than that he should risk annoying the daughter of a man like Elliot Scott. And she was no slouch herself, but an assistant curator at the Smithsonian. He should be so lucky. Well, one thing was certain—working for her would look good on his résumé, if nothing else. And, he reminded himself, if he did a good job he'd have two Dr. Scotts owing him a favor.

He nodded to himself. No doubt about it. If he did a good job, his future was assured. He went back to the computer and typed in his reply. Before he could hit the send button, he heard a knock at the door.

Who could that be? he wondered. All his friends were gone for the summer. Better spell check this before I send it, he thought.

"I'm coming," he called out, annoyed at the interruption. Whoever it was couldn't be very important.

8

Ned Duffy, armed with three pints of rye, looked up at the *New York World* building at 63 Park Row and shook his head in disgust. It had been ten years since he'd graduated from obits, five years since he'd landed the crime beat. Sweet Jesus, he thought as he pushed through the door and climbed the stairs to the city room, what was happening to his career?

Steeling himself, he stepped into the cavernous city room and his jaw dropped open. This time of day the newspaper office was usually crammed with reporters, copy boys, rim-birds, and rewrite men. Now there was only the city editor, Green, the paper's city hall reporter, Don Newmark, and a dispirited looking copy boy whose name Duffy couldn't remember.

"Close your mouth," Green shouted, "and get to work. The Death Notices and obits are piling up."

"We can't fill the paper with obits," Duffy hollered back as he headed for his desk.

"Dispatches from the front," Newmark proclaimed. "Our brave boys are over there fighting in the trenches and New York is hungry for news of them. That's the front-page stuff. Major General Graves has arrived in Vladivostok to take command of our troops in eastern Russia. You can fill in the back pages with the obits and Death Notices."

He handed Duffy a sheaf of papers an inch thick. "The morticians must be saving them up. I've knocked out twenty-five so far and haven't gotten anywhere. Go through the rest of these and see if there's anyone who's important." He scooped up an armful of Death Notices and dumped them on Duffy's desk.

"Why are there so many?" Duffy asked. "There are plenty of old folks dying in the dead of winter, but this is September."

He started shuffling through the pages. "Here's one, William Randolph, father of four, age twenty-six." He shuffled some more pages. "Joseph Collins, son of Robert and Elaine, age eighteen, killed in the line of duty late of the Forty-third Infantry. The Forty-third is stationed at Fort Dix. Newmark, haven't you noticed, Fort Dix is in New Jersey. Since when have the Huns invaded New Jersey?"

"He isn't the only one from the Forty-third," Newmark replied. "You must be mistaken. They must have been shipped overseas."

"Christ, I know where the Forty-third is stationed," Duffy said.

"He was in the Army and now he's dead. Do you want to tell his nearest and dearest that he *wasn't* killed in the line of duty?" Newmark leaned over his desk and Duffy realized that he was drunk.

Green, a small, wiry man whose battered eyeshade had been handed down from his predecessor, pounded his desk to get their attention. "There are worse things than compiling death notices, as reporters who slight their city editors soon discover."

"Now, Professor Death," Green continued, "if you'd be so good as to start earning your keep. Otherwise, you'll be here all night."

"It would take six of us to catch up," Newmark snapped.

"Just write," Green said, "and keep the philosophy to yourself."

"I've been at it for hours. I'm wrung dry. I've run out of euphemisms for *dead*."

"We're not writing literature here," the city editor shot back. "Stick to *passed away* and be done with it."

"*Croaked*," Duffy said. "That's got a ring to it."

"*Dead as a doornail*," Newmark countered.

"*Gone under*," Duffy said.

Green snorted. "You'll never make editors if that's the best you can do." He tapped the side of his head with a nicotine-stained finger. "*Cashed in his chips*, that's more like it. *Pushing up daisies*."

"*Rubbed out*, as we say on the crime beat," Duffy added.

Green raised his coffee cup.

Newmark raised his coffee cup in reply. Duffy was pretty certain that it contained something stronger than caffeine. "To death," they chorused.

Green said, "Now, if you don't mind, gentlemen, we have a paper to get out even if it won't be worth reading except by the next of kin. And consider yourselves lucky. Conner's wife called in a while ago. I've got his obit to write."

Duffy swallowed rye until his throat caught fire.

"Conner was younger than me, wasn't he?" Duffy asked. "What happened?"

"Did you ever meet his wife?" Newmark answered. He rolled his eyes. "That was one gorgeous woman. If you ask me, she as good as killed him."

Green banged his desk again. "I'll be the one doing the killing if I don't see some action."

"So fire me," Newmark said, draining his bottle dry. "Just what the doctor prescribed."

For an instant, Duffy was tempted to do the same, but

the thought of a hangover stopped him. He needed to be on his toes.

He was just buckling down to work, when the city editor's phone rang. Duffy eavesdropped.

"City desk," Green answered. "Go ahead." As he listened, his lips cracked into a broad smile. "We're on it."

Green slammed down the phone, leapt to his feet, and whooped, "We've got a story for once. A subway wreck with real deaths."

"Where?" Duffy said.

"It's the Brighton Beach line at the Malbone tunnel. The BRT is running a rescue train from Astor's personal station and they'll take a reporter if we can get one there in ten minutes."

"Who covers it?" Newmark asked, lurching unsteadily to his feet.

"Duffy," Green said, "you're the soberest. Newmark can stand by for rewrite if he doesn't fall over before you get there."

A chill went through Duffy. Nothing much got past Green. He'd have to try to be more careful. As he headed for the door, Green called after him, "Get a taxi if you have to. I don't care what you spend. I just want that story."

"My bike will be faster."

"It had better be," Green said. "Don't bother to come back if they leave without you."

9

Nick's love of airplanes stopped short of commercial flying. But E-Group's 757 was unlike anything she'd ever seen. It was decorated as tastefully as Berkeley's Faculty Club. Individually lighted oil paintings glowed from the walls, as did the deep-piled Oriental carpeting that ran down a central aisle wide enough for a cocktail party. Add to that massive leather passenger seats that folded into luxurious beds and E-Group's Boeing rivaled the best *Architectural Digest* had to offer.

Even so, Nick hadn't slept during the flight. To her, a red-eye was a red-eye. A long red-eye at that, a nonstop from Washington to Seattle, where they'd refueled for the last leg to Anchorage, Alaska. At the moment, if her watch was correct and the pilot on schedule, they were two hours from touchdown.

The man sleeping across the aisle hadn't helped her mood any. Gordon Hurst had been added to the expedition at the last moment as an adviser, or so Dr. Alcott had assured her. But last night when she'd tried to talk to Hurst about why he hadn't told her, he'd been distant and cold. He'd begged off, saying he needed his rest if he was to be fresh for the expedition. Well, judging from the engine-rivaling snores coming from him, he'd be a hell of a lot fresher than she was. She wondered what Alcott had told him his exact role would be.

She rolled over to be rid of the sight of him and saw the window shade on the bulkhead next to her glowing red. Holding her breath, half-expecting an engine fire, she slid it open and was greeted by the rising sun.

Nick pulled back her blanket and sat up fully clothed. No one else in the cabin was awake. She folded her blanket and stood up. Before she had time to stretch, the flight attendant was at her side. At the push of a lever, the bed became a chair again.

"Are we on time?" Nick asked.

The attendant nodded toward the cockpit. "Here's the co-pilot now."

Up the aisle, the copilot was stopping at each chair to wake the passengers. No impersonal, hard-to-hear intercom for E-Group, thought Nick.

When he reached her, he said, "Ms. Scott, you'll just have time for a cup of coffee before we land."

Nick put her watch to her ear.

"Our orders were to get you there as soon as possible," he explained. "We've burned enough fuel for a round-trip but we're an hour and a half early." He touched his cap and moved on to the next passenger.

Their party had now swelled to seven. In addition to Hurst, the other newcomers were Karen Royce, a doctor who'd been recruited because of Wes Erickson's age, and Lew Tyler, a documentary cameraman, who'd been described to Nick as a strong back who could pitch in if the excavation site demanded it.

But the notion seemed ridiculous. Tyler looked fit enough, but he'd be busy filming most of the time. Besides, he was untrained. Nick would have to depend on herself and her digger, Mike Barlow. And she couldn't imagine Dr. Alcott getting his hands dirty, or Fred Ivins, E-Group's vice president, using a pick and shovel either. Karen Royce was close to Nick's age, but asking an MD to do manual labor seemed out of the question. That left Hurst. He was young and fit enough, but Nick thought of him as an academic with no real field experience. Or was he coming along to direct the digging?

Across the aisle, Gordon Hurst was up and doing stretching exercises. He was wearing a light blue jogging outfit and white running shoes with matching blue stripes. When he caught her eye, he smiled cheerfully and said, "I can practically smell Alaska already."

Grunting noncommittally, she headed for the bathroom to escape his fresh-faced eagerness. One look in the mirror told her more than cold water would be needed to soothe her bloodshot eyes. The rest of her, jeans and tan work shirt, looked no more rumpled than usual. To hide her cowlicked hair, she crammed on her Cubs cap as tightly as possible.

Fifteen minutes later their 757 was shunted onto an auxiliary taxiway that led to a private terminal, where portable boarding stairs stood waiting. The moment the plane came to a stop, Ivins hustled forward, cracked open the door, and then stationed himself beside it like an overeager tour guide.

"Let's go," he said, making a hurry-up, circling motion with one hand, "we've got a long trip ahead of us."

Tyler, their cameraman, was first out of the plane, so he could film their arrival. Outside, the sky was bright and cloudless, the morning crisp and invigorating, not much different than a fall day in Albuquerque.

Three huge, bright yellow Ford sports utility vehicles were parked nearby. Each was equipped with a sleek, slipstreamed cargo carrier attached to its roof rack. Three men were clustered around the lead vehicle, which had photographs spread over its hood. One of them, Nick hoped, was her digger.

Ivins ushered everyone toward the lead Ford, while Tyler circled the group like a border collie, recording their every move.

"This is our guide," Ivins announced as soon as they'd settled into a semicircle around the front of the car. "Terry Kelly."

Kelly, a tall, lean man wearing a brown park service uniform, tipped his Smokey-the-Bear hat in recognition.

"He's lead ranger at the Szczesiak Wildlife Refuge," Ivins continued, "and an expert on where we're going."

Kelly grinned, a self-effacing expression that wrinkled his leathery, weather-beaten face. "I'm a relative newcomer to Alaska. It's Gus here who knows every nook and cranny." He indicated the man next to him. He had classic Inuit facial features, though he was taller than most, Nick thought, six feet at least, with vivid blue-green eyes. He, too, wore a park service uniform, though his hat was adorned with an eagle feather. "His real name is Auqusinauq and he was born not far from where we're going," Kelly continued.

"It will be my pleasure to take you to the land of my fathers," the Inuit said.

Kelly turned to a young man who was standing a little behind the Inuit. "This is Mike Barlow. He tells me he's your digger."

"He's a grad student at the university," Nick interjected. She saw a tall, fair man whose blond locks seemed in danger of springing away from his head in all directions. Blond stubble on his face gave his visage a generally blurred impression. He looked like a hundred other grad students that Nick had worked with. "Glad to finally meet you, Mike. I tried getting hold of you yesterday, but was unable to."

"Gee, Ms. Scott. I didn't know. My hard disk crashed. I haven't been able to scrape together enough money to get it fixed."

And you don't answer your phone, Nick thought. You'd

better be more reliable than you seem or I'm going to kill Elliot. She stepped forward to shake Barlow's hand. He looked like he would be more at home with a tape recorder than a shovel. She was pleased to notice that his hands were hard and callused. "It doesn't matter." She waved a hand at the loaded cars. "It looks like E-Group thought of everything. We can compare notes on the way."

"Whatever you say, Ms. Scott."

Ivins gestured impatiently. "We can introduce everyone properly later, but first let's take a look at the aerial photos of our target area. They're less than twenty-four hours old. What do you think, Mister Kelly? Is it a viable area?"

"I've been there, but like I said, Gus is the expert."

At a nod from Kelly, the Inuit fished a map from his pocket, unfolded it, then laid it on the hood next to the photos, which had been arranged to form a continuous image of the target area, the Hammersmith Mountains.

"This is the best map we've got," Kelly said. "We've compared it to your aerial shots. As far as we can see, nothing specific shows up, though it's rough country, rough enough to hide a hundred airplanes."

"Hold it," the cameraman said. "I want close-ups." He pushed forward with his camera.

Ivins ignored him. "It was too much to hope that our airplane would be in plain sight, but let's have our fighter pilot take a look." Ivins cleared a space for Erickson.

Seen in harsh daylight, Erickson seemed more fragile than ever, Nick thought, though flying a red-eye did that to just about everyone. Even Dr. Alcott, immaculate in a safari outfit, looked frayed.

Erickson moved from photograph to photograph, now and again pausing to touch a particular geographical landmark with his forefinger. "I remember three mountain peaks in particular," he said finally, "saw-toothed peaks."

Kelly and Gus exchanged looks. Ivins spotted the eye contact and asked, "Does that ring a bell?"

Before Kelly or the Inuit could answer, Erickson said, "This looks right." He touched a photograph. "Or maybe this one." He stabbed another. His finger was following a single ridgeline.

"That's a lot of country," Kelly said.

Ivins bent over the photograph, his finger retracing Erickson's course, a matter of inches. "How far can it be?"

"Don't be deceived by scale," the ranger answered. "Those were relatively low-level photos but we're still talking maybe a five-mile area."

"That doesn't sound so bad."

"Tell me that after you've been on the ground."

"All you've got to do is get us there."

Gus snorted and looked away. Kelly said, "What Gus is trying to say is that there's only one road that goes anywhere near that area, and it's not much of a road. The proper way to travel in this region is on foot. Considering the amount of equipment you have here, I understand why that's impossible."

Ivins slapped the Ford's fender as if playing to Tyler's camera. "Lack of roads won't be any problem with these machines. They're top of the line, four-wheel drive with special suspension. They'll go anywhere. Trust me."

Kelly shook his head. "Trail blazing is strictly forbidden in the refuge. If we leave the road, any road, we do so on foot. If we see a bear on the road, or anywhere else for that matter, we stop and wait for it to move on. In the refuge, bears have the right-of-way. We don't feed them, approach them, or molest them in any way."

Ivins held up his hands in immediate surrender. "It's your bailiwick."

"One other thing," Kelly said. "I'm the only one permitted to carry a firearm in the refuge. If anyone's carrying, please speak up."

"We're strictly peaceful," Ivins said.

"But are the bears peaceful?" Alcott asked.

"We've never had a human attacked here in the refuge," Kelly answered. The comment got him a look from Gus. "My associate reminds me that we don't have many visitors, so that statistic may be misleading. Let me just say that bears are wild animals and should be treated with caution and respect at all times. It's the female of the species you have to beware of, especially if they have young. They have powerful maternal instincts and constantly tend their young. A female will even attack a dominant male if he gets too close to her cubs."

"I thought animals had their young in the spring," Ivins said.

"Bears have been known to keep their cubs with them for up to three years. So if we come across a female with cubs, do exactly as I say. And don't be deceived. After three years, a cub can be almost as large as its mother. So if you see two or three bears together, it's safest to assume that they're a family group."

"Have you ever had to shoot a bear?" Erickson asked.

"No, but there've been a few tourists I wouldn't have minded shooting," Gus interjected.

"On that note," Ivins said, "I think we'd better get moving. How far is it to the refuge?"

Kelly collected the photos and handed them to Ivins. "Not far, two hundred miles, give or take. We've got decent roads most of the way, so with luck we'll be there by nightfall. Now, I think you'd better check your gear before we take off."

Ivins said, "E-Group, Anchorage, took care of that before delivering the vehicles."

"So they told me, but once we're on the road there's no opportunity to recover from an oversight. Supplies are hard to come by this late in the summer."

Ivins turned to Karen Royce. "Doctor, if you'll give me a hand checking your supplies. You, too, Nick, let's go over our checklists."

Each of the three Ford Excursions had huge cargo compartments in addition to the streamlined carriers on top. Each vehicle had been loaded with such precision that Nick hated to meddle. The food had been packed into metal, insulated containers. Similar containers held a portable satellite dish, a gasoline-powered generator, and, judging by the Red Cross markings, enough medical supplies to cover just about any eventuality. Add to that sleeping bags, tents, stoves, survival clothing, tools for excavating, and half a dozen five-gallon cans of gasoline and Nick had a definite feeling of overkill. Compared to her father's low-budget expeditions, this one had been arranged with military precision. Of course, now that their ranks had swollen to ten with the addition of Kelly, Gus, and Barlow, they were more like a small army than an archaeological dig.

"Well," Ivins asked, "are we missing anything?"

The doctor shook her head.

"Ms. Scott?" Ivins prompted.

"If you ask me, we're overloaded." She saw Hurst smiling at her, no doubt remembering their discussion about the length of her equipment list.

"It's best to be prepared," Kelly said. "And don't be fooled by Anchorage." He and Gus peered up at the painful blue sky. "Or the good weather either. This may look like back home, but it's not. Up here, the weather can change like that." He snapped his fingers.

"We're not tourists," Nick told him. "We weren't expecting to see igloos and totem poles."

"Speak for yourself," Ivins quipped.

Kelly ignored the comment. "An hour from now we'll be in another world."

"A far harsher world than you are used to," Gus added.

10

Frost coated Nick's sleeping bag, crackling when she sat up. The entire party, laid out like dusted body bags, had spent the night on the ranger station's wood-planked porch. The Szczesiak National Wildlife Refuge didn't run to creature comforts, even for the few hardy tourists who were allowed access. Only Kelly would winter there, and then strictly as a precaution against poachers. Even Gus planned to winter in Fairbanks, the big city, as he called it.

The station itself was no more than a log cabin, maybe twenty feet square, furnished with bunk beds for two, a trestle table with picniclike benches attached, storage cabinets massive enough to hold a winter's food supply, and a huge, pot-bellied wood-burning stove. The cabin, though surrounded by forest, stood on high ground, with a panoramic view of thousands of acres of wilderness.

Fully clothed, Nick crawled out of her sleeping bag, fished her desert boots from the bottom, and stepped over sleeping bodies, descending the front steps into dazzling sunshine. The day was as bright as yesterday, the sun as warm as an Albuquerque morning. But in the shade, frost still powdered the ground. Last night, she remembered, the stars, unfettered by city lights for hundreds of miles, had been dazzling.

The ranger station was surrounded by a forest of hemlock and spruce. To get there, they'd crossed grasslands and tundra, before passing through thick stands of white birch that marked the refuge's outer perimeter.

The air, so fresh it stung the nostrils, tantalized her. It was like something from her childhood, from her first excursion into Anasazi country with her father. A sudden gust of wind erased the memory, replacing it with the smell of bacon.

She looked back at the cabin to see smoke rising from the chimney and Kelly fanning the door.

"Bacon and eggs in five minutes," he bellowed and retreated back inside, leaving the door ajar to spread the aroma. Judging from the jostling on the porch, bacon was better than a bugle call.

After breakfast, Kelly spread a large-scale map of the refuge across the trestle table, then used a Day-Glo highlighter to trace the route they would be taking. It followed a dotted line, not a proper road, the ranger clarified, and ended at the base of a section of the Hammersmith Mountains. Tyler's camera followed the ranger's every move.

"Now, if you'll step outside," Kelly said, "I'll show you where we're going."

Once everyone had gathered on the porch, Gus pointed north. "That's where."

The mountains were only a line of purple haze.

"Hold that pose," Tyler, their cameraman, said. "I'm on a zoom."

A look crossed Gus's face that reminded Nick of someone about to swat an annoying insect. But it passed quickly as Gus peered up at the sky, shaking his head in obvious disapproval. "The weather's not going to hold forever."

Nick repressed a smile. Probably Gus was playing mind games with Tyler, or maybe even hamming it up for the camera.

"Nothing lasts forever," she said. "We only need two weeks."

"In this land, two weeks can be a lifetime. I would hope that it doesn't represent yours."

Nick refused to be intimidated. "The future is a mystery to all men."

"But I think, not to some women. Is that not right, Kelly?" Gus asked.

Kelly laughed and changed the subject. "Wes Erickson and I had a long talk last night. As a result, we're going to start our hunt at road's end. Now, if everyone will step back inside I'll show you on the map. I want everyone oriented to the ground. Get lost up here and the weather can kill you."

Back at the table, Kelly tapped a fingernail over the point where the road—a dotted line—ran into the mountains. He dabbed a spot of Day-Glo on the map. "This represents where we currently are. This road passes through a forest of black spruces. And we might be in luck. Gus thinks that this area, over here," he marked another spot with Day-Glo, "best matches Mr. Erickson's memory. You can see that it is near the road's end. If we're wrong, we'll be on foot. The area within the forest consists of a tangled undergrowth of moss, fern, grass, and berries. I'm not sure about how much headway we could make off the road."

"What about the white area on the other side of the mountains?" Hurst asked.

"A glacier field. God help us if your airplane is out there."

"How far away from here is road's end?" Alcott said.

Kelly stepped to the open door and squinted toward the purple haze. "If we had a good road, we'd be there for lunch. Unfortunately, the summer has been exceptionally warm. The road was never in great shape to begin with; now we've developed several sinkholes due to the collapse of the permafrost. With luck, we'll make camp before dark."

They piled into the Fords, with Gus, Erickson, Dr. Royce, and Alcott in the lead car. Nick was disappointed to find herself assigned, with Hurst, to Kelly's car. She would have preferred to ride with Barlow, but he'd been assigned to the car bringing up the rear of the caravan with Tyler and Ivins.

Hurst, she noticed, waited until she got into the front seat before selecting a rear seat for himself, where he immediately stretched out. Kelly glared at him in the rearview mirror. "We'll be going through some beautiful country, Mr. Hurst."

"Wake me when there's something to see besides trees."

"I thought you were a historian," the ranger persisted.

"Military historian," Hurst said.

"And you, Ms. Scott?" Kelly asked.

"Historical archaeology is my field."

Without taking his eyes from the trail ahead, the ranger questioned her with a shrug.

"Think of it as starting with Columbus in this country and going from there, but my specialty is airplanes."

"How does that differ from Mister Hurst?"

"My airplanes are usually in pieces," Nick answered, "though we hope to find our dive bomber pretty much intact."

"Even if it's buried under the snow?"

Behind her, Hurst sat up and asked, "Why do you say that?"

"If it was above ground, Gus would have seen it, or at least known about it from his people. So where else could it be?"

Nick felt a surge of excitement. The last thing she wanted was an above-ground airplane exposed to the elements.

"I've been stationed here five years, Doctor Scott," Kelly continued, "and I still get lost once in a while. The refuge is vast, most of it untouched by man. If I stay here another twenty years, I still won't know it completely. As for Gus, it's hard to say. But the man never gets lost, even in country he's never set foot in before. I think he has built-in radar, like migrating birds."

"Please, call me Nick."

Kelly nodded.

Hurst said, "Nick, it looks like we're in luck. The plane is buried."

Bastard, Nick thought, what does he mean *we*. She remembered how Hurst had avoided answering her questions on the plane and her distrust increased. Sweetly, she said, "It depends."

She pretended to be studying the passing landscape, a forest of spindly birch.

"Depends on what?" Hurst asked after a lengthy silence.

Nick half turned in her seat to stare him in the eye. "On just how deeply it's buried. You must remember our discussion about the Lost Squadron. Did you come to help dig or what? I'm just a little unclear about what your duties are on this trip."

"I'm strictly an observer, really. My interest in military aircraft is no secret around the museum, so why wouldn't they invite me along? Probably they hope I'll give them a mention in my next book."

"Who exactly would you mention?"

"That depends on the outcome of our search," Hurst replied. "Your search, I should say," offering an olive branch. "Just think of me as someone who's along for the ride. Surely, you don't think the plane is actually two hundred and fifty feet down."

Only two people could have authorized Hurst's addition to the expedition, she thought, Paul Evans or Dr. Alcott. Her money was on Alcott, though his motive escaped her. When it came to recovering buried aircraft, she had the expertise, not Hurst. Yet for all she knew, he was a personal friend of one of them.

She returned to the topic of how deep the plane was. "A landslide is a possibility, the laying down of natural sedimentation another. The best we can hope for is burial under a permanent snowfield that's not too deep. That way we avoid the erosion caused during melting and runoffs, but still recover the plane."

"Makes sense," Kelly said. "It would also explain why Gus has never seen anything, though he did say there are stories about an airplane crashing somewhere in these mountains."

Nick caught her breath. "Why didn't you say so before?"

"I would have if Gus had a location. But it's only a story. Gus is full of them. Mostly they're about ghosts and spirits."

"I'd like to hear them anyway."

"You can try asking Gus. With him, you never know. If he likes you, that's one thing. If he doesn't"—Kelly shrugged—"you wouldn't know he speaks English."

The vehicle directly behind them honked twice, a prearranged signal to stop. Kelly repeated the signal for the car ahead. Once the caravan halted, Lew Tyler climbed onto the roof of the rear Ford and attached himself to the cargo carrier.

"He wants to get some establishing shots on the road," Ivins called to the others. "Five minutes ought to do it. Keep your speed down so we won't raise any dust."

Watching the cameraman through the rear window, with the Fords bouncing in the washboard ruts even at five miles an hour, Nick wondered at the man's sanity.

"Gus must be having kittens," Kelly said. "He thinks we don't have much time, because the weather's going to change on us."

"I talked to the national weather bureau before we left Washington," Nick said. "They told us we had a week of good weather, at least."

"I got the same forecast," Kelly said, goosing the Ford.

"You don't sound convinced."

"Like I said, Gus has radar." He glanced at the rearview mirror and grinned. "That ought to make Gus happy."

Nick checked the back window again. Dust was billowing around Tyler, who was bouncing up and down like a greenhorn on a bucking bronco.

Nick said, "It doesn't look like it's rained here in months."

"It hasn't."

Kelly honked the horn and began braking. "That's enough time wasted." He turned to Nick. "Doctor Scott, can you please get your cameraman back inside?"

He's not mine, she thought, but kept it to herself as she stepped out of the Ford to relay the ranger's instructions.

A minute later, the caravan was on its way again, traveling at a steady, spine-shattering fifteen miles an hour.

"How long to get there at this speed?" Nick asked.

"Like I said before, nightfall."

"Jesus," Hurst muttered. "My kidneys won't make it."

"We'll be stopping for lunch early." Kelly glanced at his wristwatch. "Maybe in an hour, when we reach our emergency hut."

"What kind of emergencies are we talking about?" Hurst asked.

"Up here, the cold. What else? You get stranded by a sudden storm and you'd better get undercover fast. Otherwise you're bear food."

The emergency hut was a replica of the ranger station, log cabin construction only on a smaller scale. Three outhouses side-by-side would have had more room.

A lunch of bacon sandwiches had been packed in advance. Whoever had done it was in love with mayonnaise and cholesterol. Even so, Nick followed her rule for survival and ate two sandwiches, washing them down with real Coke, as opposed to her usual diet soda. *On digs,* Elliot preached, *never pass up an opportunity to eat or relieve yourself.*

But Wes Erickson, she noticed, managed only a couple of bites before abandoning his sandwich. He'd been moving stiffly, like a man in pain, ever since getting out of the car, and their journey was less than half over.

What he needed was a walk to limber up, Nick thought, and offered her arm just as Dr. Royce did the same.

"How can I refuse?" Erickson responded. "A man my age doesn't get many offers from good-looking women, even if one of 'em is a lady doctor."

"We'll have none of your flattery." The doctor slipped her arm in his. "We had an agreement, remember. You stick to the rules and I stay out of your way."

"With women, there's always a catch." He grinned for Nick's benefit and squeezed her hand.

"Rule one," Dr. Royce went on, "keep up your strength and get your rest."

"A man my age shouldn't be eating bacon."

"That's sound advice for anyone, but right now you need calories." She dipped into the pocket of her immaculate jacket, which didn't have so much as a wrinkle and could have passed for a lab coat had it been white instead of tan. "I brought along a supply of energy bars. They're not Milky Ways, but they're not bad." She peeled the wrapper halfway and handed the bar to him.

Nick approved. Had she been on one of her father's digs, her pockets would have been crammed with similar high-energy packets. She mentally kicked herself for not stocking up on some.

"I've got plenty to go around," the doctor said, recovering a second bar from her jacket. She smiled as she handed it to Nick.

Nick blushed. I couldn't have looked that hungry, she thought.

"What about yourself?" Nick asked as they started walking along the road over which they'd just driven.

"Don't worry. There's a box of them in each of the cars. I'm not a field person myself, but as soon as they told me we'd be digging up an old airplane out in the middle of nowhere, I figured we might have to eat on the run. I didn't realize we'd be bringing along tents and stoves and cell phones."

Nick studied the woman out of the corner of her eye. She had to be in her late thirties, which put her ten years out of medical school. But she didn't show the wear and tear of the doctors Nick knew. In fact, if Nick had seen her on the street, she would have guessed Karen Royce to be a businesswoman of some kind, maybe an attorney. Her layered haircut had probably cost more than Nick spent on food in a week. Her figure, now hidden beneath her coat and tailored trousers, had made Nick feel lumpy in comparison.

Nick probed, "I'm surprised you were able to take time off from your practice."

"I thought you knew. I'm strictly research, one of the many minions at E-Group."

"What kind of research?" Erickson asked, eyeing his energy bar suspiciously.

The doctor patted him reassuringly. "I'm a true crusader. I'm trying to save humanity with wonder drugs."

They hadn't gotten more than thirty yards when Kelly shouted. "Let's go. We've got a schedule to keep."

As they started back toward the cars, Nick saw Kelly and Gus conversing. Not actually conversing, she decided as they got closer, since Kelly was doing all the talking with Gus nodding when he wasn't looking up at the sky and shaking his head.

Nick left Erickson in the doctor's care, and joined the men, both of whom were now peering up at the intensely blue sky. Surely, they were being overcautious. Hold it, she told herself. You don't know the country. Don't make assumptions. Most of her experience came from desert digs, where dry heat was the finest preserver of artifacts.

Both men stopped talking at Nick's approach.

"How long is this dig of your going to take?" Kelly asked.

"There's no way of telling, not until we find the plane."

"Gus says we have three days, maybe four, of good weather."

"Then what?"

"A storm will come," Gus said.

"How big?" she asked, remembering the Hopi's ability to time their dances with rain.

"It's too early to tell," he replied.

"What's usual this time of year?"

"Up here the Tlingit Indian calendar begins in August, when the birds come from the mountains and the animals prepare their winter dens. It is now September."

"You're not Tlingit, though, are you?"

"Thank you for knowing the difference," Gus said.

"You still haven't answered my question. Are you saying winter can start anytime?"

Gus glanced at Kelly, whose answering expression was unreadable.

Gus licked his hand and held it up. "The wind has changed.

There's more moisture now. The bears are getting ready for their winter sleep. It is a sure sign. They are like clocks."

"What Gus is saying," Kelly said, "is that you'd better be good at your job. Now, let's move out and stop wasting time."

11

Abruptly, the five-hundred-pound bear stopped eating and rose up on her hind legs, her nose twitching as she tested the air. A low growl rumbled in her throat, alerting her two cubs, who immediately abandoned their find of ripe chokecherries and stood poised, either to flee or attack.

The scent was faint, miles away, carried on the wind.

The great bear fell back onto all fours and moved toward her cubs, who were well camouflaged deep in the berry thicket. If they stayed where they were, they'd have enough to feed on for the rest of the day, and now that winter was coming every day counted.

One of the cubs shifted restlessly, rattling the berry branches. She snorted a rebuke, but the cub ignored her and went back to chomping noisily on berries. Her snort became a growl and the cub backed off, though at four hundred pounds it was nearly her equal. Next spring her cubs would set out on their own and she would winter alone.

Her ears pricked. A sound, as far away as the scent, alerted her. What it was she didn't know. Caution, rather than fear, made her edge closer to her cubs. In these mountains, the great bear had no equal, except for a rogue male, and even a rogue wouldn't challenge a female with cubs.

Yet, without knowing why, she sounded a warning and began ambling toward the high country where her den was already prepared. The cubs followed obediently.

Instinct told her that something had changed and that they wouldn't be safe until the snows came and buried their den for the winter.

12

Nick was surprised when the road ran out. There was no warning. One moment they were in the trees, which were casting deep shadows in the late afternoon light, and in the next they came to a stop at the foot of a rocky, treeless plain dominated by boulders the size of Buicks. Beyond the plain, maybe a half mile away, rose the Hammersmith Mountains. The road made no provision for a turnaround; it merely ended, like a driveway.

Anxious to stretch her legs, Nick flung open the car door and stepped into a chill wind blowing off the mountains. It was as sharp as the blue granite peaks looming above her.

More car doors opened. Soon everyone was gathered around the lead vehicle.

"Christ," Erickson said, staring up at the peaks like everyone else. "They look like teeth. I don't remember them that way."

"You're looking up," Nick pointed out. "The last time you saw them was from the air."

"They are the jaws of *Nanuk*," Gus said.

"The jaws of God," Kelly interpreted.

Gus smiled as if amused by Kelly's translation.

Call them what you like, Nick thought, getting to them isn't going to be easy, not for a man Erickson's age anyway.

"I don't see where a plane could land," Nick said. "It looks too rough."

"You can't see them from here, but there are snow-filled valleys along the base of the mountains," Gus said.

Erickson shook his head. "Nothing looks familiar. I must have made a mistake."

"Good God," Ivins snapped irritably. "You're the one who picked this spot from the photos."

"They were taken from the air," Nick reminded him, "just the way Mister Erickson saw them in the first place. It's no wonder he doesn't remember this place from the ground. In any case, we'd be fooling ourselves if we expected success on our first try. Look around. This mountain range runs for miles." Unfortunately, she added to herself, there was only the one road leading to the Hammersmiths, and now that she was on the site, she knew a long hike in country like this was out of the question, especially if they wanted to be in and out quickly.

"You're right, of course," Ivins said. "Sorry. I got excited there for a moment."

Kelly spoke up. "It's going to be dark in an hour. When that happens the temperature's going to drop ten degrees. So let's set up the tents." He indicated a clearing in a nearby stand of birch trees. "Gus and I have camped here before. The trees make a good windbreak."

The wind, Nick realized, had her shivering. She checked the darkening sky. "I hate to waste an hour of daylight. If you can get along without me, I'd like to look over as much of the ground as I can."

"A good idea," Ivins said eagerly. "You do that while the rest of us pitch in here."

"Nobody goes off on their own this close to dark," Kelly said, his tone making it an order. "If fact, let's get the rules straight right now. No one goes unaccompanied in the refuge. That's the rule even in summer when we have tourists. Their number is strictly limited, so that we have enough park personnel to escort them at all times. Gus, you go with Ms. Scott, but stick to the immediate area for now. We'll tackle the mountains first thing in the morning."

Gus pointed to a low, windswept rise about a quarter of a mile away. To get there without crossing the rocky plain, they'd have to backtrack through the trees. "That's our best lookout point," he told Nick.

"I'd like to go with you," Erickson said.

To Nick, the man looked exhausted. At the same time, his eyes had a spark to them Nick hadn't seen since the morning he addressed the Collections Committee at the museum. She looked to the doctor for guidance, but the woman was already fetching an armful of lightweight parkas from one of the cars. She handed one to Erickson and told him, "Zip it up and put on the gloves you'll find in the pockets."

"Don't fuss, Doc," Erickson told her, but did as he'd been ordered.

"Call me Karen, please. Anything but Doc." She distributed parkas to Nick and Gus when Hurst intervened. "Why don't I go along and keep an eye on your patient, Doctor? I need to stretch my legs and work out the cobwebs anyway."

Judging from the grin on Hurst's face, Nick suspected he was more interested in keeping an eye on her than acting as Erickson's nurse. No doubt he thought she'd hide the airplane from him if she got the chance. She smiled to herself. Come to think of it, she just might.

Kelly spoke up. "Mister Hurst, if you don't mind. I'm sure

that Gus and Doctor Scott can look after Mr. Erickson. You're going to be needed here."

"Don't worry, Gordon," Nick said. "If we find anything interesting, you'll be the first to know."

Gus slung binoculars around his neck and led the way into the sparse birch forest, following what Nick assumed to be a game trail. It was wide enough for her and Erickson to walk side-by-side. She kept a firm hold on his arm. The spongy soil made the footing tricky; it also told Nick they were walking on tundra, with permafrost only a few inches beneath the surface. There, nothing ever thawed. There, an artifact would be safe.

In the photos, the Hammersmiths had looked as impressive as the Colorado Rockies. But seen from the foothills, Nick guessed the highest peaks to be no more than three or four thousand feet. The passes between them looked a good thousand feet lower. What the mountains lacked in height, they made up for in jagged ruggedness.

She called to Gus. "How high are they?"

Without looking back, he ducked his shoulders, a kind of shrug, and said, "The maps say seventy-five hundred tops."

"They don't look it."

"The road's been climbing steadily all day. Where we stand is about three thousand feet above sea level. That makes the mountains another four, the passes over them maybe three thousand feet above where we're standing."

"What's on the other side?"

"A field of glaciers," the Inuit answered.

"That's right," Erickson said. "I remember now. When I shot down the Val, the land had patches of green on one side of the mountains and was all white on the other. The pilot headed for the green. I would have, too."

But he landed on the snow, Nick thought, not glacier ice. From the air, the ice would have glared and looked as hard as concrete.

What had looked like rising ground from the road was more of a humplike fold in the landscape, but it was high enough to get a clear look at the mountains. Gus handed Nick the binoculars. Seen in magnification, the ground at the base of the Hammersmiths was made up of a series of three deeply cut ravines, probably gouged into the land by glaciers from another age. The one ravine in her direct line of vision was snow filled.

She offered the binoculars to Erickson. "Take a look and tell me if it seems familiar."

The light was fading quickly now and the old pilot took a long time before responding. "Yes, it was a spot like that where he landed."

"In the snow, is that right?"

The old pilot nodded. "It looked soft enough from the air."

She turned to the Inuit. "What do you think, Gus? Could an airplane land out there?"

"Only a fool would try."

"If he had no choice, what would you say?"

"We always have choices. Better to dive into the mountain and be done with it quickly."

Erickson lowered the binoculars and sighed deeply. "Seeing this place again, from the ground, makes me think you're right. But then, I'm an old man now. Pilots are young men. They think they're immortal until the crash comes."

Nick asked, "Is there always snow in those ravines?"

"I've never seen them otherwise," Gus told her.

She was tempted to ask how often he'd been here, then decided against it. What was the point? Either the Val would be salvageable or not. Gus's answer wouldn't change that.

As she took back the binoculars, the peaks caught fire in the last rays of sunlight. More than ever they reminded Nick of teeth protruding from a prehistoric jaw.

"Unless I'm mistaken," she said, recalling a class she taken on arctic cultures, "*Nanuk* is a variation of Nanook. Both mean bear, not God. Not the teeth of God, as Kelly said."

Gus nodded. "I was right about you."

"About what?"

He smiled. "I've known shaman who say they can look through a man's eyes and see into his soul."

"Are you claiming to be a shaman?" she asked.

"What do you think?"

Typical shaman-speak, she thought. Hopi, Navajo, or Inuit, it didn't seem to make any difference. They were all the same. When they weren't answering one question with another, they spoke in riddles and enigmas.

Two could play that game, she decided and asked, "What does Kelly think about your spiritual insight?"

"He'll think we're staying away too long." Even as Gus spoke, the fire began fading from all but the very tallest peak, which now stood out like a blazing, molar-shaped beacon.

"That's it!" Erickson said excitedly, shifting from foot to foot while pointing at the fiery mountain. "I remember now. When I circled low over the Val I had to be careful of that peak. You see, part of it looks like an elk's tooth, just like my father used to carry on his watch fob. We're close, I know it. We're close to my Val."

"How close?" Nick asked.

"It's out there where we were looking just now, in one of those ravines."

"Which one?" Nick asked.

Erickson turned to Gus. "How far are we from the ocean here?"

"A few miles, no more."

"Then, that one," Erickson said, pointing to the one on the southern side of the peak. "Or maybe the next one over from Elk's peak."

"That still covers a lot of ground," Gus said, "and all of it belongs to Nanuk. This place is home to the bears we protect. That peak belongs to them, and only they know its name."

"What do the maps call it?" Nick asked.

"Mount Hammersmith," Gus admitted.

"We were over the coast when I jumped my Val," Erickson continued as if he hadn't been listening. "By the time we reached this point, my Jap was going down. He didn't have a lot of time. That's why I know he put down in the first soft spot he saw."

Gus shrugged.

"When you get to be my age," Erickson added, "you remember the past better than what you did yesterday. I called it Elk's peak when I got back to base and reported my kill, but there was nothing like that on any of the maps we had, which weren't much in those days."

"Then that's where we'll start in the morning," Nick told him.

"Come," Gus said. "They are lighting a fire for us."

Nick hadn't realized how dark it was until she turned back toward camp. If it hadn't been for the bonfire, she would never have been able to find her way back.

As they approached the camp Nick realized that the fire had nothing to do with the wonderful smell of food that was engulfing the camp. One of E-Group's high-tech stoves was responsible for that.

As soon as Nick reported the news that Erickson felt certain of the crash site, Ivins and Alcott led the applause. She noticed that Hurst had the grace to join in.

"Where is it?" Kelly asked.

Gus pointed into the darkness and Kelly nodded as if he could penetrate the night. Everyone else had to wait for morning.

"How's this for comfort in the wilderness?" Ivins shouted. Folding chairs had been set up around the fire. A few feet farther back from the flames, tents as high-tech as the stove had been erected in a circle.

Tyler threaded his way among them, viewing the entire camp only through the lens of his camera. Nick wondered if he would eat viewing his meal through the lens.

As plates were being passed around, Kelly said, "There are rules you ought to know about camping in the refuge. As good as that chicken smells to us, it's even more so for the bears. They can smell that for miles. We just have to hope that there aren't any close by, or that those that might be are well fed."

The moment Kelly paused for breath, Tyler asked, "Do you think they'll come after the chicken?"

"Bears love nothing better than raiding unattended camps. So someone should be here at all times. The fire will help keep them away. What we have to worry about mostly is food storage and garbage. Everything should be kept in sealed containers, including the garbage. But if bears do wander into camp, the best thing to do is lock yourselves inside the cars. Bears will usually go away after a while."

"And if they don't?" Ivins asked.

"Let's worry about that if it happens," the ranger answered.

Even by firelight, the look of disapproval on Alcott's face was readable. "I think we should be ready for all contingencies."

"Gus and I will be standing watch."

At the mention of his name, the Inuit, who'd been feigning sleep in one of the camp chairs, opened his eyes and said, "Bears will be in their dens soon. As I have said, winter is coming early this year."

He rose, stretched, and stared up at the night sky as if expecting proof. Hopi shamans often did the same thing during rain ceremonies, Nick thought. Often as not, the rain clouds obliged.

But at the moment the sky was so clear the Milky Way was as dazzling as a light show. Nick blew into the air. The temperature had dropped far enough to make her breath smoke, but that often happened at this time of year in Albuquerque, when the temperature dipped into the forties at night. Surely it wasn't any colder here.

Gus wrapped his arms around his chest as if warding off the weather.

No, she told herself, the man was playing mind games with the tourists. She'd checked the long-range weather forecast twice, once before they took off, and again when they refueled in Seattle. The National Weather Service had promised unseasonably warm temperatures for another week at least.

She was about to enlighten the assembly when Hurst handed her a steaming plastic plate. "You'd better eat that chicken before the bears beat you to it."

13

Ned Duffy cursed to himself as he pedaled frantically toward Astor's private station. Sweat poured from him. Each ragged gasp for breath felt like his last. His lungs were on fire, his heart pounding hard enough to explode from his chest. His mouth was so dry he couldn't spit, his tongue so parched he couldn't wet his lips.

"You're turning into an old man," he wheezed.

He'd been too long in precinct houses and city rooms, he told himself, smoked too many cigars and drunk too much whiskey to cover a real story.

He was on the verge of collapse when a cop the size of a Greek wrestler stopped him at the entrance.

"No vehicles allowed," the cop bellowed, his face as red as a hard-core drinker's.

Duffy lurched off his bicycle, abandoning it where it fell, and staggered toward the stairs leading down to the station.

"No, you don't," the cop said, collaring him with a hamlike arm, "no civilians allowed. Especially civilians the likes of you."

"Press," Duffy managed to say.

"I've heard that one before."

Duffy reached for his press card, though many a detective had warned him against making any such move when confronting a harness bull.

"Now, there," the cop said, tightening his grip around Duffy's neck. "Let me do that for you, lad."

"O'Malley at headquarters will vouch for me," Duffy gasped.

"Sure, everyone knows O'Malley," the cop answered but picked Duffy's pocket anyway, coming up with Duffy's card and the dollar bill he kept nestled beside it.

"Ned Duffy of the *New York World,* it says. Now, would that be you?"

"That's me," Duffy replied, silently counting the minutes and forcing himself to appear calm.

"Maybe I recognize the name, at that," the policeman replied, returning the press card. He then palmed the dollar before releasing his grip on Duffy's neck.

Duffy flung himself down the ornate staircase to the subway landing. Under any other circumstances he would have paused to admire the ornate tile work and elaborate furnishings of the private station. The light from the crystal chandeliers was more than sufficient to see the men milling about the track.

"Duffy, from the *World,*" he called out.

"And not a moment too soon," one of the men yelled back and pushed him forward. "Here you go," he said and thrust Duffy up to what looked like the handle of a gigantic pump perched on a platform covering the tracks.

"What is this?" Duffy asked, as the man swung along beside him and grasped one end of the handle.

"It's a handcar, Mister Reporter from the *World,* and you'd best be pumping along with me if you want to get to your story."

Duffy looked around him and saw two more men grab the long handle at the other end.

"We're away," the man next to him shouted. "Push lads, push as if your lives depended on it, because there're other lives that do."

The handcar started to move and Duffy grabbed hold of the handle more to prevent himself from falling off the vehicle than for any other reason, but soon found himself straining to depress the pump.

"Where's the relief train?" he managed to gasp.

"This is it," the rail man answered. "The power's out down the line and this is the only thing that can get us there. The old tracks are still wooden on that stretch, as long as the BRT is operating under the dual standard. The cars being wooden too, there's nothing ahead of us but kindling. It's a bad business, my lad, and you'd best pump like mad to make it worth the effort to bring you. I had to leave a good man behind to make room for you. If your paper hadn't taken management's part in the strike I've no doubt you'd still be trying to figure out how to get there."

Duffy heaved and wondered how the man could find any breath to speak. He pumped until he thought he would pass out from the effort. Sweat poured down his forehead and into his eyes, but there was no opportunity to wipe them. Suddenly they rounded a turn in the tunnel and were plunged into darkness. Duffy thought he could fall off the platform and no one would notice.

"Steady, lads, we've got about a mile to go, but we'd best be slowing down a bit. Don't want to come a cropper ourselves."

Duffy was grateful that the pace had slackened and he managed to say, "How do you know that the wreck's a mile away?"

"From my previous trips," the man replied. "We've been ferrying lights and equipment as fast as we can."

It was unbelievable to Duffy that any human being could

make this trip more than once in a lifetime. His arms felt as if they were being torn from their sockets with each upswing of the pump. "Do you know what happened?" he asked.

"They put a kid on the line, us being so shorthanded. The curve at the tunnel is a tricky one and I heard that they dispatched him wrong to boot. He was at the end of a double shift and trying to make up for lost time. He'll not have to worry now, I suppose. Hold up lads, we're nearly there."

Duffy saw a dim glow ahead that seemed to consist of fitful shadows. As the handcar glided to a stop he could hear men shouting and he realized there was something worse, a thin wordless keening from people who could only be too injured to scream.

His companion thrust a lantern in his hand and said, "You're on your own, now. Me and the lads have work to do."

1 4

To Nick's surprise, the weather had turned warm by morning. So much for their guides' forecasting abilities and premonitions. The air, though fresh, wasn't cold enough to cloud her breath as she blew on her coffee. Breakfast was instant oatmeal, which required only boiling water and, Gus added, his own special touch, canned cream.

Since they didn't carry enough water for dishwashing, and they couldn't use the streams because they might pollute them, the oatmeal was ladled into plastic, disposable bowls.

While the rest of the party held their breakfast at arm's length, looking skeptical, Nick dug in with her plastic spoon. One swallow and she smiled her approval.

"My father uses a similar recipe," she told the Inuit, whose only response was a raised eyebrow.

"When you dig in the desert," she explained, "milk doesn't keep because of the heat, so you use either powdered or canned."

Gus nodded. "He sounds like a practical man."

Like you, she thought. Only in Elliot's case her father could usually read the weather, though to be fair, the desert climate wasn't all that unpredictable, except for the occasional cloudburst and it was important to get that right. She checked the sky again. Not a cloud in sight, and the temperature had to be every bit as warm as an Albuquerque morning.

She shrugged. With a little luck and trust in Wes Erickson's long-term memory, a couple of days might be all they'd need to find their airplane. Besides, Elliot always said she was lucky. Of course, he'd been referring to her escapes from Elaine's food poisoning.

The moment Nick finished her oatmeal, Alcott and Ivins got down to business. Ivins, who had a metal detector slung over his shoulder like a rifle, began. "I took your advice, Nick," he announced loudly enough for everyone seated around the fire to hear, "and bought two Garrett Master Hunters with depth multiplier attachments. They told me these babies are state of the art and can find a Volkswagen ten feet down. So it ought to work for an airplane."

"I've used them before," she said. "Ten feet refers to soil. There's no telling how much depth we'll get in snow."

"They're nicknamed Bloodhounds," Alcott added as if the detectors had been his idea in the first place. "Now, where are we going to start?"

Nick's surprise must have shown, because Alcott quickly added, "Don't worry, my dear, I know my limitations and hauling heavy equipment in this kind of country is one of them."

"Don't look at me, Ms. Scott," Ivins said. "I wouldn't want to steal your thunder." He turned to look back at one of the cars, where Gordon Hurst was unloading the second Bloodhound.

"I thought it best that you and Mister Hurst work together on this," Alcott said. "After all, you're our experts when it comes to military aircraft. Gus will show you the way and Tyler will record your efforts for posterity."

Nick clenched her teeth to keep from voicing her annoyance. She'd been planning to work with Barlow, her digger, or Gus, who knew the ground. The last thing she needed was an out-of-shape academic like Hurst slowing her down.

Alcott waved Hurst over. When Hurst reached them, Alcott said, "Well, Nick, show Gordon where you're going to start looking."

She gestured toward Mount Hammersmith. "Last night, Mr. Erickson thought he recognized that peak. We'll start at its northern flank and work south. There are a series of snow-filled valleys out there. He thinks that's where the Val landed."

Alcott rubbed his hands together. "Then time's a wasting, as they say."

"Not so fast," she said, doing her best not to gloat. "Don't you think I'd ought to show Mister Hurst how to operate his Bloodhound first?"

"No need to worry about me," Hurst told her. "I won't hold you up." To prove his point, he switched on the metal detector and swept it back and forth across the ground as if it were second nature.

"I'm impressed," Nick admitted.

"It's a hobby of mine." Hurst grinned. "Though mostly I use my detector at the beach, looking for treasure that tourists leave behind. But I don't have anything as good as a Bloodhound."

Nick reached for the Bloodhound, but Hurst stepped back and grinned. Alcott smiled and said, "No need to worry, my dear, there's plenty for all." He signaled to Mike Barlow, who already wore a backpack and was holding another magnetometer. "Barlow will carry yours."

"Mike," Nick asked, "do you know how to use a Bloodhound?"

He nodded.

She was embarrassed that she didn't know exactly what he was familiar with. She still hadn't had a chance to talk with him and now he was acting more like an employee of Ivins's than hers.

Ivins patted Barlow's backpack. "Attached are entrenching tools, an ice axe and snowshoes. Inside, we've packed canteens, power bars, matches, flashlights, binoculars, replacement batteries for the Bloodhounds, an extra two-way radio, and even Swiss Army knives. Anything else you need, say the word."

Nick nodded at the mountains. "We're not going more than half a mile." She assessed her own pack; it was much lighter than those she carried on her father's expeditions.

"Maybe so," Gus interjected, "but it's a long half-mile."

Nick must have betrayed her skepticism, because he added, "Save your breath. You'll need it."

Kelly said to Gus, "I'll light a beacon a half hour before sunset."

The Inuit nodded impassively.

Five minutes later, Nick realized Gus's comment had been an understatement. What he called a long half-mile had to be five times that. Distance as the crow flies had nothing to do with the serpentine route they had to take across the rocky plain on their way to the mountains. When they weren't wading through loose shale, they were scrambling over and around boulders that Nick had first thought to be the size of Buicks. Seen close up, many were as big as bungalows.

At times the five of them had to wind their way like soldiers through a mine field, often as not doubling back the way they'd come in order to get around some particularly nasty obstacle. Forward progress became a crawl. Her backpack, which had seemed so light at first, now seemed to increase its weight with each step she took.

The warm weather, which Nick had thought a good omen, now had her sweating and exhausted. Leg cramps had her clenching her teeth. Tyler, staggering under the weight of his camera, looked even worse than she felt. He'd lost all color in his face and was sucking air so hard he wheezed.

She thought that if she had been carrying a Bloodhound she'd never have been able to keep up with Gus's determined pace. As it was, she wondered if she'd have the strength to work, or even think straight, by the time they reached their objective. Hurst, she felt certain, was also nearing the point of collapse although he was keeping up a brave front.

Give it up Gordon, she thought. I'm five years younger and in better shape.

She managed a backward glance at Barlow, who was bringing up the rear. He looked unfazed, moving as easily as if he were out for a stroll. She said a silent prayer of thanks for Elliot's old boy network. She thought about asking Barlow to add Tyler's camera to his load, but it didn't seem fair since he was already carrying a Bloodhound. That left Gus, but the ranger was here as their guide, not their dogsbody.

Even so, Nick was about to ask for his help when Gus called a halt. "We're through the worst of it," he announced.

Nick raised her eyes. Directly ahead the rocky barricade gave way to a flat, debris-strewn moraine that hadn't been visible from her reconnaissance vantage point the night before. Crossing it was a trail of solid ground, free of scree, that appeared to run all the way along the base of the mountain to their first objective, now less than a quarter of a mile away.

Gus slipped off his pack to reach his canteen. Nick did the same, forcing herself not to suck it dry as she collapsed onto the ground.

"How long do you think it will take to excavate this plane of yours?" Gus said after what appeared to be a single swallow.

"That depends on how deeply it's buried."

"Are we talking one day, two, what?"

"I'd only be guessing," Nick answered, massaging the knots that were cramping the backs of her thighs. "This terrain is not going to make it any easier."

She checked her watch. The trek in and out was an hour and a half each way, minimum. A bitch of an hour and a half.

She said, "There's no guarantee we're in the right place."

"That's true. The old man was certain, but memory is a trickster."

"Let's hope not," Hurst gasped.

"Even if he is right," Nick added, "we should move the camp closer to the site before we start digging. Otherwise, we lose half of every day traveling in and out."

"That is not possible," Gus said. "Now, we must move out again."

Nick groaned as she got to her feet.

"I don't have the energy to groan," Hurst said.

Gus nodded at Barlow. "And you?"

"I'm fine. You show me where to dig, I'll dig."

"Shit," Hurst blurted, "if a Val flew over right now, I wouldn't have the strength to wave."

Nick realized that they hadn't heard a word from Tyler. He was on his feet, but seemed to be tugging ineffectually at his camera strap.

"The spirit is willing," he gasped out and then shook his head.

Gus picked up the camera and shouldered it as if it weighed very little. He grasped the cameraman's arm and said, "Come, walk with me."

The party proceeded at a somewhat slower pace and within minutes they topped a rise and stood looking down into the ravine Nick had seen through the binoculars the previous night. It was much narrower than it had first appeared, maybe a hundred yards across. Its snowfield was broken by outcroppings of sharp rock, minireplicas of the toothlike peaks above. The open space available for landing was no larger than an aircraft carrier's deck, but that was exactly where the Val had come from.

"Jesus," Hurst breathed, "landing here would be impossible."

"Think about it," Nick said. "This wouldn't be any harder than landing on a pitching deck. And look at the snow. The summer is nearly over and it still hasn't melted. Erosion will be at a minimum. This is a good site."

"You mean if that old pilot of yours hasn't sent us on a wild-goose chase." Hurst clenched his teeth as he rubbed the shoulder where he'd been carrying the Bloodhound.

But Nick was feeling no pain. One look at the potential dig site and her adrenaline had kicked in. Her cramps were gone and so was her exhaustion. She dug the pair of binoculars from her backpack and scanned the valley. It showed no telltale signs of a crash, or even a helpful airplane-shaped hump in the snow, though Nick hadn't expected any such luck after so many years.

"How deep's the snow?" Hurst asked.

"There's only one sure way to find out," Gus answered with a wry smile. "Do you want me to lead the way?"

"I'd rather you and Mike stayed here on the ridge," Nick answered. "Gordon and I will use our footprints as guides to make sure we've covered all the ground." To Hurst, she added, "We'll walk side by side, just far enough apart for our sweeps to overlap across the valley."

"You call this a valley?" Hurst said. "It's more like a canyon."

Nick smiled, wondering what Hurst would have thought about the desert canyons favored by her father's beloved Anasazi.

Gus said, "For Mister Hurst's sake, let's hope the other valleys are more to his liking."

"I thought you knew this area," Hurst complained.

"I have been here before, but that was a long time ago. There was no sign of a plane then."

It took Nick and Hurst nearly two hours to cover the first valley. From time to time their metal detectors fluctuated slightly, but never enough to suggest anything more than a deeply buried mineral deposit, or maybe ore-bearing rocks that had been washed down into the valley during a storm. Tyler kept shouting at them to look up for the camera, which they both ignored.

By the time they rejoined Gus and Barlow at their second target, the ridge above the adjacent valley, Nick's legs were shaky from the strain of working in snowshoes. But the rest of her was still high on adrenaline.

"Did you find anything promising?" the Inuit asked.

"Just beautiful country," Nick replied.

"It is good to see beauty, even when one is working."

"Shit," Hurst muttered. "No airplane is worth this." He collapsed onto a rock and tugged off his snowshoes.

Nick checked her watch. It was two o'clock, giving them a little more than four more hours of remaining light.

She turned to the Inuit. "Do you think it's possible to cover the other two valleys before dark?"

"You're crazy," Hurst said.

"We should eat first," Gus said. "Then we'll see."

Two power bars and instant hot chocolate warmed up with canned heat from their packs restored Nick's strength, though only time would tell if her legs would hold up.

"I'm ready to give it a try," she said.

"And you, Mister Hurst?" Gus asked.

"The more ground we can cover the better," Nick pleaded.

"You think I don't know that?" Hurst snapped. He rose to his feet. "I'll do my best."

"Show me how to work that Bloodhound of yours, and I'll help you," Gus said.

"Which one of us?" Hurst asked.

Gus shrugged. "That's up to you."

"It's my dig," Nick said. "And if it's all the same, I think Mike ought to come with me."

Hurst looked as if he was about to object, or so Nick thought, but he finally nodded and said, "Why not?"

Gus said, "The next valley's a steep one, but there is a good bear trail."

Gus's trail took Nick's breath away. Clinging to the side of the canyon wall the way it did, she thought it more fit for mountain goats than bears. But it served its purpose; it got them onto the snowfield quickly enough. This time, the metal detectors didn't produce so much as a tremor.

By the time they were in position to tackle the third valley, Nick was full of self-doubt. What if the plane was buried too deeply? When she'd failed to get a reply from Barlow as to the composition of the ice, she'd omitted the low frequency ground radar from her list. It's too late for regrets, she told herself. She changed the batteries in both detectors and then tested them to make certain that they were operating correctly.

"There's nothing wrong with the magnetometers," she told the others. "Our sites are bad, that's all."

"Or maybe we should be using low-frequency ground sonar like the kind that found the Lost Squadron," Hurst called out.

Nick ground her teeth but said nothing.

"We have two hours of daylight left and you're tired," Gus said. "You should leave the next valley until tomorrow."

Hallelujah, she thought. The man was human.

"Then again," the Inuit added, "the next valley is the one where I would land if I were a pilot."

"Why didn't you say so before?" Nick said.

"Would you have skipped the other two if I had?"

"Probably not," Nick admitted. "If I don't keep moving, I'll never make it. Come on, Mike, if you're up to it, let's finish and go home."

"I've shot all my film," Tyler wailed. "You've got to wait until tomorrow."

What a relief, Nick thought. The constant requests of the cameraman had been getting on her nerves. "We can do a re-creation, if we find anything," she snapped to shut him up.

By the time they descended onto the snowfield's icy crust, the temperature was dropping with the sun and the wind started gusting.

"We must start back in thirty minutes even if you haven't covered all the ground. The return trip isn't going to be any easier, or faster, and none of you are as fresh as you were this morning."

"What about yourself?" Nick asked.

"When one is born Inuit, one learns how to walk. But even I could not carry you back, if you broke an ankle in the dark."

"A half hour it is," Nick said.

They started their search at the top of the ravine, where the snow ran up against the mountain itself, and worked their way downhill. Nick and Barlow swept the snow from side to side, while Hurst, Tyler, and Gus followed in their wake. The cameraman kept up a steady stream of complaints about the shots that he was missing. They'd reached the halfway point when time ran out.

"Time's up," Gus announced.

Nick nodded, though she dreaded making the return trip tomorrow with so little ground remaining to be covered. But Gus was right. Traveling in the dark wasn't worth the risk.

Sighing, she made one last sweep and got a solid reading.

"I've found something," she shouted, expanding her search area by a step. The reading grew more intense. She backed away and signaled Barlow to give it a try. His metal detector confirmed her find.

"Is this it?" Gus asked. "Have you found it?"

Nick looked up and down the snowfield. A desperate pilot would certainly aim dead center in his landing zone, which was just about where they stood. "There's no way of telling until we start digging," she said calmly, though her heart was pounding with excitement at the prospect of what tomorrow might bring.

Hurst snorted. "If we're unlucky, we might find gold."

15

The following morning the expedition started out at first light. The group was augmented by Alcott. Royce, Ivins, and Erickson remained behind under the watchful eye of Ranger Kelly, who'd kept Nick up the night before, lecturing her on camp-site management in the refuge, which also applied to dig sites. "Even if your airplane is recovered," he'd told her, "the site will have to be restored. All signs of digging have to be erased." She'd intended to do that anyway.

Looking at the site again, she understood why he was so protective. Yesterday, the valley of snow lay pristine and untouched. Today it was littered with footprints. An hour from now, it would be gouged with trenches.

Their cause was good, she reminded

herself, the rescue of a piece of history. But first she had to reconfirm the Bloodhound's reading.

One sweep told her that she was on the money, though she told herself not to get too excited. Hurst's joke about gold might have been prophetic. Even so, her instincts had her trembling in expectation.

Forcing herself to breathe deeply, Nick scanned the immediate area. The readings matched the size of a single-engine airplane. At the point where the readings were strongest, she drove a peg into the snow.

"Mike," she called, "double-check me on this."

"No," Alcott insisted. "Let Gordon do it."

Unwillingly, Nick backed off far enough for Hurst to survey the area with his Bloodhound.

"We're on target," he reported, grinning for the camera.

Together, they marked off a square, pegging each corner and then stringing colored tape to outline their proposed dig site. Tyler filmed their every move, while the rest looked on.

"What now?" Hurst asked.

"We start trenching around the perimeter and then work our way toward the point where we got our strongest readings, probably the engine and fuselage. By coming in from the sides, we avoid damaging the plane any more than absolutely necessary."

"You're sure it's here, then?"

"I won't be sure until I see it," she said.

"How long will it take your way?" Alcott said.

"We're in luck there. The warm weather has melted the top layer of ice so we'll be digging through relatively soft snow." She dipped into the snow at her feet. "Slush is more like it. With any luck, I'll know where we stand by the end of the day."

"How deep are you going to have to dig?"

"That's hard to say. Since we got a reading with the magnetometers our target can't be buried too deeply. Let's hope we don't have to hack our way through compacted ice."

"Wouldn't it be faster to drill an exploratory hole where your metal detector was most active?" Alcott persisted.

"That sounds like a good idea to me," Hurst added.

Nick concentrated on holding on to her temper. "Doctor Alcott, who knows how fragile our Val might be after so many years?"

"Time could be a factor if the weather changes," Alcott said.

"Look at the sky," Nick said. "Not a cloud in sight." Out of the corner of her eye, she saw Gus smile. "Wouldn't you agree, Gus?"

"I think you'll do what you want," the Inuit replied.

Oh, thanks a lot, Nick thought. She'd have to go for a compromise. "Mike, dig us a test hole in one corner. Let's see exactly what we're going to be up against."

Barlow went to work without a word. The snow was much softer and much wetter than Nick had anticipated. As a result each shovelful was heavy and hard to shift. After two feet without hitting ice, Nick stopped him. The sooner they got that plane out, the better. Water would be trickling down through the melting snow, causing erosion. There was a real possibility that they would not be able to extricate the plane. If that happened, the plane would be immersed in water that would refreeze when winter came. By next year the Val might not be worth salvaging. Perhaps it was already too late.

"That's far enough," Nick told Barlow. "We'll risk going in right on top of the airplane."

"It's your dime," he said.

Normally, she would have insisted on a slow, methodical excavation. But she was under the gun in more ways than one. Not only was the weather against her, but she was low woman on the museum's totem pole. And there was also E-Group's investment to think about. Worse yet, any mistake she made was being filmed for PBS. If she wasn't standing on top of the Val, TV land would see her wasting time over a mere mineral deposit, which wouldn't help her reputation any.

Stop, she told herself. Do your job and to hell with the consequences. The trouble was, the Val had already crash-landed once, so there was no telling how much of it would be salvageable after all these years. She groaned silently. It was a no-win situation.

"The airplane will have to be restored anyway," she said to no one particular.

Blasphemy! she could hear her father saying. Had she uttered such a remark in one of Elliot's classes he would have flunked her. But then, thousand-year-old Anasazi pots were beyond restoration.

As she and Barlow dug, the hole had to be constantly enlarged the deeper they went. It was a slow, tedious process of digging a little and then spending a great deal of effort tamping down the loose snow. To pass the time as she was pressing the snow against the side of the pit, Nick said to Barlow, "Tell me about your thesis work."

"If you don't mind, I'd rather not talk about it," he replied.

Nick knew how competitive the academic world was and how ideas often get stolen, but she was disappointed that Barlow didn't trust her.

"However," he continued, "I wouldn't mind talking about you." He thrust his body next to hers against the wall of the pit.

Nick felt he was a little closer than the work required. "I think you'd better dig while I pack," she said stiffly.

He grinned at her and Nick had to admit to herself that there probably was a good-looking man lurking beneath the adolescent fuzz all over his face.

"Okay, Boss lady." He moved away and resumed digging.

By the time they reached six feet down, the pit was nearly as wide as it was deep. Even then, it was barely large enough for two people to work side by side. To reach that depth, they'd switched teams twice, with Gus and Hurst pitching in. After that, Gus worked on his own, spelling Nick and Barlow. Even Tyler stopped filming after a while to lend a hand. He was in the hole with Gus, helping to shovel snow into one of the canvas bags they'd brought along to used as buckets, when the Inuit's shovel struck metal.

"Out!" Nick commanded. "Both of you."

The moment the two men scrambled from the hole, Nick

eased into the pit and went down on her knees, using her hands to scoop away the snow. Her gloved fingers touched metal. She held her breath and dug carefully.

"It's a wing," she announced a moment later. "We've found our Val. Judging by the shape of it, I think we're close to the fuselage, no more than a foot away."

"How does it look?" Hurst asked.

"See for yourself." She backed against the edge of the pit.

Hurst whistled.

"Like brand new," Alcott said.

"We're lucky. By next year global warming would have exposed the site. After that, the Val would decompose quickly."

Nick radioed base camp to report their find, then sagged against the snow wall, suddenly exhausted. She dug an energy bar from her pocket, then she caught herself. *Never eat on site* was one of her father's ten commandments. Eating led to littering or worse yet, crumbs and morsels left behind for scavengers, who'd been known to wreak havoc on many a dig site.

She stuffed the bar back into her pocket and reached for one of the handholds they'd cleared in the snow. Gus leaned over and grabbed her arms. The Inuit lifted her out of the pit as if she weighed nothing.

"How much light do we have left?" she asked, retrieving an energy bar and taking a bite.

Gus looked at the sky.

"It's noon," he said.

Alcott looked at his watch. "The man's right," he said.

"If we all work together," Nick said, "we should be able to uncover most of the plane by dark."

"Look at yourself," Alcott said. "You're done in."

"I'm fine," she assured him, cramming the last of her bar into her mouth.

She glared at Hurst. "What about you?"

Hurst inspected his hands, but kept them to himself. "I'll do my part."

Barlow, she knew, was a professional.

"Mister Tyler?" she probed.

"I guess I can keep on digging, but I'm missing some great shots." He sounded done-in.

"A well-shot documentary on PBS will enhance the museum's stature," Alcott interposed.

And do wonders for its fund-raising, Nick added to herself. "I think you'd better stick to your job," she told the cameraman. "Gus, leave this to me and Mike. We'll keep on working here while you escort Doctor Alcott and Mister Hurst back to camp."

"I told you, I'd do my share," Hurst objected.

"I know that, Gordon, but if your hands get any worse, you'll be useless."

Gus shook his head. "My orders are to keep everyone together."

"Why don't we all go back," Alcott suggested. "Now that we know the Val's here, I should let the outside world know." He stamped his feet in the snow. "Besides, it's starting to get cold."

Nick hadn't noticed in the excitement. But he was right. The wind was picking up, and with it the chill factor. The only way to keep warm was to dig. "Gus thinks bad weather is coming. Isn't that right?"

The Inuit nodded.

"So," Nick went on, "if we continue to dig you can go back and get Mister Ivins to make arrangements for the chopper tomorrow." Nick shivered in the wind. "Gus, what kind of weather will we have tomorrow?"

"It will hold."

"There, you see," Alcott said. "There's no need to suffer out here."

She nodded at Barlow. Together, they dropped back into the hole.

"This is the only place around here that's out of the wind," she said. "I suggest the rest of you head back to camp and get yourself something hot to drink."

Gus stepped to the edge of the pit and glared down at her. "You are a very stubborn woman."

"You should meet my father."

"Just be here when I get back." He shouldered one Blood-hound; Hurst took the other. Tyler hesitated and then said, "I think I've already got the most important shots." He shouldered the camera and followed after the others.

"We need to keep warm," Nick said. "Let's enlarge the excavation along the wing."

"I can think of other ways to keep warm," Barlow replied.

Nick ignored him and started to dig. There obviously was a side to Mike Barlow's personality that Elliot had never been exposed to. She was relieved when he joined her at what she considered a safe distance.

Nick's initial estimate had been correct. They'd dug their pit within inches of the fuselage.

By the time Gus returned, they'd uncovered six feet of the fuselage and with it the rear half of the cockpit, which was filled with snow. A cannon shell had blown away much of the Plexiglas. What glass remained was pock-marked with bullet holes, just as Erickson had remembered.

Gus joined in, hauling out buckets of snow as Nick cleared the rear-gunner's position. Within minutes, her fingers found what she hadn't been expecting, the gunner's body, in remarkable condition considering how long it had been there.

"We'd better get him out before he starts to defrost," she said.

"Look at your breath," Gus said. "It's getting colder. He won't be defrosting today."

Nick blew, clouding the air. "Tomorrow, then."

"I wonder why the pilot left him sitting here?" Barlow said.

"Maybe he didn't have a choice," Gus answered, nodding to the peak looming above them. "There's a mountain sits on top of this place."

"Yes, you're right," Nick said, rummaging in the snow until she found a small tree branch that had been wedged into the cockpit. "This plane was buried by an avalanche. We were lucky. It kept our artifact in a deep freeze for more than fifty years."

"And the pilot?" Barlow asked.

"He wasn't so lucky," she said.

Gus snorted. "That would depend on whether the avalanche killed him or the bears did."

16

The moment they abandoned the dig and started back to camp, exhaustion threatened to overwhelm Nick. Until then, the excitement of her find had her running on full adrenaline. Now, every muscle in her body ached from hours of digging, most of it while stooping over. Her hands were numb with cold, her feet worse, as if they'd frozen into blocks of ice. Barlow didn't look any better. Gus was impossible to read.

They'd all worked nonstop until they'd uncovered the entire fuselage. Tomorrow, all that remained was to free the wings and possibly the undercarriage, if any of it had survived. Then all they had to do was coordinate with the chopper to carry their trophy back to Anchorage. One more day of pushing herself, one more day of hiking back and forth across a rocky plain worthy of Dante's vision of hell.

Collapse felt imminent when Nick smelled smoke, and for an instant she wondered if hell wasn't closer than she'd imagined. Then she raised her head to see their campfire blazing less than a hundred yards away. With the smoke came the smell of hot food.

"I hope Kelly has relented," Gus said.

"About what?"

Gus, who was leading the way, stopped so suddenly she walked into him. "He is terribly upset with us. With me for leaving you two alone out there, and with you for asking me to do it. I told him it was the right thing to do in the circumstances, but Kelly is like a big brother when it comes to his refuge. He's very protective."

"I feel the same way about my dig sites," she said. "Now, let's get moving. I need to put my feet up in front of that fire."

"That makes two of us," Barlow echoed.

Applause greeted them when they walked into camp. Ivins and Erickson led the tribute, though Kelly, Nick noticed, kept his arms folded over his chest. Hurst wasn't clapping either, but then he was probably suffering from the blisters Nick suspected he had developed. Her boss, Alcott, was smiling gleefully. As an afterthought, he snapped her a thumbs-up, something she hadn't expected from someone so proper. Of course, there was Tyler filming their return.

The moment Erickson stopped applauding, he rushed forward to hug her, practically enveloping her in his parka. "You've made an old man very happy," he said into her ear.

"Your memories made it possible." Over his shoulder, she saw Gus and Kelly huddling off to one side. Judging by the look on Kelly's face, he didn't like what Gus was saying.

"And my pilot?" Erickson said, stepping to watch her reaction. "Did you find him?"

"Not yet, but his rear gunner was there, still strapped in his seat."

The old man's shoulder's slumped. "He's got to be near by. It's impossible that he walked out."

Nick had been thinking about the pilot on the walk back. Considering the mentality of Japanese officers during World War II, suicide seemed a distinct possibility, assuming the avalanche hadn't killed him. A traditional suicide, with its inevitable smell of blood would have attracted bears, just as Gus had suggested. Even without blood, exposed bodies didn't last long in the wilderness.

"Will you keep looking for him?" Erickson asked, then shook his head. "I'm sorry. I realize that's not practical. I guess I was hoping he'd be in the cockpit, keeping company with his gunner. But considering how brave that man was, he probably did try to walk out of here. I would have."

Erickson took a deep breath before adding, "He'd want us to bury his gunner."

"Of course." Nick dug into her pocket. "I found the gunner's identity disk." She handed it to Erickson. "We'll send it to the Japanese government."

Ivins cleared his throat. "While you were out there making us all famous, Ms. Scott, I spoke to Jon McKenna, E-Group's chairman." Ivins brandished his cell phone. "He sends you his congratulations on a job well done."

"There's a lot of work left to do."

"The plane's there. What else do we need to know?"

Nick was about to point out any number of complications when she spotted Alcott fidgeting to catch her attention.

She took his cue. "The museum is fully aware that Mister McKenna's generosity has made this possible."

That appeared to make Alcott happy.

Ivins dismissed her comment with a casual wave of his phone. "I know for a fact that Mister McKenna is a man who believes in rewarding favors properly."

Alcott, still smiling, said, "The museum is always appreciative of Mister McKenna's efforts on our behalf."

"He gave me the distinct impression," Ivins went on, "that he's intending a reward beyond anything you ever imagined."

"Excuse me!" Kelly said loudly as he approached them where they were gathered around the fire. "There're a few things to be considered before congratulations are in order. For one thing, Gus tells me we've got a body on our hands." He glared at Nick. "Is that right, Doctor Scott?"

"You knew we were looking for an airplane that had crashed with its crew."

"I expected the bodies to be long gone, eaten."

Erickson winced.

"Now that you've got one," Kelly continued, "you can't just bury it. Burials in national parks require permits, which are seldom granted, I might add, and never in this refuge. Otherwise, we'd have bodies all over the place."

"He was already buried," Nick told him.

"Until you dug him up. Now he's your responsibility."

"Why not blame the Japanese?" she shot back. "Or Mr. Erickson here?"

Alcott stepped in. "We all work for the government, Mister Kelly. It's merely a matter of sorting through the red tape."

"There're the bears to be considered," Kelly persisted. "You left an exposed body out there. What happens if they get to it? How do I explain that?"

"I'm sorry," Nick said. "I didn't consider that." She'd been too tired, she realized now, to think straight, too cold, too tired, and too excited by her find. "I'll take full responsibility if something happens to the body."

"I doubt if the Japanese government will raise a fuss after all these years," Alcott said.

Nick hoped he was right. When it came to bodies, archaeologists had to walk a fine line. Thousand-year-old bodies usually were fair game. Bodies a few hundred years old, especially among the Indians, tended to have descendants still living, many of whom took delight in calling archaeologists nothing but grave robbers. Dead less than a century old were definitely taboo.

Next to Nick, Erickson hugged himself. "It makes me cold thinking of him alone out there."

"We left him in the cockpit," she told him. "That should afford some protection."

"Not good enough," the ranger said. "Someone will have to go out there and bury him. Me!"

Gus laid a restraining hand on Kelly. "Let it go, Terry. You know I won't let you go alone, not in the dark. If we go together, who'll watch over these folks?"

"I could order you to stay behind," Kelly told him.

The Inuit smiled indulgently. "You could."

The ranger shook his head in obvious frustration.

"My mother told me a story about the mountains here," Gus said, "the mountains where old sins cast long shadows, she called them." He nodded to himself. "That body has been there since before we were born, yet its shadow touches us all."

More shaman-speak, Nick told herself, but that didn't stop gooseflesh from crawling up her spine.

17

Duffy followed the bobbing lights to where a small knot of men were huddled in consultation. His companions from the handcar were long gone.

Coughing, Duffy put down his own lantern and pulled out his notepad and pencil. "I'm here to cover the wreck."

"More like a disaster," one of the men told him.

"Tell me what happened."

"You'll have to ask the brass."

"Who's in charge?" Duffy asked.

"If you find out, let us know." The man turned away.

"Is it okay if I take a look for myself?" Duffy said.

"Just stay out of the way. We've still got people trapped in here."

As Duffy inched his way along the tunnel, his sweat turned cold. Hair prickled on the back of his neck. He grabbed his flask to ward off the chill but stopped halfway to his mouth when he realized what had spooked him. It was that sound again. The one he'd first heard and pushed out of his consciousness. Dear God, he thought, that can't be coming from human throats.

Louder cries, unintelligible but frantic, boomed down the tunnel, breaking the spell. A moment later a BRT workman stumbled down the line at a dead run, waving a lantern.

"Cut the power, for God's sake!" he shouted.

"It's off," someone shouted back.

"Some bastard turned it on again. People are being electrocuted in there."

"I'll take care of it," a voice roared back and Duffy saw a light bob back up the line.

The BRT worker who'd sounded the alarm disappeared back along the tunnel. Duffy looked around, expecting to see action, but no one was taking charge.

To hell with them, he thought, this was the biggest story of his life. He took a deep breath and ran toward what he thought was the wreck, following the bobbing lantern light and praying to God he didn't step on the third rail.

Abruptly, the lantern disappeared. Duffy lurched to a stop, his hand groping in the dark. When his fingers touched concrete, he sighed with relief and flattened himself against the wall. Without thinking, he started edging back the way he'd come.

Then he heard the sounds, picks and shovels. He felt the vibration through the wall, too. If men were working, there had to be light somewhere. With clenched teeth, he reversed direction, shuffling toward the sounds, keeping his back to the wall. Sporadically, men's shouts echoed through the tunnel. Once, he thought he heard a woman scream.

The moment he felt the tunnel begin to curve, he saw the light, dim at first, but growing with every shuffling step. He pushed away from the wall and picked up his pace.

A few yards later the curve ended and there, in the light from dozens of lanterns, Duffy saw the wreck. If that mound of wood and splinters had once been a subway train it was now impossible to tell. Men, a small army of them, were trying to clear a path through the debris.

God in heaven, he thought, what was that smell? Even as the question flashed in his mind he knew the answer: burning flesh. He gagged. Some reporter. By force of will he hurried ahead, sticking close to the wall.

"The power's on," someone shouted at him.

"They're on their way to turn it off," he yelled back but kept well clear of the electric rail.

"Hey, you. Watch where you step."

Jesus, the mound of rubble he'd been about to step over was a body, or pieces of one anyway. Duffy swallowed hard and stepped over the third rail to get around it.

"Are you going to just stand there?" a workman yelled from where he was sitting with his back braced against the tunnel wall. One of his shoes was off, his ankle obviously broken. His knees were bloody and his hands even bloodier. A lantern stood beside him.

"I'm a reporter," Duffy answered.

"Who gives a fuck?"

Duffy hesitated. His editor was waiting for a story. If Duffy didn't deliver, he'd be out of work.

"What do you want me to do?" Duffy said.

"Look for survivors."

"In there?" Duffy asked incredulously, nodding at the mass of splintered wood and glass shards that had once been a rail car.

"You have to climb over it, for Christ's sake. What are you anyway, deaf?"

Before Duffy could answer, the man added, "You'll hear them when you get closer." He tilted his head to one side as if listening. "Screaming for help or to be put out of their misery."

Duffy took the man's lantern and moved, doing his best to pick his way through the razor-sharp glass shards and splintered wood. But soon he had no choice but to scramble on his hands and knees, dragging the lantern and clenching his teeth in agony as splinters ripped his flesh. Around him, other men were making their way over the twisted wreckage.

God, what had he been thinking? Report the news, that was his job, not participate in it. And how the hell was he going to write if his fingers were cut to hell? Dictate it to Newmark, that's what. And then Newmark would share the byline. Duffy groaned at the thought of it, but kept on going.

His groan was answered by a woman. "Please, help me." It seemed no more than a whisper, and for a moment he thought he was imagining things.

He froze in place and raised the lantern, which swung back and forth on its handle, casting shadows that slithered over the mangled wreckage.

"Where are you?" he called.

"I'm buried under something," she answered. "But I can see your light."

She sounded close by, to his right.

"Are you hurt?"

"I think my arm is broken. I can't feel my legs. Maybe they're broken too. I'm trapped, I can't move at all."

"Watch my light. I'm going to move toward you." He edged to his right, but no matter how slowly he moved debris shifted beneath his weight.

"My name's Ned. What's yours?" He held his breath, waiting for her answer.

"Mary."

A little more to the right, he thought. "Keep talking, Mary, so I can find you."

"Now I lay me down to sleep," she said, almost a sob.

Definitely to the right, but to get there, he'd have to climb over a mass of twisted rails.

"If I should die before I wake," she continued, "I pray the Lord my soul to take."

Duffy sucked in a deep breath, grabbed hold of a knife-sharp edge, and pulled himself over the obstacle.

Mary screamed.

He froze in place. "What's wrong?"

She gasped, "You're . . ."

Dear God, she sounded directly beneath him. Keeping as still as possible, he moved the lantern back and forth.

"Mary, do you see the light?"

She didn't answer.

He set the lantern to one side, and began digging. His fingers, fit for nothing more strenuous than writing, were no match for the splintered wood and glass as he tunneled into the rubble. He clenched his teeth until he thought they'd shatter. It was either that or scream. But somehow, he kept digging, the sound of her prayer echoing inside him, spurring him on.

He didn't realize he'd touched her until she said, "Ned, I can see you."

When he saw her face, his pain no longer mattered.

18

With a hot meal in her stomach and her feet roasting in front of the fire, Nick felt like a new person. She also felt foolish for allowing herself to be spooked by a fireside ghost story, which was all Gus's talk about old sins and long shadows amounted to. No doubt he and Ranger Kelly had planned it together, so they could get a good laugh out of frightening the tourists.

Speak of the devil, she thought, as Kelly and Gus reappeared in the firelight. They'd been out scouting the perimeter, or so they'd said, but she couldn't help imagining them marking the trees like territorial dogs. Moving in unison, they sat on either side of her.

"We wanted to speak with you privately," Kelly said, hanging his hat on his knee.

Not knowing what to expect, Nick pasted a smile on her face and said nothing.

Kelly continued. "I owe you an apology. I came on a little strong earlier. By uncovering that body, you were only doing your job."

"And you were doing yours," she said. "No harm done."

"The thing is, Gus and I have been talking. You seem to be the only one here with any kind of real experience."

Nick didn't know what he was getting at, but the last thing she needed was to get in the middle of some political feud.

"Doctor Alcott is my boss," she reminded him. "He's in charge of this expedition. If it's a decision you want, talk to him, not me."

"Not the money man?" Kelly said, nodding in Ivins's direction.

"His company is our sponsor, if that's what you mean. The expedition is strictly a Smithsonian operation."

Gus clicked his tongue. "Money talks, but the blood talks stronger. See for yourself." He was looking directly at Ivins, who was by the cooking stove with his arm around the doctor's shoulder.

"They both work for E-Group. They've probably known each other for a long time," Nick said.

As she spoke, Ivins and Dr. Royce snuggled together.

"On a cold night like this, sharing a sleeping bag is a good way to keep warm," Gus said.

Kelly fidgeted. "Let's stick to the point. We came to you, Ms. Scott, because we think you have your head screwed on straight."

"Thank you, I think."

"While you were out there digging today," Kelly continued, ignoring her sarcasm, "I kept an eye on you through the binoculars. Once I caught a glimpse of bears."

"Where?" Nick said.

"In the rocks. I lost sight of them after a few moments, but I had the feeling they were following your trail."

"It could be they were heading for the high country," Gus

put in, "and we just happened to be in their way. If they'd been tracking us, we'd have seen a sign of them by now."

"I hope you're right," Kelly said to Gus. He paused, then hesitantly said, "Doctor Scott, I respect you enough that I think you won't mind if I ask you if you or the doctor are, uh, if this is a special time of month for either of you ladies." Nick was amused that the ranger had turned a bright beet red.

"I'm sorry," Nick said. "I can't speak for Doctor Royce but I can assure you I'm not in that part of the estrous cycle."

"Bears are highly sensitive to the smell of blood," Gus added.

"You act like they might attack," Nick said.

Kelly shook his head. "They never have, not here in the refuge. But there was a case in Yellowstone. For sure, they know we're here. That's the problem." Kelly toyed with his hat. "Bears are unpredictable. If they take it into their minds to come into camp, we'll have to abandon the site."

"You just said they won't attack."

"I said they haven't so far. But that's not the issue. This refuge exists for one reason, to ensure the survival of the Hammersmith's bear. Here, as I told you before, they have the absolute right-of-way. Should they want this site, we'll have to move."

"That's crazy."

The ranger shifted his hat from one knee to the other. "Surely, you wouldn't want to further endanger a species already on the verge of extinction."

"I was thinking of scaring them away, not shooting them."

Gus snorted. "She's got you there, Terry."

"We have our orders," Kelly persisted.

"She does work for the Smithsonian," Gus reminded him. "So maybe we can bend the rules."

Kelly opened his mouth as if to object, then broke into a grin. "If you say so, but just how do you suggest we go about scaring them?"

"Sometimes loud noises will scare a bear," Gus said. "Sometimes a bear is scared of nothing. *Siudleratuin* is not afraid."

"Here we go," Kelly said. "I'd better warn you in advance, Ms. Scott. Gus's name, Auqusinauq, means teller of myths. Teller of tall tales is more like it, if you ask me."

"You may call my stories myths if you want, but what I tell you now is true. Once, long ago, but not so long that a man's lifetime wouldn't stretch that far, my people came to a place like this." With one arm, he gestured expansively. "They built a village despite the warnings of a wise old man, whose memory went back before long ago, to when he'd found what he called the book of the dead. 'I found it,' he counseled them, 'very near here. Here, the dead come alive and walk.' But the old man's eyesight was failing, so the people thought he couldn't tell one place from another and they ignored him and built their village. But no sooner was it finished than people began to sicken and die.

"A meeting was called and the people gathered together to ask the old man's advice. 'What can we do?' they asked him. 'Nothing,' he told them. 'It is too late.'

" 'We can leave,' they said. 'We can go back to where we came from.'

"The old man shook his head. 'We have come to a place where the spirits of the dead, the *Siudleratuin* walk,' he told them. 'And we haven't come by chance. The *Siudleratuin* lured us here, so they wouldn't be alone. They want our spirits to walk with them.' "

Gus paused, nodding to himself.

"And?" Nick prompted.

"They died and walk here still."

"If they all died," she said, "no one would have been left to tell the tale."

"She has you there," Kelly said, nodding at Nick.

Gus tilted his head to one side and clicked his tongue. "The dead crave company."

"I suppose you mean us?" Nick said.

The Inuit shrugged. "Your airplane. Perhaps they lured it here to crash and keep them company."

"I'm not a tourist, Gus," she said. "Your story doesn't scare me. I've been hearing ones just like it all my life from my father."

The Inuit stared up at the star-filled night. "My people have a saying. One is not alone. Always remember that, Ms. Scott."

With that, he got to his feet. After a moment's hesitation, Kelly stood and said, "Don't let Gus worry you. He and I will stand a bear watch tonight. Sleep well," with that the pair of them crossed the fire-cast terminator and disappeared into the night.

"One is not alone," Nick murmured to herself, but decided not to dismiss it as more of Gus's cryptic shaman-speak. A people like the Inuit, who lived and hunted in a desolate, arctic wilderness, needed to believe they weren't alone. Just as we all do, Nick reminded herself as the spill-gate opened and a flash flood of memory washed over her.

"I'm always alone," her mother had complained so often it had become her mantra. Usually, it marked the beginning of one of Elaine's black moods of depression. During those times, she seldom left her bed, surrendering everything, housework and cooking, to Nick.

"Alone, alone," she'd croon from her bed. "Your father knows I'm afraid to be alone, but still he leaves me. He runs away from me like you do, Nicolette."

"I always come back, mother." Usually Nick ran only as far as her father's office on campus.

"That's because you have nowhere to go."

"Elliot comes back, too."

"Only so he can leave me alone again," Elaine answered. "One day I won't be here when he comes back."

How could she leave, Nick had wanted to ask, if she never left her bed? But she'd kept the question to herself.

"When I'm dead he'll be sorry," Elaine said. "You, too, my girl. You'll all be sorry."

"Yes, mother."

"Don't you want to know why I'll be dead?"

"No."

"Do you ever wonder what it's like to be dead?" Elaine asked.

Nick had fled her mother's bedroom and then the house,

though her father was beyond reach on one of his Anasazi digs. Even so, she was determined to run away until dinnertime at least. But where to go? She'd come away with no money, so there was nothing to do but walk. The park was close by, but Elaine had warned her about going there on her own, especially now that she was nearly a woman, as her mother put it.

Three blocks from home, Nick saw Billy Meeks working on his car. At least, those were his legs, encased in grimy jeans, protruding from beneath his old Ford convertible. He was two years ahead of her in junior high, too young to drive legally, and the envy of the student body because of his car.

Rumor had it that he had once served jail time for car theft. Whether Elaine had heard the rumor Nick didn't know, but Billy and his friends were definitely on Elaine's list of undesirables. Nick hadn't believed the stories until she'd overheard Billy in the cafeteria, boasting that he could hot-wire any car ever made.

She was about to pass by when he slid out from under the car and sat up. "I saw you coming, kid."

He looked her up and down, stopping at her bare legs, which pleased and embarrassed her at the same time.

"I'd take you for a ride," he added, winking, "but I've got to get this baby ready for a hot date tonight."

Nick glanced toward the house and was relieved to see Billy's mother watching them from the window. Nick waved.

"Look at her," Billy said. "The old lady loves spying on me."

So did Elaine, Nick thought, but this was one time she took comfort from such company. Besides, the sight of Billy had given her an idea. She said, "Some of the kids at school say you hot-wire cars."

"Why are you asking, kid?"

Because she had a plan. "Most of us don't believe it."

"Believe it, kid. But hot-wiring ain't easy like you see in the movies. You don't just twist a screwdriver in the ignition. But if I can pop open the hood, I can start anything."

"Could you teach me how?"

"Why would I do that, kid?"

"Because I'll pay you," Nick said, already imagining herself hot-wiring Elaine's car, which seldom left the garage, and driving away to meet her father.

"How much?" he asked.

Nick had twenty dollars saved to buy her next model airplane. "Twenty dollars."

"Christ, kid, if you were a little older, I'd make you pay on your back. Now, beat it."

Nick's face flushed, but she didn't back off. "I was right, you don't know how."

"Look, kid, why would you want to hot-wire a car anyway?"

She glanced at the house again. "To get away from my mother."

Billy stared at her for a long time. "Okay, kid," he said finally, "just don't tell anybody where you learned how."

"I promise," she said, crossing her heart.

She had kept that promise, too, when the police arrested her for driving Elaine's car without a license.

Nick shook her head at the memory and headed for her tent. As she was about to zip herself inside, she saw Gus silhouetted in the moonlight, standing bear watch.

19

The great bear stood perfectly still. Behind her, her cubs did the same. There was no restlessness this time. They sensed her caution, her alertness, and sat quietly, though their noses twitched expectantly at the delicious smells coming from the camp. The fire fascinated them, as did the men sitting around it. But the great female knew better. Men could bring food or death. It was a lesson her cubs had yet to learn.

She moved closer to her cubs, aware of their growing restlessness. Soon the smell of food would get the better of them and they would risk foraging near the men. She couldn't allow that. Not yet, not until an opportunity presented itself.

She snarled, little more than a whisper in the night, and her cubs hunkered close to the ground to wait. After a time, the fire burned low and the men, all but one, disappeared into their tents. And still she waited, until the embers died away and the man vanished into the shadows. He remained, though. Her nose told her that. She'd smelled him before, though never this close to her den. The familiarity of his smell reassured her. Her ears told her he was still awake.

If the camp was to be entered and food found, now was the time. The men, even the one she recognized, might never hear her or her cubs. She tensed her muscles, weighing the danger. His smell had never brought harm before, and the promise of food was so tantalizing.

She was about to move forward when the man moved. He was coming her way. Probably, he would never see her in the dark, not as long as she remained perfectly quiet. But she didn't dare put the cubs to such a test.

She backed away, signaling the cubs to follow. Men were careless. Sooner or later, they'd leave their food unprotected.

20

Ivins was miserable. His idea of roughing it was a Holiday Inn. He hated creeping out in the dark. Anything could be out there. He decided to risk taking the Glock. More firepower would have been nice on a moonless night like this, but the assault rifles had to stay hidden for the time being. Still, he didn't like the idea of going up against anything really large with a mere nine-millemeter pistol, even one that held seventeen parabellum rounds in the clip.

Think about the money, he told himself. Millions. That was worth taking one hell of a risk. Besides, he wasn't going far. All he needed was enough distance to give himself a little privacy. He'd keep the firelight in sight at all times. That way there was absolutely no chance of getting lost.

He sauntered over to the last Ford Excursion in line. Once there, he pretended to examine the satellite dish on the roof, even though he knew it was working perfectly. Hell, that was the first thing he'd tested. Finally, moving casually, he opened the car's rear door and made a show of rummaging around.

When a glance over his shoulder showed him no one was paying the slightest attention, he triggered the mechanism, popping open one of the hidden panels in the door. Inside was a Glock and two fully loaded magazines. Each Ford had a similar cache. To get the Ford's assault rifles, he'd need time and a screwdriver. Besides, how tough could a bear be? Seventeen rounds of nine-millimeter ought to knock down just about anything.

He stashed the Glock inside his parka and leaned against the Ford, eyeballing the camp. No one was looking his way; no one had a clue.

Grinning, he ducked around the Ford and kept it between him and the campfire as he worked his way into the forest. Once out of earshot, he tested his cell phone–satellite connection. He smiled with relief at the dial tone. Technology was great as long as you had the big bucks to pay for it.

McKenna answered immediately. "Are we encrypted?"

"Yes, sir," Ivins answered.

"Even so, keep it simple. We don't want some Cal Tech hacker blackmailing us."

"Yes, sir. We've found our initial target."

"And?" McKenna demanded.

"It's just a matter of time. We don't have an exact coordinate, so it's hit-and-miss until we strike it rich."

"Any complications?"

"The park rangers are pretty damned hard-nosed about their rules and regulations, trying to keep us under their thumbs."

"I thought we'd planned on that contingency?"

"Yes, sir. But I thought it best to keep everyone sweet as long as possible."

"Your point's taken."

Ivins smiled and ducked his shoulders, making himself smaller, as if he were still in McKenna's presence.

"Anything else?" McKenna asked.

"Yeah, the weather."

"I don't understand. I've been keeping track of it here. It reads like you're on the beach in Miami."

"That's the trouble, sir. Our expert says the warm weather is thawing everything. You know what kind of exposure that means."

"You're paid to take risks."

"I'm not complaining for myself, but I thought you ought to know that we might have to go to one of our contingency plans."

"Keep the details to yourself. Just get the job done. Otherwise . . . you don't want to think about otherwise."

"Yes, sir," Ivins responded, but the connection had already been terminated. He bit his lip in frustration. What if it were already too late? There'd be no millions. All this would be for nothing. McKenna was back at corporate sitting in the center of his web like the bloated spider that he was. Let him wait for Jarvis. Ivins would do what was necessary.

21

Nick had intended to get an early start, hoping to have the Val fully uncovered and on its way back to Anchorage by the end of the day. But Wes Erickson made that impossible the moment he insisted on going along.

"I have to stand on the spot where they crashed," he announced just as Nick, Mike Barlow, and Gordon Hurst were about to leave for the site. "I must say a prayer where that brave pilot stood, saluting me as I flew overhead." The speech left him breathing through his mouth.

"I'll need a shot of that," Tyler, their cameraman said, and began strapping on his backpack.

Nick looked to Alcott for support but the curator just shrugged and concentrated on his coffee mug. Gus looked unconcerned. Kelly was nowhere to be seen.

"Doctor?" Nick said, seeking a second opinion.

Royce blandly replied, "I've just given Mr. Erickson a quick physical. For a man his age, he's in remarkable condition. I see no reason why a walk would harm him."

Nick couldn't believe her ears. She wasn't fooled by the old pilot's ramrod posture. As far as she was concerned it was pure bravado. His pallid, unshaven cheeks were the true measure of his stamina. What was the woman thinking? Then again, maybe she was right. Maybe exercise was the best tonic. Nick shook her head. The doctor didn't know what it was like out there.

"It's a hell of a long hike," Nick said to Erickson, trying to dissuade him. "Not to mention the return trip."

"I'd listen to her," Hurst chimed in. "It's no picnic."

Erickson shook his head. "A man my age doesn't get many second chances."

Ivins spoke up. "I think we have to remember that all of us here are in Mr. Erickson's debt. Without him, we wouldn't know about the Val."

Nick sighed. Taking him along would slow them up by an hour at least, but Ivins was right. The Val belonged to Erickson more than anyone else.

"At least the weather's holding," she said, eyeing the sky, which now had a scattering of high, harmless-looking clouds.

"Holding's hardly the word," Ivins responded. "It feels like summer."

Nick nodded at the Inuit. "What do you think, Gus?"

"Nearly fifty degrees, I'd say. Unusual for this time of year."

"Will it hold?"

He shrugged. "Yesterday, I would have bet on cold weather by today."

"We'd better get started, then."

Gus shook his head. "No can do. Kelly's out looking for bears and I have to stay with the camp."

"That's impossible," Nick protested. "We can't afford to waste the time."

"Do you think that you can you find your way?" Gus asked.

"Of course I can," Nick said. "I've been there twice."

"Kelly will be mad, but you can get a start. I expect him back any time now. It shouldn't be hard for me to catch up with you. That old man isn't going anywhere very fast."

"If it's me you're worried about," Erickson angrily interjected, "don't bother. I'll keep up."

"Let's go, then," she told him.

Twenty minutes later, Erickson had to stop to rest. After that, the intervals between rest stops slipped to ten minutes. Nick kept looking behind her for Gus's tall form, but he never showed up.

It was nearly noon before they reached the Val. By then the warm weather had done most of the work for them, melting the wings free of snow and exposing the ruined undercarriage.

The first thing that Nick noticed was that the remaining snow appeared trampled and the body of the gunner was missing.

"Where's the body?" Hurst muttered.

"Look at the snow, it's all churned up. There appear to be some drag marks further along the ravine."

She noticed that Barlow was already examining the sides of the ravine.

"Bears?" Hurst whispered.

Nick nodded, clenching her teeth and wondering if they should turn back. Kelly would be furious.

Erickson didn't seem to notice. He stepped close to the fuselage and ran his hand over the metal skin.

"Wait, Mister Erickson," Tyler called out. "Let me get the shot set up." Erickson obliged.

"Can you just put your hand out, like you did before?" Tyler continued.

Erickson smiled and stroked the plane. "The last time I saw this plane was on the film from my gun camera. This kill made me an ace, you know. They would have killed me if they'd gotten the chance."

Erickson smiled at Nick. His eyes shone. "Thank you for bringing me here, Miss Scott."

Before she could respond, the two-way radio clipped to her belt crackled to life.

"Nick!" a voice shouted. "Come in!"

"Go ahead," Nick answered, turning up the volume so everyone could hear.

"This is Alcott. We thought you ought to know that Kelly is missing, lost maybe."

"How could he get lost in his own park?" she asked, remembering that Gus had said Kelly was out reconnoitering for bears.

"All I know is that Kelly never came back. The Inuit went out looking for him, leaving the rest of us here on our own." Judging by the rising pitch of his voice, panic was just around the corner.

Nick looked at Hurst, who appeared as perplexed as she felt. What did Alcott expect her to do about the missing ranger?

But since he was her boss, she said, "Would you like us to come back."

"Gus told us to stay put here. He said he didn't want anybody else getting lost, especially with bad weather coming."

Nick jerked her head up, expecting storm clouds, but nothing had changed. What clouds there were looked benevolent enough. Hurst and Barlow looked at one another, mystified.

She said, "What did Gus say we should do?"

"Nothing."

"Then I think we'd better stay here, don't you?"

"I thought you ought to know, that's all," Alcott said, annoyance creeping into his voice.

"Let us know if anything changes," Nick said to placate him.

"He said something about spirits, too," Alcott added. Even through the radio's crackling static, the curator sounded spooked. "The spirits of the dead are definitely on the move, Gus told us."

Sure, Nick thought. What better way to keep tourists in line and afraid to wander off than to scare them with ghost stories. When she got back to Washington, she promised herself to research Gus's so-called *Siudleratuin*. Probably he was nothing more than the Inuit version of the Bogey Man.

"Don't worry, Doctor. We'll be back well before dark," she radioed.

"On second thought," he replied, "I think you ought to come back here immediately. There's safety in numbers."

"We've run into a bit of luck," she said to ease his mind. "The snow's melting fast. Because of it, we'll have the Val fully cleared in two hours, maybe a little less. We can be on our way home soon."

"The Inuit could be right about the weather," Alcott responded, "so I insist you bring Mr. Erickson back here to camp before anything happens."

"Give me that radio," Hurst said.

Nick hesitated and then handed it to him. He was as eager as she was to continue and Alcott seemed to respect his opinion more.

"Nick's right, Donald," Hurst shouted. "We're almost done here. Besides, Gus and Kelly could come back any minute. Then we'd be making the hike back for nothing."

"I'm alone, for Christ's sake."

"What?"

"Ivins and Doctor Royce went out looking for Gus and Kelly and left me alone."

"How long have Ivins and Royce been gone?" Hurst asked.

"Ten minutes this time."

"What do you mean, this time?" Nick said loud enough to be picked up by the radio.

"They were off somewhere when I woke up this morning."

"Stand by for a minute," Hurst said, turning to Nick. "What do you think?"

"I think Alcott should have stayed behind his desk in Washington," she answered.

"That's not helpful."

She looked at Barlow, who shrugged and said, "You're the boss."

Nick gestured at the cameraman. "What do you say?"

"Me?" Tyler shrugged. "Do what you want. I'll just keep filming."

Nick stared at the sky again, praying the weather would hold one more day. To Hurst she said, "If it stays this warm, most of our preliminary work will be done for us by tomorrow."

He looked at the sky and nodded. "I see what you mean. Besides, Alcott is your boss." He handed her the radio.

"We're on the way, Doctor Alcott," she transmitted.

"How soon will you be here?" Alcott asked.

"It took us two hours to get here this morning."

She glanced at Erickson, whose ashen face said he needed to rest, not walk. The old pilot forced a smile. "I'll do my best to keep up, Miss Scott."

"We'll keep you informed of our progress," she told Alcott, hoping that would keep him calm.

"Thank you, Nick," he answered. "Your father was right about you."

Christ, Nick thought, Elliot had meddled in her job hunt after all. If she hadn't been conserving her strength, she'd have raised hell.

22

She was the most beautiful girl, Ned Duffy thought, he'd ever laid eyes on. Even through the dirt and grime and blood her skin shone with a translucent whiteness that reminded him of his mother's face. A thick strand of auburn curl lay plastered to her badly cut cheek. Duffy wanted to kiss it. Instead he grabbed his flask and retrieved a handkerchief from his pocket. To his surprise it was clean. He soaked it with whiskey and dabbed the cloth on her lips. At the taste of alcohol, her eyelids fluttered.

"I need a stretcher here!" he shouted.

"Stretcher!" someone relayed down the subway tunnel, where rescue workers were digging frantically.

"Mary, can you move?" he asked,

afraid to touch her now that he'd cleared the debris from her body. His hands were bloody, the nails ripped from half his fingers.

She started to reach out to him and gasped in pain.

"I'll get help," he said. "Don't move."

"No," she said through her tears. "Don't leave me alone in the dark again."

"Where's that stretcher?" he screamed.

"Hold me," she whispered.

Gently, he laid his ruined hand on hers. Her skin felt icy. What if she was dying? What if he was killing her by not going for help?

He leaned close to her face. "Mary, I have to find you a doctor."

Her head shook ever so slightly. "It's only my arm. It feels like it's broken."

He looked down at her legs, realized her skirt had ridden up, and carefully covered her. She forced a smile, like that of an angel, he thought, and shifted her feet.

"Thank God," he breathed, remembering a man he'd once seen paralyzed when a streetcar ran over his spine.

Two men arrived carrying a stretcher, its canvas webbing bloody from previous use. Grime caked their sweating faces.

"Be careful," he told them. "She has a broken arm, maybe worse."

She fainted the moment they lifted her.

"It's for the best," one of them said.

"The longer, the better," the other one added.

Duffy started to scream at them, but realized they were right the moment they began picking their way through the rubble. With each step they took, the stretcher rocked her body back and forth. Had she been conscious the pain would have been excruciating.

He trotted alongside, trying to steady the stretcher, but without success. By the time they reached one of the waiting ambulances, the two bearers were staggering with exhaustion. The ambulance, with double tiers for two on each side, held four. Mary made three. The other two occupants were deathly silent.

"Are they dead?" Duffy asked.

"They weren't when we loaded them."

"How many runs have you made?" he said, thinking like a reporter again.

"Who knows? We lost count."

"Who drives?"

"We take turns."

"Let's go, then."

"Sorry," one of them said. "We've got our orders. We don't go without a full load."

With that, they headed into the tunnel again, one on each end of their folded stretcher.

Duffy reached for his notebook without thinking. Pain shot up his ravaged fingers. Holding a pencil was impossible, writing unthinkable. He'd have to phone his editor and dictate what he knew.

Beside him, Mary whimpered. The sound was more unbearable than his fingers.

Her eyes opened, staring up at the wooden rack that was only inches from her face. "Where am I?" she asked, her voice barely a whisper.

"In the ambulance."

"Are we moving?"

"Not yet. They're going back for another."

"Do something for me," she begged.

"Anything."

"Get word to my husband. He can be found at Thirty-two Brooklyn Street. His name is Samuel Lovett."

Duffy's heart fell.

Fool, he told himself. What had he been thinking? He was nothing but a down-at-the-heels reporter, a drunken one at that, not some knight riding to the rescue.

In need of fresh courage, he reached for his flask.

23

Halfway back to camp, Nick, who was bringing up the rear of their single-file, snail-paced trek, glimpsed a flash of movement out of the corner of her eye. Breath caught in her throat as she pivoted toward it, half-expecting to see a bear. Instead, there was Gus, hidden from the others behind a boulder, a cautioning finger pressed against his lips. Her relief at the sight of him was momentary only, quickly giving way to alarm. Why was he behaving this way?

"Wait up," she shouted to the others. "I need a break. Nature calls."

The moment she reached Gus, he pulled her further behind a gargantuan boulder, where it was impossible to be seen by the others.

"What's wrong?" she asked him.

His hand jerked in the air, signaling

a warning. His voice was a low, hackle-raising whisper. "I need your help."

Before she could ask why, his hand was across her mouth, his head tilted to one side as he listened intently.

She twisted to free herself. But his grip tightened and he breathed, "Kelly is dead. I need you as a witness."

"What?" she tried to shout against his hand.

"I don't want the others to hear." His grip relaxed.

"A witness?" she whispered. "To what? What happened?" Fear constricted her lungs and started her panting.

"It looks like an accident but . . ."

"What are you saying . . ." she gasped ". . . that he was killed deliberately?"

"I want you to see the body before I move it."

"You shouldn't touch it."

"If I don't, the bears will," he answered.

She tried to swallow but couldn't. "Why me, Gus?"

"Because you see clearly. Until then, the others mustn't know."

She stared at him, wondering if he'd gone over the edge or if Kelly really had been murdered. All this secrecy could only mean one thing, he suspected someone in the camp. Paranoids suspect everyone, she reminded herself.

"What do you want me to do?" she said.

"Go back to camp, wait a few minutes, and then wander off alone."

"Where?"

"Don't worry. I'll find you."

Without another word, he turned and disappeared among the maze of boulders.

The remainder of the trip back was slow and painful. Erickson's earlier exhilaration at seeing the Val had given way to labored breathing so tortured that Nick feared each step might be his last. Finally by midafternoon, he grew so tired that she and Barlow half-carried him between them. Even with that, the old pilot's legs gave out the moment they tried to stand him in front of Dr. Royce, now back in camp along with Ivins.

"You should have taken more care," the doctor said, glaring at Nick.

Nick clenched her teeth to keep from reminding the doctor of her earlier diagnosis, that a walk would be good for the old pilot.

"It's my fault," Alcott said.

"Well, the harm's done now," the doctor said. "Mr. Erickson needs rest. Help me carry him to his tent."

Dr. Royce's idea of help was to walk beside her patient, while Barlow and Hurst did the carrying, their arms locked underneath Erickson to form a fireman's chair.

Alcott trotted alongside, the fingers of one hand fluttering nervously. "Mister Erickson," he pleaded, "I hope you don't blame the museum."

Erickson didn't answer until he was lying inside his tent. "I blame your Miss Scott for making me feel young again. I wouldn't have missed this day for anything. If it had killed me, that would be fine by me."

"That's enough talking," the doctor said, fitting her stethoscope into her ears as she knelt beside her patient. "Now, if you don't mind, we need some privacy."

"We won't be far," Ivins said and led the exodus to the fire, which was blazing high despite the balmy weather and the fact that darkness was still hours away. Once seated, Ivins and Alcott looked at one another as if waiting for a signal to speak.

Alcott began. "Nothing's changed since we spoke on the radio. Kelly hasn't come back and Gus is still out looking for him."

"It's been hours," Hurst complained.

Furtively, Nick checked her watch. Nearly three hours of daylight left. Even so, she wanted to get away on her own as quickly as possible for her meeting with Gus. The last thing she wanted was to take a chance on missing him and getting lost in the dark, especially in bear country.

"What happens if they don't come back?" Hurst persisted.

"That doesn't seem likely," Alcott said. "The fact is, I'm surprised they've left us alone this long in their precious refuge."

"And with bears on the loose," Hurst added.

"Dear God," Alcott blurted. "Maybe they've run into trouble."

"Did anyone hear shots?" Nick asked. All heads shook in the negative. "Then maybe we're worrying for nothing." Fat chance, she added to herself, remembering the stricken look on Gus's face. The trouble was, she could think of no reason why anyone would harm a man like Kelly, who was only doing his job, albeit zealously.

"I think we're right to be worried," Hurst said. "They treat this place like it was sacred. The last thing they'd want would be for us to be out here on our own."

Ivins nodded. "Since we are on our own, what happens now?"

"We can leave the day after tomorrow if we have to," Nick said. "Thanks to the weather, we didn't have to dig through the ice. As of now, the Val is clear of snow and just about ready to go."

"I'll alert the chopper to stand by."

"Thank God for that," Alcott said. "I wouldn't want to get stuck out here without a guide."

Nick watched Ivins's face, looking for some kind of reaction, some hint that he might be responsible for Kelly's death. After all, Ivins had gone missing from camp, along with the doctor. She said, "I'm sure Kelly and Gus will be back soon."

"Even if they're not," Hurst responded, "it's no big deal. If need be, we can jump in the cars and drive back the way we came."

Nick said, "I don't think we can drive away and leave our guides behind."

"I see your point," Hurst conceded.

Alcott pointed a finger at Nick. "I hope you're not suggesting we go out looking for them. Two people lost is quite enough."

"Mike Barlow and I will do the looking if it comes to that."

Ivins snorted. "They were right about you, Ms. Scott. You know your business and your mind."

Who was right? Nick was tempted to ask, but didn't bother. Probably Elliot had been up to his tricks with E-Group, too.

Dr. Royce joined them. "Our pilot is sound asleep," she announced, holding her hands out toward the fire. "I think that's all he needed. His vitals are fine. Now what have we decided to do about our missing guides?"

While the others brought the doctor up to date, Nick studied the faces around the fire. As far as she knew, she and Barlow were the only ones with experience coping in country as rough as this. Ivins looked like your typical executive, fit only for running on his office treadmill. Hurst, though a scholar, had surprised Nick on that first day, never complaining about his blistered hands, but she didn't think he was equipped for the long haul. As for Alcott, Nick guessed he was more concerned with dieting to keep up appearances rather than physical fitness.

Their cameraman, Tyler, looked sound enough, though his experience was limited to shooting documentaries on location, a far cry from surviving scorching summers during one of Elliot's Anasazi digs. That left Dr. Karen Royce to consider. If she was anything like Nick's doctor, she dispensed advice on physical fitness rather than following it.

Then again, Nick reminded herself, you didn't have to be an athlete to be an archaeologist. In most cases, you didn't have to hike any further than your own museum.

Hold it, she told herself. Stop thinking about appearances. If Gus wasn't crazy or hallucinating, someone in the group was dangerous. And good enough to ambush a man like Kelly, who was on his own ground, and the only one among them who was armed.

But why would anyone bother? It wasn't as if they'd discovered gold. The Val was collectable enough, but hardly worth a fortune, not in its present condition. In fact, the only fortune involved would be the money it took to restore the dive bomber to its original condition.

Any possible motive escaped her. That brought her back to Gus. What if he was crazy? If so, she'd be even crazier if she went out to meet him alone.

24

Nick hadn't gotten more than fifty yards from camp when Gus appeared out of nowhere. One minute she'd been picking her way through a stand of spindly birch, careful to keep her bearings, and in the next he'd materialized close enough to touch her arm, startling her so badly she started to scream. But he clapped his hand over her mouth so quickly she didn't have time to utter so much as a whisper, his grip a paralyzing reminder of just how strong he was. He could have snapped her neck and no one would have heard a thing.

"Quiet," he murmured.

She tried to nod but his powerful fingers held her fast.

"Sorry," he whispered, releasing his hold. "We'd better move before someone comes looking for you."

"Where are we going?" she whispered back.

He shook his head and signaled her to follow him. He was wearing a bulky backpack, with a heavy coil of rope attached.

She took a deep breath and fell in behind him as he moved quickly, sure of his way. They were heading in a northerly direction toward the mountains, though their path was anything but direct as it wound its way into the high country.

She glanced over her shoulder at the afternoon sun to reaffirm their direction. As she did, the sun slipped behind a cloud, whose shadow chilled her to the bone. Without the sun, she'd have to navigate by dead reckoning if she got lost.

They broke out of the trees just as the sun reappeared, setting fire to the Hammersmiths directly ahead of them. By now the camp was well to their left, blocked from view by the knoll from which Nick had first glimpsed potential dig sites. From where they stood, the path ran in a relatively straight line toward the mountains and, at a guess, toward her dig site.

"How far does this trail go?" she asked.

"All the way to your airplane, if that's what you're wondering about. And beyond."

"Are you saying we could have skirted the rocks if we'd come this way?"

"Kelly didn't want anyone using it."

"For God's sake. It would have saved us hours, not to mention aching muscles, and damn near a heart attack for Mr. Erickson."

"I've seen bears on this trail many times. Kelly didn't want you interfering with them. Besides, he thought it might be dangerous if you came this way."

"If it's so dangerous, why are we here now?"

"It's the quickest way and there are now other dangers. Kelly told me he was coming this way to look for bears. I looked for him here when he didn't come back." The Inuit gestured at the ground over which they were walking. "I found the tracks of someone following Kelly."

"Who?"

"A man," he said, without slowing down. "Perhaps another,

146

if the other stepped in the first man's tracks. The ground is not good. Let's hurry. I want to get back to camp before someone decides to follows us." The pace he set left her panting.

She glanced back the way they'd come. Until that moment, she hadn't realized how steeply they'd been climbing. When she turned back to Gus, he was already on the move again, forcing her to trot to catch up.

Less than ten minutes later, they passed within shouting distance of the Val.

"How far?" she asked breathlessly.

"You see the rockfall up there?"

She craned her neck. The rockfall looked to be a quarter of a mile ahead, all of it steeply uphill.

"That's where he is, on the other side of the fall, where the ice begins. This high up, it isn't melting."

Beyond the rockfall, the trail appeared to snake its way into a *v*-shaped pass between the peaks.

"Is this the way over the mountains?" she asked.

"It's the only way over the Hammersmiths. The other passes are too dangerous."

Kelly's body lay at the bottom of a shallow crevasse, maybe twenty feet deep, whose sides were sheer ice. He was face down, his legs canted grotesquely.

"He might still be alive," she said, not believing it for a moment.

Shaking his head, Gus shrugged off his cumbersome backpack, which hit the ground with a heavy thud.

"What the hell do you have in there?" she asked.

"Enough to survive on my own if I have to."

She eyed the backpack more closely. It had to weigh fifty pounds, maybe more. Even so, it couldn't have held enough food to survive a winter.

"How long could you survive?"

"Until I die of old age," he answered.

"If you say so."

They were standing on a narrow extension of a glacier, squeezed like glue between two massive slabs of granite. The trail ran parallel to the crevasse, from which cracks ran like veins feeding an artery.

Gus opened his backpack, removed an ice axe and drove it into the ice to anchor his rope. "Nick, I'm going down to get him. You stay here. I may need your help."

With that, he lowered himself over the side quickly, hand over hand like an acrobat. Once at Kelly's side, Gus removed his gloves and touched his friend's neck. Nick held her breath until Gus looked up at her and shook his head. After that, he turned Kelly, closed his eyes, and then began tying the rope around Kelly's feet.

Watching him work, Nick felt her teeth chattering. The cold was bad enough, so was her fear, but neither matched her anger at seeing a man like Kelly having to be hauled out of an icy grave by his heels.

When it was done, she felt sick. She also wanted to shout her frustration at Gus for scaring the hell out of her. He'd all but said Kelly had been murdered, but examining him, Nick saw no indication that his death was anything but an accident. She told Gus so.

"My friend wouldn't die in a place like this," he replied.

"He's here, isn't he?"

"He shouldn't be. Look around you. You're a scientist. This area is unstable. Anyone with Kelly's experience would know that. He wasn't the man to take chances. Here"—he gestured at the granite slabs hemming them in—"he would have kept to the trail. This wasn't an accident."

"You can't be sure of that," she said.

"I thought you saw clearly. You're missing the obvious."

Nick looked around and saw nothing. "What?"

"The bears were here," he responded cryptically.

Ever since reaching the ice, Nick had been watching for any kind of tracks. All she'd seen was Kelly's, or those she assumed belonged to the ranger. Before that the rockfall had revealed nothing.

"Even if they were," she said, "what difference does that make? Bears didn't attack Kelly. If they had, there would have been marks on his body."

"A spirit, a *Tornaq,* leaves no mark, not unless it wants to. But you are right. The bears were here before Kelly died." Gus reached out as if to touch his friend, but stopped short. Then he raised his head and stared up at the darkening sky.

Until that moment, Nick hadn't realized how late it was.

He said, "Winter is coming."

The sky showed no sign of it, she thought. What cloud cover there was, was high up and sparse.

"The bears know," Gus continued. "They know it's time to hibernate. Even your scientists don't understand how they know, but they do." As he spoke, the wind gusted over the ice, making Nick shiver.

"It's time," Gus said. "We must carry Kelly back to camp before the snows come."

We! Nick thought. The man weighed a good two hundred pounds.

"You said I was missing the obvious."

Gus smiled grimly. "Kelly's gun is missing. That changes the balance of power."

Before Nick could respond, Gus hoisted Kelly onto his shoulder and started down the trail, moving as agilely as if carrying no load at all. Nick grabbed Gus's heavy backpack and hurried after him, trying to shake off the growing fear inside her.

25

Nick's fear had given way to exhaustion by the time she and Gus reached camp. At the sight of the two of them stumbling out of the trees, Gus bent double under the burden of Kelly's body and Nick stoop-shouldered from carrying the Inuit's backpack, the others stood stunned. Dr. Alcott's face reminded Nick of a death mask, while Wes Erickson merely looked older than ever as he leaned heavily on Fred Ivins, whose head was shaking from side to side as if denying the sight before him. Gordon Hurst's mouth opened and closed without producing sound. Dr. Royce looked too dumbstruck to react. And even Tyler forgot to film the event.

Mike Barlow recovered first, lunging forward to steady Kelly's body so that Gus could lower the ranger to the ground. Only then did Gordon Hurst think to help Nick out of the straps that had been cutting into her shoulders for the past hour.

"Good God," Alcott said. "What happened?"

"An accident," Gus rushed to say, staring at Nick, his eyes narrowed in an unspoken warning.

She rubbed her shoulders to hide her annoyance. What did he think she was going to do, blurt out what they both suspected?

She said, "He fell into a crevasse."

Alcott motioned to Royce. "Doctor, would you take a look at Mister Kelly?" His tone sought a second opinion.

Karen knelt beside the body. "His skull is crushed," she reported. "Most likely he died of a cerebral hemorrhage."

"And?" Alcott probed.

The doctor spread her hands. "And what?"

"Is there anything else you can tell us?"

"That will have to wait for the autopsy," Royce answered.

"Is that necessary in the case of an accident?" Ivins asked.

"It's usual."

Nick jumped in. "In light of that, Mister Ivins, I think it's time you called in that helicopter of yours."

"We're allowed one flight only," he reminded her.

"The Val's ready to go. All we've got to do is attach a sling. Mike and I can do that in an hour." She glanced at Kelly. "Your chopper can take them both back at the same time." She turned to the doctor. "Unless you think the police will want to examine the body here."

"I wouldn't advise that," Gus said. "It's not wise to bring in more people to the refuge, not this late in the year."

Ivins examined the darkening sky. "I can have the chopper here three hours after daybreak tomorrow."

Alcott intervened. "I wouldn't want to rush things. Our Val is too valuable."

"I agree," Hurst said. "I'm sorry Mister Kelly is dead, but panicking isn't going to bring him back."

"Panicking?" Nick said, furious. "Recovery is my responsibility. You have no right saying that. When I say the Val is ready I—"

Gus interrupted her. "It's better if you all leave the refuge as soon as possible. If Terry Kelly were alive, he'd say the same thing. He'd insist upon it."

"Are you ordering us out?" Ivins asked.

"If need be."

Erickson pushed away from Ivins to stand beside Nick, surprising her. "I've lived to see my Val," he told them. "Frankly, it's more than I ever expected. Finding the Japanese pilot I shot down would have made it perfect, but I realize now that was never a possibility. Nature buried him in her own way."

"You'll all end up buried here if you don't leave," Gus said.

"Does that include yourself?" Ivins snapped back.

The Inuit shrugged.

"I was about to add," Erickson said, "that Mister Kelly should be taken home as soon as possible. It's the proper thing to do. It's time for me to go home, too, I think." He sighed deeply. "I realize now that I shouldn't have come. I no longer have the strength for such journeys."

The old pilot bowed his head. The gesture seemed to overbalance him. He would have toppled over if Nick hadn't grabbed his arm.

"That settles it," she said, easing him onto a camp chair. "If you haven't already, call your chopper, Mister Ivins, the sooner the better."

"Of course."

"Meanwhile, what are we going to do with Kelly's body?" Alcott asked.

"I will place it where the bears cannot reach it," Gus relied. But Nick thought that she heard him mutter, "All bears but the *Siudleratuin*."

26

The ride took forever, or so it seemed to Ned Duffy. He tried to supervise Mary's removal from the ambulance but the orderlies brushed him aside.

"You'd best see to those hands," one of them told him. "There's a nursing station along the way, they'll take care of you there."

Duffy grimaced. "I need a telephone, if there is one."

"Your editor will be proud of you, seeing to your story before your wounds. There's one on the wall outside the director's office." The orderly pointed in the opposite direction.

But it wasn't the *World* that Duffy called. Duffy knew someone in all the station houses of the five boroughs, and Kleinst, the man at the Brooklyn precinct house, promised to send someone around to look up Lovett. It had cost him two seats to next year's series.

"Now you'd be making a mess on our nice clean walls and that's not allowed," a voice said to him.

Duffy turned around and looked down on a nurse barely five feet tall. "They told me that you'd come in with a woman from the train wreck and would be needing help so I've come to get you. I can't be spending my time waiting around for people all day." She grabbed him by the arm and led him down the hall.

"I had to make a telephone call," Duffy tried to explain.

They arrived at a small, windowless examination room.

"Now let's take a look at those hands. Well, we'll have to go after those splinters, but first a little carbolic."

Duffy winced with pain.

"Now hold still," the nurse told him, "and don't be such a big baby."

"I ought to be with Mary. . . . uh, Mrs. Lovett," Duffy corrected.

"Then hold still," the nurse replied with a hint of exasperation in her voice. "The sooner I'm done here the faster you can leave. It's not like I don't have really sick people to attend to."

"I'm sorry," Duffy said and winced again as another sliver was drawn from his hand. For the first time he looked at the nurse, really looked at her and noticed her drawn face and dark circled eyes. "You must be at the end of your shift and I've held you up," he said in a placating tone.

"Don't I wish," she sighed. "I've been on for eighteen hours and it looks like at least six more to go."

Duffy was astounded. He knew that young doctors who were residents were asked to work as long as thirty-six hours at a go, but he'd never heard of such hours required of nurses. "Is it because of the wreck?" he asked.

"We're that shorthanded," she replied and for the first time Duffy noticed a hint of the Old Sod in her voice.

Duffy could deepen his brogue when he wished and did so now with a hushed conspiratorial whisper. "Funny, we're that shorthanded at the paper as well. In fact, now that I think of it his mates mentioned that the train operator was pulling a long shift too. Everyone seems to be shorthanded. Don't you think it strange?"

"Not in the least, all things considered." The nurse looked around, as if a third person could be concealed in the tiny room. "We took in twenty on Monday, thirty yesterday, and more than that today. Eight of our own are lying right here in the wards. And this is only the beginning."

"The beginning of what?" Duffy asked.

"First the war, and now *she's* come. There'll be more before it's over."

"Who's come?" Duffy asked. He was starting to feel weak and wondered if the entire conversation was a dream.

"*She* has," the nurse insisted. "We're not supposed to say anything, but it's *her*. They keep denying it, but I know what I know."

"Her?" Duffy asked weakly and involuntarily pulled back his hand.

"Here, now," she said, roughly retrieving his hand and dousing it with more carbolic, "I've said enough."

"Oh shit," Duffy cried, "that hurts."

"As it should, me boyo. Trying to get me to say things as I shouldn't." She swiftly wrapped his ravaged hands and turned to go.

"Wait," Duffy pleaded. "You can't leave me like this." He gave her his most ingratiating smile.

"Can't I just," she said, then paused for a moment. "You can go see Doctor Welsh in a couple of days to see how your hands are coming."

She lowered her voice until Duffy was straining to hear her. "And while you're in the neighborhood, go talk to that lying rascal, Royal Copeland, who's head of public health in this fine upstanding city. Ask him about *her*."

Seeing the bewilderment on Duffy's face she added, "Ask him about the Spanish Lady."

27

Nick and Mike Barlow used the bear trail to reach the Val the next morning. Gus had objected at first, giving in only after she'd assured him that by avoiding the long trek through the rocks they'd save enough time to be out of his hair all the quicker. Even so, he'd insisted on accompanying them far enough, he said, to be certain they didn't run into any bears. Hurst, on the other hand, who Nick had thought would insist on coming too, had instead said, "I'll leave it in your capable hands." His lack of interest had made Nick uneasy.

They made the trip without talking. Nick didn't feel like conversation and she was thankful that Barlow had proved to be the silent type.

Once on site, Nick immediately saw that last night's freeze, yet to thaw, had left the Val coated with a shimmering glaze. The ice, as thin as it was, magnified a spider web of hairline fractures she hadn't noticed before. They were concentrated at the point where the wings attached to the fuselage, the area of most stress, as was to be expected after so many years in a deep freeze.

When she pointed them out, Barlow squatted on his heels next to the wing and shook his head. "If we move her, she could fall to pieces on us."

Nick agreed. It was better to remove the wings now, since they'd have to be detached eventually for the trip back to Washington. The trouble was, they didn't have the time to start removing rivets.

"She'll have to be restored anyway," she said, squatting beside him. "So we'll have to risk moving her as is."

"You're the boss."

It was also her reputation on the line, and she was about to violate one of Elliot's ten commandments. *An artifact is a piece of history. Treat it with reverence and respect and never, never, risk damaging it.*

"Let's fit the sling," she said, noticing that her breath came out like smoke. She blew a frosty contrail.

Barlow blew smoke for himself. "I guess the Eskimo was right about the weather going south on us." He nodded at the horizon, where clouds were building rapidly.

"Inuit," she absentmindedly corrected. "That settles it," she said, following his gaze. "We don't have time to do anything fancy."

Barlow nodded. "We were lucky to have so much good weather. Otherwise, we'd have been chopping through solid ice to reach this baby." He ran his hand over the forward edge of the wing.

Nick crossed her fingers for luck. Then they went to work, fitting the sling into position underneath the dive bomber. The moment they finished she started to shiver. Working had kept her warm, and her mind occupied. Now the plummeting temperature was turning her sweat to ice.

She dug out her radio, blew on her fingers, and punched the transmit button. "This is Nick, over."

"Ivins here."

"We're ready for the pickup."

"Bad news, I'm afraid," Ivins said. "I just talked to Anchorage. The chopper can't make it."

"The weather?"

"No, mechanical problems. It will take a couple of days to fix it."

"Did Anchorage give you a weather report?"

"Cloudy, they said. A minor cold front coming through, nothing to worry about."

Nick felt a surge of relief. A couple of days would give her time to detach the wings. "What does Gus say about the weather?"

"Jesus, isn't he with you? He and Erickson?"

"Erickson?"

"I know," Ivins said. "The old man shouldn't be out in cold like this. Hell, last night, he looked done in."

Erickson had still been asleep when Nick and Barlow left camp.

"And this morning?" she asked.

"I'll give him credit," Ivins replied. "He looked chipper enough."

"And the doctor agreed?"

"Erickson insisted."

Nick looked at Barlow and shook her head. The bear trail was a much easier route than the trek through the rocks, but it was still a long hike.

"He said he wanted one more look at his Val," Ivins added, "and the doctor gave her okay."

"What did Gus say?"

Barlow tapped her on the shoulder. "Speak of the devil."

Gus wasn't more than fifty yards away. Erickson was beside him.

Nick gave a sigh of relief. "They've just arrived," she reported to Ivins.

"We'll have a hot meal ready by the time you get back," Ivins said. "Out."

Since they now had the time, Nick had hoped to get a

start on the wings, but at the mention of hot food she realized just how cold she was. Besides, her fingers were too numb to be trusted to anything as delicate as rivet removal. She stamped her feet, then decided to keep moving and went out to meet them.

"I'm sorry to be such a bother," Erickson said as soon as she was in range. "But I had to be here one more time. I had to stand where that Japanese pilot saluted me." He took her arm. "Maybe we could stand there together, Miss Scott?"

"Of course."

He guided her to a point adjacent to the cockpit, then planted his feet deliberately.

"I'm sorry we couldn't find him for you," she said.

"It was a foolish hope on my part. Look at this place. There's no place to hide, no place to take shelter."

He sucked a quick breath and tapped gloved fingers against his forehead. "I'm an old fool. He might have gone over the mountain."

He pointed at the peak looming above them, its saw-toothed granite pinnacle like that of some prehistoric carnivore. According to Gus, Nick remembered, there was only one pass over the Hammersmiths. The chance that a downed Japanese pilot would have discovered such a passage seemed remote, if not impossible.

"I know what you're thinking," Erickson said, "but I saw something when I flew over this mountain. Maybe my enemy did too."

"What?"

"A cabin of some kind. That's where I would have headed if I'd crashed here. Maybe that's where we'll find his body."

Nick shivered at the thought of trying to make such a journey, probably without food, and with no hope of food once there and therefore no hope of long-term survival.

"Why didn't you tell me this before?" she asked.

"Maybe I shouldn't have said anything now." He stared up at the mountain. "What's the point? I can't bring back my youth, or the dead."

28

Nick tried to question Erickson during the trek back to camp, but it was all the old pilot could do just to keep his feet moving while Gus and Barlow supported him between them. As far as Nick was concerned, it was time Erickson went home. Certainly, there was nothing to be gained by having him wait around two days for the choppers to arrive.

She told Alcott just that as soon as they reached camp. "He needs rest," she clarified, pulling him aside, "and the cold weather isn't going to help him any. Besides, we can spare one of the cars to take him back."

"Who did you have in mind to drive him?" Alcott asked suspiciously, as if she were including him among the infirm. His bulky parka made him as round as a snowman.

"Doctor Royce, of course. He's the reason she's here."

"Not having a doctor might put the rest of us at risk," Alcott countered.

Rather than argue with her boss, Nick nodded at Erickson, who was being helped into one of the camp chairs in front of the fire. The man's face was ashen, his chest heaving.

At the sight of him, Alcott relented. "I see what you mean."

Even as the curator spoke, Ivins fetched Erickson a hot cup of cocoa, then sat beside him, holding the cup to his lips. The old pilot managed a single sip before pushing the cup away.

"After all," Alcott added, "we've accomplished our mission and Mister Erickson has seen his Val." He cocked an eyebrow. "I imagine you're thinking the same applies to me."

"We could all go home if our chopper was airworthy," she responded diplomatically.

He snorted. "Not bad. We'll make a civil servant out of you yet. Now, let's see what Ivins has to say, since it's his vehicles we're talking about. Money talks, you know."

Nick followed her boss to the fire, half expecting him to genuflect in front of E-Group's representative. But Alcott surprised her. "Fred," he said, the first time she'd heard him address Ivins on a familiar basis, "I think it's time us old fogies got out of your hair." He tipped his head at Erickson.

"What did you have in mind?" Ivins asked.

"I thought maybe the doctor could chauffeur Mr. Erickson and myself back to Anchorage. I hate to admit it, but I just don't have the stamina I used to. Besides, there's the problem of Kelly's body. We could take it out of the refuge."

Good for you, Nick thought. Alcott was giving the old pilot a way to bow out gracefully. The curator was full of surprises.

Ivins shrugged. "It's your expedition."

"What do you say, Wes?" Alcott asked as he dropped into the chair next to the pilot. "Why don't the two of us go back to town, hole up in a nice warm hotel suite, and relax while the young folks freeze their butts off out here?"

"Are you sure you won't be needed here?" Erickson asked.

"From now on, it's all grunt work and best left to the peons. Isn't that right, Nick?"

"I might as well go too," Tyler said. "I've got the shots of the plane being dug up."

"You'd better stay to film the chopper retrieving it," Alcott insisted.

That was more like it, Nick thought. More in character for Alcott, at least her assessment of his character.

The cameraman looked crestfallen, then suddenly smiled. "But if I were already in Anchorage I could film the chopper arriving with the Val in tow."

"That would be fantastic," she said. "And, in this cold, I wouldn't stay myself if I didn't have to."

Erickson wrapped his arms around his chest. "I thought it was just me and my old bones. How soon do you think we could leave?"

Alcott looked to Ivins who said, "I suggest you hold off until morning. Otherwise, you'll be driving in the dark or pitching camp in the middle of nowhere. If that's all right with Gus, of course."

The Inuit knelt in front of Erickson so he could look him in the eye. "I think you should leave as soon as possible."

"You don't mind us splitting up the party, then?" Ivins asked.

Gus rose to his feet. "I think it's out of my hands." He walked away.

Nick stared after him in astonishment. With Kelly dead, the refuge and everything in it, including the expedition, was his responsibility. Or had Gus given up that responsibility on the glacier when he told her that Kelly's missing pistol had shifted the balance of power?

Ivins interrupted her thoughts. "I'd say it's time we drank a toast to Wes Erickson for bringing us all together and giving us the chance to witness history in the making." He beckoned to the doctor. "Would you bring us the medicinal brandy, please."

"Medicine recognizes no such prescription, I'm afraid," Karen said.

"Let's just say, then, that I anticipated our success." Ivins dipped into the recesses of his voluminous parka and, like a magician pulling a rabbit from a hat, came out with a flask from one pocket and a stack of disposable cups from another. "Will you do the honors, Doctor Scott? I don't think our medical doctor is comfortable with my medication."

As Nick poured meager shots, which Ivins dispensed like a Santa bursting at the seams with good cheer, she found herself looking for suspects. But even the shiftiest of the lot, Ivins, had no motive she could think of. And his shiftiness, she thought, was all in her mind, since she had a natural distrust of people who represented big money.

Add to that the possibility that Gus was imagining things, and she didn't know whom to trust. Or not trust for that matter.

She took a deep breath. Until she had proof otherwise, she would treat Kelly's death as an accident. As far as she could see, no one had a motive to kill him, and no one gained by his death. As for the missing pistol, it was probably at the bottom of the crevasse right where an accident would have left it.

She nodded to herself. That made more sense than suspecting murder. So be it, she told herself, but that didn't stop her from keeping a close eye on the faces around the fire. But everyone looked innocent enough as they toasted victory. Even the doctor ignored her own medical advice and joined in. Seconds were poured.

The brandy, she noticed, had restored the color to Erickson's cheeks.

Nick slid into the chair that Ivins had abandoned next to Erickson.

She said, "The doctor's right, you know. Brandy won't keep you warm in this kind of weather."

Erickson stared into his cup, closing one eye as if drawing a bead on it. "Maybe so, young lady, but it's doing a damn good imitation. Haven't you ever heard of antifreeze?" His eyes twinkled.

"Tell me about that cabin you saw on the other side of the mountains."

The sparkle faded from his eyes. "I wasn't thinking straight before. It was probably a fallen tree I saw."

"I thought pilots were trained observers."

"It's been a long time and my memory isn't what it used to be. Maybe it's just wishful thinking on my part, wanting to believe that the man I shot down had a chance."

Some chance, Nick thought, an isolated cabin hundreds of miles from anywhere.

"Besides," he went on, "pilots are trained to stay with their planes. Rescuers can spot a plane from the air easier than they can a man alone."

"You told me you would have tried to reach the cabin had you been in his place."

"I . . ." Erickson broke off to glance in Ivins's direction.

As far as Nick could tell, Ivins had eyes only for Karen, who was standing so close to him they could have both fit into a single parka, or possibly a sleeping bag judging by the way they were eyeing one another. Nick felt a stab of envy.

But Erickson's eyes looked as if they were seeing something else entirely.

"What's wrong?" she asked him in a whisper.

The brandy flush faded from his cheeks. His hands trembled. "Sometimes I forget I'm an old man. Inside, I feel the same as always, I feel young, but my body has betrayed me." He sighed so deeply his throat rattled. "It betrayed me today when I went to see my Val. I . . . maybe I'd better tell you after all. Maybe . . ." His eyes, which had been riveted on Nick, shifted focus behind her.

She jerked her head around to see Ivins and Karen break apart and head their way.

"That's two brandies you've had, isn't it?" Karen said to Erickson.

He nodded.

"Alcohol lowers the body's temperature, so I want you in your tent and resting until dinner. Otherwise, I won't be responsible."

Erickson touched Nick's arm and said, "I am tired. We can talk in the morning before I leave for Anchorage."

With that, Ivins and the doctor hustled him away impatiently. Probably they were in a hurry to get their charge tucked in, so they could share that sleeping bag, Nick thought.

29

By early evening, Ivins and Karen had been missing for hours. When Nick checked their tents, their sleeping bags were not there, confirming her suspicion that the pair were lovers. She just hoped they realized how quickly the temperature was dropping.

Nick looked in on Erickson, who was sleeping. Hurst and Alcott, both bundled in parkas, were sitting close to the fire, playing chess, while Barlow and Tyler were working over the camp stove.

Gus was sitting off to one side, perched on a log, whittling. When Nick joined him, she realized he'd positioned himself just beyond the fire's warmth.

"In case you haven't noticed," she told him, "it's getting colder."

"If you don't get used to the heat, you don't miss it when it's gone."

"Tell me that when it drops below freezing."

"It's freezing now."

"Have you checked the thermometer?"

"I don't have to check."

"Will you stop with the phony mysticism. In case you haven't noticed, you're wearing a park service uniform, not the robes of a shaman."

"Not all shaman wear robes."

"Will you please listen to me for a moment?"

"I don't have much choice," he answered without looking up from the amorphous wooden figure in his hand. It was human in shape, maybe three inches tall, with no distinct features.

She backed up a step closer to the fire, hoping he'd follow. But he stayed put.

"Ivins and the doctor are missing," she said.

"I'm surprised you didn't see them leave."

"I thought they were in their tents, or sharing one of them, anyway."

"Did you?" His knife kept whittling, shaving at the figure's waist.

"It's almost dark," Nick pointed out.

He nodded.

"I know they wanted to be alone, but don't you think it's time we went looking for them?"

He looked up from the now wasp-waisted figure. "Is that what you think, that they're lovers?"

"What else?"

His knife began creating breasts. "Because I'm surprised that a woman of your intelligence would reach such a conclusion."

"I can recognize love when I see it," she replied hotly.

"Can you?" He showed her the figure, now obviously female.

"I hope that's not supposed to be me," she said.

"It is a charm against spirits. It will bring you luck." He tossed it to her.

She caught it reluctantly. "Now what about helping me find our lovers?"

"You still insist on that, do you? That you can recognize love when you see it?"

She nodded.

"Your hair is like the fire, it glows. Yet you keep it so short. In my culture a woman's hair is her glory. Why do you keep it so short?"

"It's convenient," she snapped. Besides, she thought to herself, it's a penance.

Suddenly Gus leapt to his feet, kissed her on the lips, and then danced out of range before she realized what was happening.

"What are you trying to say?" she asked, wondering if the figure in her hand was a love offering.

He smiled. "Maybe I just want to alter your perception of things."

"The next time you try that, I'll kick you in the balls."

"If there is a next time, I'll ask first."

By dark Nick was seething with anger, most of it directed against herself. She should have insisted on a search for Ivins and Karen while it was still light. Worse yet, she should never have allowed herself to be distracted by Gus's kiss.

Now all she could do was stoke the bonfire and hope the beacon would lead them home. While she did that, Gus, maddening as ever, continued to whittle.

She was about to alert Alcott and Hurst, intending to challenge Gus's fitness to be their guide, when the Inuit rose from his log and ambled her way.

"I carved you another charm," he announced.

"One was quite enough."

He shook his head, condemning her. No doubt he'd seen her toss the first one on the bonfire.

"You appear to be an educated man," she said.

"So?"

"Then why do you cling to such beliefs?"

Gus smiled. "Some things you don't learn from books."

"For God's sake," she snapped at him, "it's Karen and Ivins you should be worrying about."

"They're safe enough."

"They're lost out there in the dark."

"I don't think so." He pointed in the direction of the mountains. "Take a look for yourself."

Not more than fifty yards away, two strong lights were bobbing in the night, heading toward camp.

"Unless I'm mistaken," he said, "here come your lost lovers, who weren't so lost after all."

Nick bit her lips. The man's calm tone infuriated her.

"Here," he said, thrusting the newly whittled figure into her hand. "You never know when you might need a wooden charm. Now let's see what your *lovers* have been up to."

For an instant, she was tempted to hurl his latest carving into the darkness. Then caution, or maybe it was superstition, got the better of her, and she tucked the totem into her pocket and followed him toward the bobbing lights. She could dump the carving later, if the mood suited her.

Gus hesitated at the edge of the firelight as if suddenly uncertain of who might be approaching. Talk about superstition, Nick told herself. Probably the man saw spirits everywhere, though why spirits would have the need for flashlights she couldn't imagine. But she stayed behind him just the same, as did the others who came to join them.

"Sorry we're late," Ivins called out the moment he stepped into the light. "We went for a walk."

"Time got away from us," Karen added.

Their faces were flushed.

"Let's get you two over by the fire," Alcott said. "You must be frozen."

Barlow fetched mugs of steaming coffee. The commotion woke Erickson, who crawled out of his tent to see what was happening. Everyone packed as closely together as their bulky parkas allowed to hear what had happened. Barlow came up behind Nick and rested a proprietary hand at the nape of her neck. "Bet they found a way to keep warm," he whispered in her ear. Nick shook off his hand and forced her way between Erickson and Hurst. She felt chilled, and not by the bitter wind that had come with the night.

"We didn't have time to get cold," Ivins said as he wrapped both hands around his coffee mug. "We were too excited."

So much for Gus's mystical insight, Nick thought, stamping her feet. She'd been right all along. They'd kept themselves warm making love. She craned her neck, looking for Gus so she could gloat. But he was back on his log, whittling, and apparently paying no attention. Come to think of it, with the temperature as low as it was now, it would take more than sex to keep you warm. Even warming at the fire was a losing battle, toasting her on one side only. If it got any colder, she'd have to turn in circles, like a chicken on a spit.

"Isn't that right, Doctor?" Ivins said, blowing on his coffee. "The cold wasn't a factor."

"That wouldn't be my medical opinion." Her chattering teeth stopped her from saying more.

Alcott spoke up. "You had us half-scared to death. We thought you were lost, or worse."

"You'll forgive us when you hear what we found," Ivins said.

Erickson grasped Nick's hand.

"This is your lucky day, Ms. Scott, you being an archaeologist," Ivins went on.

Erickson gripped tightly.

"We found you an old mining camp, or what's left of it anyway. My guess is that it dates from the gold rush days, though we'll leave that to your expertise."

"Where exactly?" she asked him.

"The other side of the mountain."

Hurst whistled. "That's some walk."

I'll be damned, Nick thought. The old pilot had been right all along.

"There's a trail through one of the passes," Karen managed through clenched teeth. "It's an easy walk, not more than a couple of miles."

That trail was where Kelly had fallen to his death. By no stretch of the imagination could it be called an easy walk, especially in the dark.

"Describe what you saw," Nick said.

"There was a cabin. Part of the roof's caved in, but there's enough left to shelter from the wind if you had to. There are some wooden sluices too. At least that's what I think they are. We'd need you to confirm that, Doctor Scott."

"Did you see any sign of life?" Erickson asked.

"Who'd you have in mind," Ivins said, "your dead Jap?"

Erickson nodded. "It was just a hope. I guess I wasn't thinking."

"Sorry, not a soul. Just the old cabin and some run-down mining gear."

"But I—"

Ivins interrupted him. "Don't start imagining things, old-timer. Otherwise, our archaeologist here won't want to do her job."

"I think I'm the best judge of what my job is, Mister Ivins," Nick said stiffly. "Besides, I'd like to hear what Mister Erickson has to say."

"That's all right," Erickson said, looking at Ivins, who was staring back at him. "It wasn't important."

Erickson was holding something back, Nick felt certain.

"It would be a shame not to investigate now that we're here," Ivins persisted.

"No," Gus said, startling Nick because he had crept up behind her when she wasn't looking. "That is where the *Siudleratuin* walk."

"We didn't see any of your ghosts, either," Ivins mocked.

"It is the place I spoke of in my story."

"Ghost story, you mean. Look at us, the Doctor and I. We've been there and come back, no harm done. It's a beautiful spot, nothing to be afraid of. Hell, if you ask me it ought to be opened up to tourists."

Gus shook his head. "My father was there as a young man. He told me it is a cursed place."

Ivins looked to Alcott. "What if I'm right? What if the camp does date from the Alaskan Gold Rush? Then who knows what artifacts we might dig up? Wouldn't the Smithsonian be interested in such a find? If you'd like, I'll get on the phone to E-Group. I'm certain our chairman, Mister McKenna, will authorize all necessary expenditures."

Alcott turned to Nick. "What do you think?"

Nick glanced at Gus, who was watching her, stone-faced. His warning was clear enough; he wanted nothing to do with the place. But the Siren song of undiscovered artifacts was too much for her.

"I'd hate to miss the chance to look over a site when we're so close," she said, fighting the urge to duck her head to escape Gus's withering stare. When she looked up again, Erickson's head moved ever so slightly, a nod of approval, she thought.

"It's settled, then," Ivins said. "We join the gold rush tomorrow."

"So be it," Alcott said.

Gus moved forward so that he could face them as a group. "I'm sorry," he said. "That site is off limits. My ancestors are buried there. It is a sacred place."

"We will not disturb your dead," Ivins said. "You have my word on it."

"Disturb the *Siudleratuin*," Gus responded, "and they will call upon the *Tornaq* for vengeance."

"Superstitious rubbish," Ivins shot back.

Gus folded his arms over his chest, a pose of pure male stubbornness.

"All we want to do is take a look," Nick said to placate him.

Gus shook his head.

Alcott said, "Whatever you do, Ms. Scott, be certain of your priorities. Our Val comes first."

"Yes, sir."

Alcott nodded, appeared to be mollified.

To Gus she said, "The weather's closing in. You said so yourself. That doesn't give us much time, so we'll be in and out before you know it."

"That won't stop you from awakening the *Tornaq*," Gus said.

Enough was enough. "Just what the hell is a *Tornaq*?"

"A spirit being," he answered, "a familiar."

"Like a witch's cat," Ivins said scornfully. "For Christ's sake. Nobody with common sense believes that kind of crap."

"The danger out there is real," Gus said. "Kelly is dead. That's proof enough."

Ivins snorted derisively. "Are you saying one of your spirits killed him?"

"Someone killed him."

Ivins's eyes narrowed to quivering slits. "If you ask me, the only danger around here is you."

Nick cringed inwardly. What if Ivins was right? Had she been kissed by a maniac? She looked from one face to the other, hoping for a revelation. When none came, she said, "Gus, do you intend to stop us from going in the morning?"

Gus shrugged, an ambiguous gesture.

"I think Kelly would have wanted you to guide us over the mountain in the morning," Nick went on. "He would have wanted you to watch over us."

"No," Gus said, "he would have known better."

30

Ned Duffy thought he was a hard man. As a reporter, he'd seen it all, or so he told himself. He was an old hand at murder, mutilation, even road accidents when crime got slow. Through it all, blood and torn bodies that had turned many a cop's stomach, he'd taken his notes and kept his objectivity, never so much as batting an eye or losing a lunch. But Mary was a different matter. He'd loved her at first sight, from the moment he pulled her from the wreckage. Mary Lovett, whose husband was standing in front of him and who was smiling at him the way no one had done since Duffy's father had been alive.

"Come this way, please," the nurse said.

Duffy started toward the door at the same time Lovett did.

The nurse raised an eyebrow. "The hospital is packed, no room for visitors. Sorry, sir, family only."

Duffy forced a smile to hide his envy.

"We've set her arm and taped her broken ribs," the nurse continued. "She's comfortable for the moment, but don't stay long. She should rest. The wards are full so we've had to curtain off a portion of the hallway. God knows what we're going to do if more casualities come in, poor things."

Both Duffy and Lovett eyed the corridor that led to Mary's bed.

"You're welcome to come and see her later," Lovett said. "I'm sure she'll want to thank you."

"I'll look forward to it," Duffy replied, surprised that his voice sounded so calm. Why couldn't Lovett have been under that wreckage? If he had been, Mary would be alone and in need of someone like Duffy.

"Wait for me, then, will you?" Lovett said, not moving until Duffy agreed.

As they walked down the corridor together, Duffy tapped the side of his head to show he'd just remembered something. "Dammit! I've got to call in."

"Young man," the nurse said, "we can't have that kind of language here."

"Yes, sister."

"There's a telephone downstairs," she relented. "You can use that if you're quiet about it."

Lovett drew the curtain far enough for Duffy to get a glimpse of Mary's face as she lay on the bed, her red hair splayed over the crisp pillow like a halo. "I'll join you downstairs in a few minutes," Lovett said.

Duffy nodded to mask the scream of protest welling inside him. Mary, why couldn't you have been mine?

The curtain was drawn. With it went the sight of her. Darkness seemed to close around him. His sigh of whiskey breath drew a look of disapproval from the sister, who folded her arms over her bosom and glared at him, refusing to leave Mary's door unguarded until she saw the back of him.

"Downstairs, you say? I thought there was one outside the director's office."

"He doesn't like people using that one." She looked at him sharply.

"My editor's waiting," he told her.

"These people have suffered enough without having to read about it," she called after him.

He fled her withering gaze only to encounter a barrage from his city editor when he called.

"For Christ's sake, Duffy, it's been so long I figured you were dead. Hell, I hoped you were dead. That way, I could have turned you into a hero. 'One of the *New York World*'s own falls in combat.'"

I am a hero, Duffy thought. Mary said so. "I'm at the hospital," he said.

"That's more like it. '*World*'s own wounded in combat.'"

"I rescued someone," Duffy said.

"You got to the actual wreck?"

"Yes."

"That's what I need, an eyewitness account. Why the hell didn't you call in sooner?"

"I rode in the ambulance with the woman I dug out."

"I take back everything I said about you. You're good. An exclusive interview with one of the victims. That'll sell papers."

Duffy wasn't about to use Mary to sell newspapers. "She's too badly hurt to give an interview," he said.

"Hovering near death, eh? We can use that. Start dictating."

Succinctly, giving Mary a fictitious name, Duffy reported what he'd seen and heard. Details Green could fill in for himself, or make them up as he saw fit, a city editor's right, he so often proclaimed. When Duffy finished, the editor grumbled for a moment, then said grudgingly, "I've heard worse. Hold on while I feed this to Newmark."

Duffy slumped against the wall and reached for his flask. For once he limited himself to a single sip, which he swished around like mouthwash before swallowing.

Green came back on the line. "I want you back in that tunnel."

"There's something funny going on"

"What do you mean funny?"

"It's not just us that's shorthanded. Everybody is, the police, the BRT, even the hospital."

"So, it's a fine summer day. People are shirking. You're looking for an excuse to take the rest of the day off. The tunnel, Duffy."

"Now?"

"Unless you prefer unemployment," Green said and hung up.

Duffy grimaced. He was fooling himself about Mary. Her husband was with her now, so what would she want with the likes of a whiskey-soaked reporter?

"Mary wants to thank you," Lovett said, so close behind him that Duffy jumped.

"Sorry. I didn't mean to startle you. Come on. Maybe I can sneak you into her room."

Duffy forced a smile. His face burned with guilt. A man like him had no right even thinking about a woman like Mary.

"She's safe," he managed. "That's what counts."

Lovett held out his hand again. Duffy accepted it sheepishly.

"I owe you a debt I can never repay," Lovett said.

For the first time, Duffy noticed the scar on Lovett's face. It ran from his right ear all the way to his chin. Some reporter you are, he told himself, but he'd had eyes only for Mary.

Lovett caught him staring. "I got it in the war." He tapped his right knee. "The face and a bad leg." He took a step to show his limp. "Crashed my plane."

"Where?" Duffy asked, though part of him, that part that envied Lovett, didn't give a damn.

"France. I was shot down. I was one of the lucky ones. I didn't burn."

Duffy cringed inwardly. He hadn't been fit to serve in the army. "I can't stay. I have to go back to work."

"Mary told me you were a reporter."

He nodded. "For the *World*."

Lovett's lips pinched together in disapproval.

"I've left Mary's name out," Duffy hurried to say.

"That's another debt I owe you."

With a shrug, Duffy turned to go.

"Dinner," Lovett called after him. "Mary asked me to invite you to dinner. Here's our address."

He handed Duffy a slip of paper.

"Why don't we make it one month from today. Mary ought to be up and around by then. Say seven o'clock."

Duffy started to say no. Seeing Mary again would only make him miserable. And she was married to a war hero, for God's sake, a wounded one at that.

"I'll be there," Duffy said, the words coming out of his mouth almost on their own.

"Good. We'll look forward to it," Lovett said.

Before leaving the hospital, Duffy carefully tucked the note containing Mary's address into his billfold for safekeeping.

31

Nick sat up with a start. Her wristwatch alarm, set for an hour before daybreak, had been right next to her ear when it went off.

Yawning, she struggled out of her sleeping bag and unzipped her tent flap. The sky was still pitch black, but there was enough glow from the fire's embers to make out her watch face. She was on time. Now all she had to do was creep over to Erickson's tent, so they could have a chat without being disturbed.

She sighed, the frigid air fogging around her face, and shivered. What she really wanted was to crawl back into her warm, cocoonlike sleeping bag and wait for someone to make coffee. But she couldn't rid herself of the feeling that the old pilot was holding something back, something he didn't want to speak about in front of the others.

She dug into her sleeping bag, fished out her warm boots, and pulled them on. Boot management was something she'd learned on one of her father's wintertime digs. Boots left in the open could freeze stiff by morning.

She struggled into her parka, which she'd used as a pillow, checked that her flashlight was still in the pocket, and unzipped her tent all the way. Then she hesitated.

Maybe she was overreacting. Worse yet, maybe the old boy was a bit gaga. She shook her head. That didn't make sense. So far, he'd been as good as his word. For starters, the Val had been right where he'd said it would be.

So why hadn't he told them about seeing the mining camp sooner? The obvious explanation was that he'd simply forgotten. Under normal circumstances such a lapse wouldn't have mattered. But now Kelly was dead, killed on the trail leading to that mining camp.

So move, she told herself. Go talk to the man. Follow Elliot's rules: Don't speculate, don't guess, don't make assumptions.

Nodding to herself, Nick crawled out of her tent. Once on her feet, she looked around, half expecting to see Gus still on watch from the night before. But there was no sign of life in camp. Even the fire, usually tended so carefully, was down to its last, anemic embers. Another few minutes and it would have to be rekindled from scratch.

She moved quietly, as much to keep from waking the camp as anything else, but she still felt like a sneak thief. When she reached Erickson's tent, she knelt in front of the flap and whispered his name.

There was no response.

She pressed her face to the nylon siding and whispered again. When he didn't answer, she felt for the zipper, though if the tent was like her own, the pull tab would be on the inside. Her fingers felt an opening. The tent flap hadn't been closed all the way. She wiggled her hand inside, found the tab, and unzipped the flap.

When she switched on her flashlight, Erickson's eyes didn't blink. Death had frozen them open.

She stifled a cry. No point in alarming the others. "Goodbye, Wes," she murmured. "I hope you're in Valhalla with the rest of the warriors." She started to stand up when a tremendous blow sent her sailing halfway across the camp. She heard Hurst shout and Karen Royce scream, then Gus was lifting her out of the tangle of brambles that had broken her fall.

"This way," he said, half lifting her, half dragging her toward the fire. He rapidly rekindled the fire and Nick nearly screamed when she saw the towering black shape illuminated by the flames. It let out a roar that Nick hoped she'd never hear again in her lifetime, but backed off.

"It was startled," Gus explained.

"It was startled?" Nick said. "What if it gets mad?"

Hurst joined them, with Alcott close behind. A moment later Barlow led a crying Tyler to the fire.

"There must be at least ten of them," Hurst said. "They're all over the place."

"There are three," Gus replied calmly. "They will circle and try to get behind us. We cannot keep the fire between them and us for long. We are distracting them from the food." He swept up a flaming brand and said, "Come," taking Nick's arm. "We will go to the cars. I'll get the old man."

"He died in the night," she said.

"It begins, then," Gus answered.

Ivins and Royce had already locked themselves in one of the Excursions. For a moment Nick thought Ivins wasn't going to let them in the car, but the doctor leaned over him and released the latch.

Gus shoved Nick into the backseat before climbing after her.

"There's no more room," Ivins mumbled. Again it was Karen Royce who detached a key from a set that were dangling from the ignition and handed it to Barlow.

"The other car," she said.

Barlow nodded and led the others away.

"We were lucky," Gus said in a whisper. "Probably, they were more curious than anything else."

"Christ's sake," Ivins sputtered. "This is ridiculous, sitting here doing nothing while those . . . animals eat our food."

"We can spare them a little bacon."

"That's not the point."

Gus leaned forward, close to Ivins, who was in the driver's seat. "If we sit here calmly and quietly, they'll go away. This time of year, bears scrounge all the food they can find before they hibernate."

"And if they don't go away?" Ivins asked.

"We'll have to wait and see, won't we?"

Ivins banged the steering wheel. "You're starting to piss me off."

"Relax," Nick told him. "There's nothing we can do anyway, though I'm sorry about leaving Erickson behind."

"What?"

"He's dead."

"I say we shoot the bears."

"With what?" Nick said without thinking. "Kelly's gun is missing, and they didn't kill him, anyway."

Beside her, she felt Gus stiffen.

"Bastard bears," Ivins muttered.

There was enough light now to see that the largest of the animals had stopped circling the fire to raise her head as if testing the air. The other two watched her closely.

Nick nudged Gus. "What are they doing?"

Ivins twisted around to face her. "They've probably figured out there isn't enough good stuff to go around. That leaves us for breakfast."

"They won't attack the cars unless provoked," Gus said.

Ivins pointed a finger at the Inuit. "I see. You're a mind reader now."

"I don't have to be." He nodded toward the fire. "They have plenty of food."

The bears had turned their attention to one of the tents.

In horror, Nick said, "Erickson. They've found Erickson's body."

"That does it." Ivins lunged for the glove box and came out with a black pistol.

"Put the gun down," Gus said sharply.

"A man has a right to protect himself."

"You swore you had no weapons."

"So sue me."

"Give me the gun," Gus said, "and I'll forget that you've broken the law."

"Fuck you." Ivins threw open the car door and began firing. At the sound, the large bear turned and charged. Ivins barely managed to scramble back inside.

The bear took out her frustration on the car, slamming into it hard enough to rock the huge Ford on its wheels. Claws raked the metal siding. A side mirror tore off.

"Jesus," Ivins said, reaching for the glove box to retrieve a fresh ammunition clip.

"It's a federal crime to shoot an endangered species," Gus said matter-of-factly.

"We're the ones endangered," Ivins snapped back.

One of the tires exploded.

"Son of a bitch!" Ivins slammed home the fresh clip.

Someone in the one of the other Fords honked a horn to distract the bear. But the sound only enraged her. She charged the next Ford in line, this time forgoing metal to attack the more vulnerable tires.

"For Christ's sake," Ivins shouted at Gus. "If I can't shoot them, do something. If you don't, we're going to be on foot."

"That's a female out there," Gus answered, "the most dangerous animal alive when someone threatens her cubs. And you tried to shoot one."

"How the hell did I know?"

"Give me the gun," Gus said.

"Not on your life."

"So be it." Gus turned to Nick and took her hand. "Remember, in this climate, food is the key to survival. If you get lost, you must eat within three days. If you don't, your strength will go and the cold will take you. Look for rabbits. They like to hide near rocks and streams. Ptarmigans are good eating, too. If your aim is good enough you can kill one with a rock. But remember, you must do that quickly, before your strength goes."

"I'm a better shot with a rifle than a rock," she told him, producing a contemptuous snort from Ivins.

"Then make a net with tree branches."

"I won't get lost."

"Sometimes it's the only way to survive."

"What the hell are you saying?" she asked him.

"I must do what my people have always done when outsiders bring evil upon our land."

"What evil?" Ivins said.

Gus ignored him and spoke directly to Nick. "One more thing, round clouds are a bad omen. When they come, a great storm is sure to follow." He squeezed her hand. "Stay here in the car until it's light. By then the bears will be foraging somewhere else. *Aksuse'*. Be strong."

Before Nick could reply he launched himself out of the Ford and slammed the door behind him. At the sound, the great bear roared and turned away from the other car. When she saw Gus, she rose up on her hind legs and clawed at the air.

Gus ran for the trees.

With a snarl, the bear dropped to all fours and gave chase. Her cubs followed.

"Jesus," Royce said. "That's a brave man."

"A dead one, you mean," Ivins responded.

32

The coming of light revealed a dead gray sky, so low Nick felt she could almost touch it. There were none of Gus's round clouds to be seen, though, just a solid, leaden overcast.

Their camp was in shambles. Half the food storage containers had been ripped open, as had the garbage bins. Two of the Fords looked like they'd been through a war. Four of their eight tires had been shredded, which left them with only one useable vehicle.

Cautiously, Nick, Royce, and Ivins opened the doors on the Ford they'd been sharing. The doors on the other cars opened, too, but no one made a move.

"Gus!" Nick called softly. When she got no response, she raised her voice. "Gus! Can you hear me?"

Not so much as an echo came back. She left the Ford. The others followed.

"The bastard probably abandoned us," Ivins said.

"An hour ago you said he was dead meat," she reminded him.

Ivins shrugged. "It was just talk."

"You're an asshole."

"Doctor Scott," Alcott said as he emerged from the neighboring vehicle, "that'll be enough of that."

"Ivins and his gun damn near got us killed," she shot back. "If it hadn't been for Gus, who knows what might have happened? Look for yourself. Thanks to him, the bears didn't get all our food."

"Keep your voice down," Alcott said, moving close beside her. "The bears might hear you."

"Let them," Ivins said, cocking his pistol. Now that it was light, Nick recognized the weapon as a nine-millimeter Glock, state of the art when it came to killing people, but she sure as hell wouldn't go up against a grizzly with one.

"You heard Gus," she said to Ivins. "These bears are on the endangered list. You shoot one and I'll testify against you. That's a promise."

Hurst spoke up. "Where's Erickson? I thought he was with you."

Nick shook her head. "I went to see him just before the bears came. He'd died in his sleep."

"Are you sure? My God, where's his body?"

Nick swallowed hard. "I think the bears found it," she replied.

Ivins said, "I suppose we need to make certain. If we investigate the trail I mentioned we can look for his . . . ah, remains."

Alcott shook his head. "I don't think that's wise in light of what's happened. In fact, I think it's time we left this place."

"We can be there and back in a few hours. The earliest the chopper can make it in will be tomorrow. We can have them haul in some tires for the car. Surely, Donald," he said, clapping

Alcott on the shoulder, "you don't want to give everything up on the verge of success?"

"Your chopper will be in tomorrow assuming it doesn't snow," Nick said.

Ivins shook his head. "In case you haven't noticed, it's warmed up. It's practically balmy. Besides, I checked the weather forecast myself. Clouds sure, but no snow." He shrugged. "Would I risk our chopper if I thought it was going to snow?"

"What about the risk from the bears?" Alcott said.

"Artifacts for your museum should be worth some risk. Besides, I happen to know that Mister McKenna is particularly interested in the gold rush era. This little extra trip could have a big payoff, Donald."

Nick could see that Alcott was wavering. "If we're going to stay, I should see to the Val's rivets," she said.

Ivins smiled. "Did I tell you that I spoke to Mister McKenna last night? We can hook up the satellite phone and contact him now if you'd like. He's a busy man but I'm sure he won't mind being interrupted."

Alcott sighed so hard it deflated him. "That won't be necessary."

Ivins thumped him on the back hard enough to make him wince. "That's the spirit. I loaded some gear yesterday. All we've got to do is get it out of the cars and be on our way."

Nick was surprised to see Ivins shoulder a heavily laden backpack, since all they intended was to conduct a quick reconnaissance. Karen, too, grabbed a fully loaded pack, as did Lew Tyler, though that was no surprise considering the amount of camera equipment he always carried with him.

When she and Hurst were handed similar packs, she raised a skeptical eyebrow.

"Just a precaution," Ivins explained. "You ought to be happy. You're the one who thinks it's going to snow."

Nick glared but donned her pack just the same. After a moment's hesitation, Hurst followed her example.

"If you people don't mind," Alcott said, his tone making it

clear that he didn't give a damn whether they minded or not, "I'll wait here by the fire. I have no intention of walking over that mountain just to see an old mining camp. If you find anything of interest, Nick, we can discuss it when you get back."

"Of course."

"What if the bears come back?" Tyler asked.

"Mike has volunteered to stay behind with me," Alcott added, the expression on his face reminding Nick who was in charge and who Mike Barlow, her assistant, actually worked for. "We'll build up the fire," he continued, "and we can always get into the cars, if they should return."

For an instant, she was tempted to argue. Other than herself, Barlow was the only one with dig experience. But then there wasn't going to be time to dig anyway.

33

Ivins set a fast pace. Even so, it took nearly two hours to reach the trail's summit. What he and Karen had called an easy walk had eaten up half the morning and left everyone gasping for breath. Worse yet, by gaining altitude they'd closed the gap between themselves and the threatening sky and were soon shrouded in clouds.

Descending the other side, they moved in single file, holding on to one another to keep from getting separated. A rainlike mist soaked them and the trail, making it slick and treacherous.

Ivins called a halt where the trail became a narrow ledge as it passed between a cliff of sheer rock on one side and a deep crevasse on the other. Just how deep the chasm was, Nick couldn't tell through the mist.

"This is no place to stop," Hurst complained, backing against the rock face. "There's not enough room to sit down."

"Kelly died in a place like this," Nick said, shuddering at the memory of the crevasse and its knifelike outcroppings of ice.

"It gets better and better," Hurst muttered.

"Wait till you see the mining camp," Ivins said to ease the tension. "It's worth it. Isn't that right, Karen?"

She blew on her gloved hands. "If you say so."

Nick noticed the edge to Karen's voice. It seemed to confirm Gus's assessment of the pair. They no longer appeared to be the lovers she had suspected. Just what was their relationship, then?

Nick was mulling over the possibilities when she heard a shout behind them. "Hello. Anybody there?"

"It's Barlow," Hurst said, then raised his voice. "Mike, we're directly ahead of you. Be careful. There's a crevasse on your left."

A moment later Barlow materialized out of the mist.

Ivins called to him.

He caught sight of them, and waved. "Thank God I've found you. Alcott's dead."

The breath caught in Nick's throat as Gus's words echoed in her head. *It begins, then.*

The moment Barlow reached them, he turned to look back the way he'd come. "The bears came back."

He raised his arm to show where his parka had been clawed to shreds. Only then did Nick see the bloodstains on the Gore-Tex.

"We didn't see them until they were on top of us," Barlow continued. "They attacked without warning, two of them. The only reason I'm here is that they started fighting over Doctor Alcott's body. The poor man."

"For Christ's sake," Ivins said angrily. "I want those animals hunted down and shot."

"Now's not the time," Karen said as she examined Barlow's parka. "Are you hurt?"

He shook his head. "That's Alcott's blood, not mine. There was nothing I could do."

"Goddamn bears," Ivins persisted.

"You're missing the point," Hurst told him. "They've tasted blood. They're man-eaters now. If they came back for Alcott, they could come after us. We've got to get out of here."

"We can't go back to the camp," Barlow said. "The bears are still there."

"Arguing isn't going to get us anywhere," Ivins said. "I say we move. It's shorter to go on than go back. We can stay overnight at the gold mine and return in the morning. By then the bears will probably be gone and the chopper will have arrived." When no one objected, he turned and led the way.

Nick stayed close to the granite wall. When that ran out so did the crevasse. At that point the trail was wide enough to walk two abreast. When she drew alongside Ivins, he grunted and said, "You see, we're out of the clouds. The trail ahead is dry. No storm."

She glanced up see that the mist had given way to clouds. They were not the ragged thunderheads that brought great storms to Anasazi country. They were round, the clouds Gus had warned her about.

34

The next day Duffy was back on obituaries, slowly pecking at the Hammond
typewriter with his bandaged hands. The
newsroom was as empty as it had been
for the previous two days. Newmark was
sitting at a corner desk leaning against
the wall, apparently sleeping. Green, the
city editor, was pacing like a caged animal.

"It's enough to make a strong man
weep," he cursed. "If it weren't for the
war we wouldn't be able to put this rag
on the streets."

"This isn't natural," Duffy complained.

"You're darn right it isn't natural.
We're already advertising to replace the
fools who think that they can abuse the
paper's generosity."

"Green, you've got to listen to me.

Something is happening. The crime rate's down. O'Malley told me that they were shorthanded at the station. The driver that caused the wreck was pulling extra shifts because they were shorthanded."

"The BRT was dealing with a wildcat strike," Green replied.

"Sure, and I noticed that none of that information got into the story, but the really odd thing was that they were short-handed at the hospital, too." He held up his hand and forestalled Green's comment. "They were pulling extra shifts before the train wreck. And one of the nurses kept whispering about *her*."

Green raised his eyebrows. "Are you sure you didn't go to Bedlam to get fixed up? Did you maybe get a knock on the head?"

Duffy shook his head. "I only heard about half of what she said, my hands hurt so much. But I'm sure she said something to me about a lady." He paused for a moment. "A Spanish lady."

"What has that got to do with . . . wait a minute." The editor snapped his fingers and dashed into his office. Duffy could see him rooting through a pile of last week's dispatches.

"Ispanka!" he shouted charging out of the office, waving a dispatch.

"You mean Eureka," Newmark said, waking up.

"No, Newmark. If you even made a pretense of staying sober, like Duffy, you'd have remembered that Reuters had informed us that the Russians were having a spot of trouble fielding their troops. They were experiencing *Ispanka,* which our Reuters correspondent kindly translates for us as the Spanish Lady."

"Duffy," Green continued, "you're not much good to me here with your hands all swathed like you were wearing mittens. Get over to Fifty-fifth Street and talk to the new guy that just took over as commissioner of public health. Copeland, I think his name is. See if you can find out what's up."

As Duffy pedaled toward Fifty-fifth Street, it felt good to be out of the office. Miraculously his old bike had been waiting for him outside the entrance to Astor's private station when he had at last dragged himself back from his second stint at the tunnel. Perhaps the presence of the cop had ensured its safety, but Duffy was cynical enough to believe that the cop would have taken it home for himself if it had been in better shape.

He stopped at the Board of Health, and rolled the old bike into the lobby, where he propped it up against the wall and removed the bicycle clips from his trouser legs. He straightened his tie and approached the receptionist, a bored young woman reading a magazine.

"Ned Duffy, of the *World,* to see Doctor Copeland," he told her.

"Do you have an appointment?" she asked without even looking up.

"I'm sure Doctor Copeland will want to see me," Duffy confidently replied.

"Doctor Copeland never sees anyone without an appointment."

Duffy leaned over and snatched the magazine away. "Oh, I think he'll see me. Tell him it's Duffy of the *World* here to talk about the Spanish Lady."

The girl glared at him and then plugged into the switchboard, never taking her eyes off him. "Doctor Copeland, sir, there's a foreign man here to speak to you about some Spanish woman."

Duffy leaned over and yelled, "The Spanish Lady."

The girl jumped, "There's no need to yell like that." To Duffy she said, "He'll give you ten minutes. Take the elevator and get off at four. Now give me back my reading."

"Why did you tell him I was a foreigner?" Duffy asked as he handed over the copy of the *Saturday Evening Post.*

"You said you were from the world," the girl replied truculently. "This is New York."

Dr. Royal Copeland was a small man who rose to greet Duffy as he entered the office. "Mister er, uh?" he grunted inquiringly.

"Ned Duffy, from the *World.*"

"Your English is excellent."

"I'm a reporter. The *World* is my newspaper."

"Oh, of course. I read the *Herald* myself. You'll have to excuse the girl, she's just filling in. We seem to be somewhat shorthanded at the moment."

"That's exactly what I've come to talk to you about. Everyone seems to be shorthanded at the moment."

The small man blinked. "You've come to talk to me about labor problems?"

"Sir, I'll not beat about the bush. It seems that there are an awful lot of sick people about. In fact, they're so sick that they can't report to work. Is the city doing anything about it?"

"Well, we have noticed a mild influenza, but it certainly isn't anything to worry about."

"And might this mild influenza be called the Spanish Lady?"

For a moment Duffy imagined that Copeland's florid complexion paled, but it could have been a trick of the light.

"That's a rather baroque term for a very common form of the grippe," Copeland said, smiling. "There was a brief epidemic in Spain early this spring, I believe. You know how xenophobic Europeans are. Each country blaming the other for some natural disaster."

"Disaster?" Duffy interjected.

"The French Pox, The Spanish Lady, what does it matter? Don't try to put words in my mouth, young man. We had our own little flurry in March, I believe. There were some incidences reported among the troops at Fort Riley. That's in Kansas, a long way from New York. I can assure you we are up on the latest conditions and there's nothing to worry about."

"Any deaths?"

"You know what they say about the influenza. The physician's friend, they call it, carrying off those who are weak or elderly. There . . . ah . . . has been some increase in the mortality levels."

"Doctor Copeland, I see a lot of obituaries in my line of business. There are so many these days that we can't keep up and they're not all elderly. Not by a long shot."

Copeland bristled. "And did these obituaries state that the individuals died of influenza?"

Duffy hesitated. "Well . . . no," he stammered. "A few maybe, mostly pneumonia, brain fever, and even grippe. But if this is something new, most local doctors wouldn't recognize it, would they, not unless your office warned them."

"I can assure you there's nothing to warn anyone about. Now I've given you just about as much time as I care to. You can quote me as saying that there's nothing to worry about, do you understand?"

"Oh, I understand," Duffy replied. "My condolences on your shortness of help. It seems like there's a lot of that going around."

3 5

The moment the mining camp came into sight, Nick felt rejuvenated. Her exhaustion gave way to heart-thumping eagerness as she jogged ahead, outdistancing the others. Her worries about Gus's storm clouds vanished. Even his warning about evil walking his sacred land paled in comparison to the prospect of an archaeological discovery. At a glance, the mining camp didn't live up to Ivins's glowing description, but Nick knew better than to judge a site by first appearances.

This one was situated atop a shallow ridge of land, the height and size of a graded highway and about a half mile long. The northern end of it, or what she assumed to be north without the sun as a guide, had been buried beneath a slide of dark shale.

Squatting atop the ridge's southern end was the cabin Erickson had seen so long ago from his P-38, plus a couple of sluice cradles, not much of a site after all. The mine itself, a rubble-strewn opening in the mountain, was a good quarter of a mile away.

Beyond the ridge and its campsite, a massive glacial plain stretched all the way to the gloomy horizon. Across that plain blew a freezing, east wind. Because of it, the temperature felt twenty degrees colder than their camp on the other side of the sheltering Hammersmiths.

Nick stopped in front of the cabin, or what was left of it, to catch her breath. The roof had collapsed in the middle, creating a sort of lean-to effect with both outer walls. There were no windows, and the single entrance had been crushed to the size of a dog door when the roof fell in.

She knelt and used a rock to dig into the soil. Close below the surface lay permafrost. Mining here would be backbreaking in the best of weather. Back in the gold rush, without modern equipment, it must have been sheer hell. As for digging for artifacts, Nick shook her head. It wouldn't be very practical.

The others arrived. Only Ivins joined her, the rest of the party took shelter behind the cabin's west wall, out of the wind.

"What do you think?" he asked her.

"Examining this site would take a week in good weather. Now . . ." She shook her head. "Miners usually don't leave much behind anyway. The best we could hope for is to find their trash."

"Let's get out of the wind and I'll prove you wrong."

"Lead the way."

The moment she and Ivins reached the others, Hurst called out, "Remind me to stick to museums from now on. The fact is, I give you permission to kick me in the butt if I so much as look at an airplane newer than a Spad."

"I told you so" was on the tip of her tongue when she spotted shovels and picks stacked carefully nearby. They, too, were out of the wind and so new they gleamed. Too new in a corrosive climate like this. She swung around to confront Ivins only to find a pistol pointed at her chest.

He winked. "Good-looking women aren't as dumb as people say." He moved away from the wall far enough to show everyone the gun in his hand.

"What the hell's going on?" Hurst demanded.

"Judging by the look on your face, Nick, you can explain it to him," Ivins replied.

"Talk to me, Nick," Hurst said.

She shrugged. "Those tools are brand new. Someone had to bring them here, and the only people unaccounted for recently are Ivins and the doctor."

"You can't have a proper archaeological dig without proper equipment," Ivins said. "Isn't that right, Doctor Royce?"

"I have mine right here," Karen answered, producing a pistol of her own, a sister of the Glock in Ivins's hand.

Ivins motioned Karen away from the wall and out of his line of fire. A calculated, professional move, Nick thought, though she still couldn't imagine their motive. As far as she could see, nothing in this derelict mining camp was worth the effort.

Ivins said, "I'm sorry we have to do it this way, but that old bastard Erickson misled us. We'd expected to find what we wanted in plain sight. If we had, you people would have been saved a lot of hard work. Sorry." He smiled to show his sincerity, but the look in his eye told Nick that he was enjoying himself.

"What the hell are you talking about?" Hurst blurted. "We came here looking for a Japanese dive bomber and that's what we found."

"I'm afraid that was a lot of hard work for nothing. The Val was only important as a reference point. Finding it proved that we were in the right place, only on the wrong side of the mountains. I'm afraid your Val's so much useless junk."

Nick and Hurst exchanged bewildered looks. Collectors and museums alike would pay a fortune for a find like that once it was restored. Tyler and Barlow looked equally stunned.

"Will you get to the point," Hurst said, "before we all freeze to death?"

"Hard work will warm you up," Karen told him. "That's my medical advice."

"Just how much digging has to be done is up to you, Doctor Scott," Ivins added. "Since what we're looking for isn't where we expected, you're going to have to find it for us."

Nick eyed the shovels and picks skeptically.

"Don't worry," Ivins assured her. "We made several trips over the past few days. Everything you're going to need is here, even your metal detectors and a portable satellite dish so we can phone in your success."

"Just what is it we're looking for?"

"Fame and fortune, what else? As for me, I'll leave the fame to someone else. What about you, Doc?"

"Cash buys you everything else."

Watching them, Nick felt like a fool for thinking them lovers. She should have listened to Gus.

"Naturally," Ivins went on, "we'd hoped our treasure would be right where the old fart said it was, but just in case it wasn't we wanted a qualified archaeologist with us. Your reputation with airplanes won you the honor, Doctor Scott. We want you to find us another one."

He clicked his tongue at Hurst. "You turned out to be a bonus, Doctor Hurst. I hope you're worth the hundred thousand Doctor Alcott insisted on paying you."

"What?" Nick said, glaring at Hurst.

Ivins ignored her. "The question is, which of you is going to be more useful, though my money is on Doctor Scott. Either way, there's plenty of hard work for everyone, I'm happy to say, because the ground is frozen solid."

"Why happy?" Tyler asked.

"Permafrost is as good as a deep freeze," the doctor answered.

"I don't understand," the cameraman said. "I'm just here to shoot pictures."

"Erickson spotted our objective when he flew over back in forty-two. The trouble is, nature's covered it up, like she does with all her treasures."

Karen interrupted. "I know you're enjoying yourself, but get on with it."

"Doctor's orders, is it? Why not? My real job is solving problems for Mister McKenna. The problem here is those damned bears and their refuge. If it hadn't been for them, we would have walked right in and taken what we wanted, or bought the place if we had to. We considered a raid, in and out before Kelly and his Eskimo knew what hit them. But Mister McKenna vetoed that. If we failed, he said, one of our competitors might get wind of what we were after."

Nick's teeth chattered, more from fear than cold. "Make your point," she said, "before we all turn into permafrost."

"I'm surprised you didn't catch onto us when Erickson spilled the beans about seeing this camp. Lucky for us, the old bastard didn't know what he was looking at."

Ivins grinned, pleased with himself. Maybe maniacs didn't feel the cold, Nick thought. As for his cohort, the doctor looked as miserable as everyone else, gun or no gun.

"What about you, Doctor Scott?" he continued. "Now that you know there's a fortune to be had, look around and tell me if you see any likely hiding places. You lead, we'll follow."

Nick's second look produced no more than her first. There was the cabin, a twelve-foot square, she estimated, and the sluice boxes. Hardly a major archaeological find.

She braved the wind and headed toward the old mine shaft but stopped a hundred yards short when she ran into a ravine, one of a series of shallow canyons that ran along the base of the mountain range. Their presence indicated periods of swift run-off.

She turned to Ivins and shrugged. "That mine's not big enough to hold an airplane. Even if it was, how would you get it there?"

"You're no better than Erickson. You don't know what

you're looking at either." He stamped his feet, whether to warm them or dance with joy she couldn't tell. "This is the site of the Flying Dutchman. Maybe you've heard of it."

Nick looked to Hurst. They both shook their heads, baffled.

"What about the Lost Dutchman Mine?" Ivins prodded.

She nodded. "A gold mine in Arizona's Superstition Mountains."

"Well, Alaska has its own version and it's going to make us billionaires."

36

Nick took one look at the metal detector Ivins had thrust into her hands and said, "Bloodhounds aren't designed to find mineral deposits."

"Gold?" Ivins shoved the second detector at Hurst. "Chicken feed. I told you. We're looking for the Flying Dutchman."

Ivins had forced Nick and Hurst to leave the cabin's shelter to go exploring, while Karen stayed behind with Tyler and Barlow.

Ivins laughed at her bewilderment. "That mine's only a namesake. What came out of it wouldn't buy you a new dress, Doctor Scott. What I want you to find is the original Flying Dutchman. It's a Junkers F.13, right up your alley if you're the expert people say you are."

Nick had never seen a Junkers F.13, but she'd read about them. It was the world's first all-metal airliner. In 1919 it vaulted Germany into the forefront of commercial aviation. Its single-engine design had evolved from the warplanes that Junkers built during World War I. But as a collectable it hardly rated armed robbery. The Val was much more valuable because of its connection with Pearl Harbor.

She asked, "Why would a Junkers land here?"

"Gold miners flew it."

"When?"

"In 1919."

"In this wilderness," Hurst said. "I find that hard to believe."

"It's here all right," Ivins answered. "We have more than Erickson's word on it. We've also confirmed it through independent research."

Hurst pursed his lips. "I'll say one thing, if any plane could make it, a Junkers could. They were great planes for their time. Did you know the Germans were still flying them on the Russian front as late as 1943? Six seaters, they were, though I imagine the Germans crammed in more soldiers than that."

Hurst leaned the metal detector against his shoulder, freeing his gloved hands so he could rub them together as he warmed to his subject. "The F.13 was made of corrugated Duralumin from nose to tail. In its time, it held several altitude and distance records."

"I knew it was a good idea to bring you along," Ivins said. "But you're not telling me anything I don't already know."

"It's what you're not telling *us* that worries me," Nick said. "Look at this place."

The narrow spit of land on which they stood was rocky and pitted, hardly a likely landing strip. But the glacial plain beyond, strewn with massive boulders, was even worse. This late in the day, under a heavy overcast, the landscape had turned an ugly gray.

Nick continued. "Why would a pilot risk landing his Junkers in a godforsaken place like this?"

"It's a long story. Right now, just find me the damned thing."

"You wouldn't happen to know exactly where Erickson saw it, would you?"

"Somewhere near the end of this ridge, if you believe the old fart."

"Which end?"

"He never said."

"It's too bad he's not here now to show us."

"Yeah, maybe we were a little premature there," Ivins said. "But once he started blabbing about this place, I figured it was time he had a heart attack."

"You killed him?" Hurst gasped.

Ivins shrugged. "Let's just say the doctor cured him of getting any older."

Hurst's eyes widened as they focused on the pistol in Ivins's hand. His expression said what Nick had already concluded, that once the guns had come out, their survival was unlikely, since Ivins wouldn't want surviving witnesses.

Nick forced a smile. "What's your Mister McKenna going to say when he finds out you killed the man who could have showed us where to look?"

Ivins gestured impatiently. "The Junkers was in plain sight in 1942."

She hugged her hands into her armpits so Ivins wouldn't see them shaking. More from cold and anger, she hoped, than from fear. The wind had picked up enough to send the chill factor plummeting. She glanced toward the cabin, where Karen Royce was guarding the others.

Ivins went on. "The old boy was very clear on that point. He described the Junkers in detail. It wasn't going anywhere, he said, because it had crashed into a rock."

Instinctively, Nick turned to study the rock slide that had buried the northern end of the spit.

"Jesus," Hurst muttered, "if it's under there we'll be digging forever."

"Let's hope not," Ivins said. "We haven't got that much food. At least, you haven't."

"That rockfall is forty feet deep in places," Nick pointed out. "At that depth, our metal detectors are useless. We won't know where to begin. Besides, if that plane is under there, it won't be worth salvaging."

"Just start looking," Ivins said.

"I suggest we walk the ridgeline first. Erosion could have sent the plane over the side."

"I did that yesterday, and didn't see anything."

"You're not an archaeologist," Nick said.

"What do you expect to find?"

"I won't know until I see it."

Ivins's eyes narrowed. "Let me tell you the rules first. If you screw up, I shoot Mister Hurst. I figure he's more expendable."

A visible inspection along both sides of the spit produced no sign of the Junkers, but then Nick hadn't expected to be that lucky. Still, procedure called for site survey before any digging began. And in this case procedure was buying them some time. It was also exposing them to a knife-sharp wind that cut to the bone.

Her hands were numb and she had a hard time holding onto the metal detector. Hurst had his Bloodhound slung over both shoulders, like a soldier so weary he no longer worried about the enemy.

"That's it," Nick said as they completed their tour. "That leaves us with the rockfall."

She checked the blackening sky. "We don't have much daylight left." Or maybe Gus's storm had finally arrived, bringing darkness with it.

Ivins, whose head was hunched into his parka, said, "To hell with this. We can start again in the morning." He gestured toward the cabin.

When they reached it, Nick saw that two tents had been erected along the outer, western wall. The tents, though out of the direct gale, billowed in back-drafts each time the wind gusted. Several containers were stacked close by, along with a couple of small cans of gasoline.

"Karen!" Ivins shouted.

"In here." Karen's voice, though windblown, hadn't come from the tents.

Ivins herded them to the far side of the cabin, where a light now shone from the opening that had once been a door. Old roof timbers had been wedged into the opening, enlarging it enough for a crawl-through on all fours.

Karen's head poked out. "The wind chill out here is a killer, so I shifted all the equipment into the tents. As soon as I back up, send them in one at a time."

Nick crawled in first, wriggling her way, wary of the squat, fragile-looking timbers that shored up what remained of the original door frame. Dislodge one, she thought, and she'd be trapped like a miner in a cave-in. But her claustrophobia was short-lived. The tunnellike entrance quickly opened up into a room shaped like a lean-to with a dirt floor. A softly hissing kerosene lantern lit the cramped space as brightly as a hundred-watt bulb.

Karen was crouched with her back against the cabin wall, her pistol at the ready. Tyler and Barlow were jammed together in the corner, their hands behind their backs.

Karen pointed Nick into the corner with them. Hurst joined Karen.

"Now turn around," Karen ordered, "with your hands behind your backs."

"They're using plastic handcuffs," Barlow complained.

"They're called restraints," Ivins clarified. "They're lightweight and tough as steel. Ain't technology great?"

Nick's every instinct told her to fight back but she resisted the temptation. Resistance would be useless in such a cramped space, especially against two guns.

"Let me do the honors," Ivins added as he grabbed Nick's wrists from behind, slipped a loop over them, and cinched it tight enough to hurt.

"You've cut off the circulation," she said.

"So?"

"I won't be much use to you if I can't use my hands."

"Let me take a look," Karen said.

"After I do Hurst."

Hurst grunted as the plastic noose tightened around his wrists.

Ivins said, "Okay, now she's all yours."

A moment later Karen said, "She's right," and loosened the restraint enough to stop the pain.

"You might as well make yourselves comfortable," Ivins said. "It's going to be a long night."

37

At the end of the day Nick was the last to eat. No doubt Ivins was proving a point by making her wait. One at a time the others had been released from their plastic handcuffs long enough to swallow down some cold energy bars. Tyler ate first, followed by Barlow, Hurst, and finally Nick.

A warm meal was out of the question, Ivins had said, because he didn't want to risk filling their lean-to with smoke. Nick didn't buy it, though, because the log walls were a maze of cracks and chinks. If they hadn't been, the kerosene lantern would have asphyxiated everyone long ago. The truth, Nick suspected, was that Ivins didn't want to risk cooking anything that might attract the bears.

"Now, is everybody comfy?" Ivins

said once they were all handcuffed again. Outside, the wind howled as if punctuating his comment.

"You're nuts," Hurst told him. "We're never going to dig up that airplane before we freeze to death."

Ivins settled onto the dirt floor, crossed his legs Indian-style, and rested the Glock on his thigh. "I'll settle for a wingtip, or even a glimpse. Hell, I don't actually have to see it. Just knowing for sure where it is will be good enough."

"What good's that going to do you?"

"I'll tell you what, we'll call it a bedtime story," Ivins said. "Now, let's see. Where to begin. Oh, yes"—he flashed a toothy smile—"once upon a time, shortly after World War One, a small band of ex–fighter pilots decided to make their fortune here in Alaska. The fact that it was a wilderness didn't bother them a bit. They'd survived a war. They thought themselves invincible. They pooled their money to buy a Junkers F.13. At the time, it was the best plane for the job, maybe the only one. It was sturdy and it didn't need much room to land or take off.

"They named their plane the Flying Dutchman, presumably a tribute to the Lost Dutchman mine or maybe that guy that kept sailing around in that opera. Anyhow they took off for Alaska and landed here."

"Wait a minute," Nick said. "You said there wasn't enough gold here to buy a dress."

"That's because they didn't have enough time to dig it out of the ground."

"Are you saying the gold's still here?"

"Who knows? Who gives a shit?"

"I don't get it."

"It's simple enough," Ivins went on. "Time ran out on them because they'd brought along a deadly female passenger. Back then they called her the Spanish Lady, their nickname for the Spanish influenza. She killed thirty million people in less than a year before she was through, including our band of pilots. We know it from the diary one of them left behind."

Ivins ran his thumb back and forth across his fingertips like a man counting money. But it was Karen who spoke. "At the

216

moment, their frozen bodies are worth more than gold to a company like E-Group. This flu virus is different from any virus mankind has seen before or since."

"What's so special about the flu?" Tyler said. "I had it last year. No big deal."

"Oh, you've never had flu like this," Karen replied. "It likes the strong, it kills the healthy. Your lungs turn to rubber and you drown in your own fluids. Most of its victims were between twenty and twenty-nine. How old are you, Mr. Tyler?"

Tyler visibly paled. Karen continued, "Once you dig the bodies up, I'll be able to extract cultures of the virus so that a vaccine can be synthesized." The rapturous look on Karen's face reminded Nick of her father when he was expounding on his Anasazi.

"Then why the guns?" Hurst asked. "If the doctor comes up with a vaccine for the Spanish flu, she'll be as famous as Jonas Salk. She'll win the Nobel Prize, for Christ's sake. Why didn't you ask for our help instead of treating us like convicts?"

Nick swallowed convulsively against the bile rising in her throat. What the hell was Gordon thinking about? These people weren't out to help humanity. If they had been, they wouldn't have killed a helpless old man, and then have the gall to admit it.

"Show her the diary," the doctor insisted.

"Don't expect to get your hands on the original," Ivins told Nick. "You of all people ought to appreciate its value as a historical document. At present, it graces the personal collection of our chairman, Jonathan McKenna. He's an authority on Eskimo art, in case you didn't know."

"I don't think a diary qualifies as art," Nick said.

"Let's call it an artifact, then. It came to the attention of one of Mister McKenna's scouts when he ran across it at an Eskimo trading post. It was cheap enough, so he bought it as a kind of memento if nothing else. When he tried to trace its origin, he was told that it had been brought into the trading post years ago by an Eskimo who said he found it at the site of an old airplane crash. But too many years had passed to trace the Eskimo, so the diary remained a mere curiosity piece for years. Then Erickson's story appeared in an Army Air Corps newsletter. That's when Mister McKenna knew he'd struck gold."

Ivins chuckled. "You see, Ms. Scott, if you'd bothered to read that newsletter for yourself, you'd not only have known about old Erickson's Val, but his sighting of the Junkers. At the time, though, the old fart didn't know what he was looking at. In any case, we suspect that the man who wrote the diary is probably still inside the Junkers."

"If he is, he might not be frozen," she pointed out.

"It doesn't matter. He buried the others close by, as you'll see from the diary. Find that plane for us, Doctor Scott, and we'll know where to start digging holes."

She shuddered at the thought.

Ivins grinned. "I thought you loved airplanes."

Nick closed her eyes and concentrated on breathing deeply to keep from being sick. In the darkness she heard Elaine, her mother, gloating. *You see what happens when a girl plays with airplanes instead of dolls. Mark my words. You'll end up like your father, running away from his responsibilities, from me.*

Someone laughed.

Nick opened her eyes, but saw no one smiling. Maybe it was Elaine's laughter she was hearing.

38

"No story," Green said.

"What do you mean, no story?"

"That *Bolshie*, Eugene V. Debs, sentenced to ten years in prison, that's a story," Green replied, holding up the previous day's front page. "Instead I get the Surgeon General saying eat good food and take salts of quinine if you're feeling ill."

"There is flu, and lots of people are sick."

"There's always flu. And our own city's Health Commissioner has said, and I quote, 'The city is in no danger of an epidemic. No need for our people to worry.'"

Duffy ground his teeth in rage. "He's lying. I could tell when I talked to him. You've got to give me more time to dig around. I've got friends at newspapers all over the country. I could call around."

"Sure you've got friends at newspapers all over the country. You've been fired from enough of them," Green retorted. "Besides, do you realize how long it would take to make those calls and what it would cost?"

"Telegrams?" Duffy asked hopefully. "Meanwhile, I could maybe get something from City Hall. Or I could go back and ask Copeland what he thinks now that the Surgeon General has warned the nation of flu."

"Three telegrams, no more, and you can spend six hours of my time, and that's it, do you understand? I'm only doing this because you did such a good job on the train wreck."

"You won't regret it," Duffy said.

"I'm sure I will."

By the end of the week, Duffy had spent more than the six hours that Green had allotted to him with no result. He'd pestered the Commissioner of Health until the man had posted a guard outside his office. No one at City Hall was returning his calls.

When the copy boy laid the three yellow envelopes from Western Union on his desk he was afraid to open them. He'd sent his own telegrams, "*Reply Paid,*" which was stretching Green's permission to wire for information.

He picked up the first telegram with trembling hands. He'd wired an old drinking buddy who had moved west to San Francisco after they'd done a stint together in Chicago. The telegram from the *San Francisco Chronicle* read:

WHERES MY 5 DOLLARS (stop)

He'd forgotten the debt. He'd have to cross San Francisco off as a possible place for employment. He groaned and crumpled up the telegram and threw it in the wastebasket. No need to let Green know that he'd even gotten a reply. At least not until the bill arrived.

He opened the second telegram, which had come from the *Philadelphia Inquirer.*

600 SAILORS IN HOSPITAL (stop)
FLU CONFINED TO NAVY (stop)

At least that was some confirmation. He closed his eyes and made a silent wish. All he needed was an additional confirmation and he was sitting on top of the story of a lifetime. He'd sent a telegram to another elbow-bending buddy at the *Boston Evening Transcript.* Duffy would have preferred the *Globe,* but he'd never been good enough to get a job there. His friend at the *Transcript* wired back:

FLU HERE (stop) 156 DEATHS TODAY (stop)
COOLIDGE WILL ASK WILSON FOR HELP TODAY (stop)

His stomach churned from a mixture of excitement and fear. The telegram had gone over ten words, but who cared if Green paid a premium. When Calvin Coolidge, the governor of Massachusetts, asked for help from a Democratic president things must be in a pretty bad way. Duffy had front-page material.

He jumped up from his desk and ran to Green's office. As he approached he noticed that Green was hunched over the typewriter with the copy boy hovering at his elbow.

"You can order them to stop the presses," Duffy said.

"For God's sake, I've already done that," Green replied. "Now beat it, can't you see I'm busy?"

Duffy was taken aback. How could Green have already known?

"You've got to read this," Duffy said, thrusting the telegram under Green's nose. "Massachusetts is hit bad. We've got to warn everyone. The Spanish Lady is coming."

"I don't care if the four horsemen are on their way. We've already got our lead story for today." He yanked the paper out of the typewriter and shoved it into the waiting hands of the copy boy. "Get this downstairs as fast as you can. Jump out the window, if you have to, but move." The boy scurried off.

"Look," Duffy persisted, presenting the telegram to Green one more time. "Massachusetts is asking for help."

"And so will you be, if you don't get out of here. This is a great day for America. I yanked the front page because our brave boys over there have just broken through the Hindenburg Line."

39

Armed with a Bloodhound metal detector, Nick crawled out of the lean-to shortly after dawn. Gordon Hurst was right behind her. Behind him came Ivins, prodding with his nine millimeter Glock.

The wind, which had howled all night, had subsided to occasional gusts. A light dusting of snow covered the ground, and yesterday's round clouds had been replaced by a dark, shapeless overcast that hung so low Nick was reminded of a shroud.

She stood up. The icy snow creaked under her boots, a sure sign that the temperature was well below freezing. Hurst rose up beside her. He, too, carried a Bloodhound.

Ivins gestured with the Glock.

"Don't just stand there, Doctor Scott. It's time you lived up to your reputation."

Nick looked at Hurst, who was hunched over, his neck scrunched into his parka, looking as cold and miserable as she was. Nick straightened her shoulders and smiled. She'd be damned if she'd give Ivins the satisfaction of seeing how she really felt.

"Come on, Gordon," she said, nodding in the direction of the rockfall, "we might as well sweep the area as we go."

"Shit," he said, switching on his Bloodhound. "With all the high-tech crap they turn out these days, you'd think they could make gloves that keep your fingers warm."

Nick grunted her agreement. Her own fingers already felt numb.

They separated far enough to keep their side-to-side sweeps from interfering with one another, and then started toward the rockfall, moving very deliberately. Halfway there, Nick's metal detector registered a minor fluctuation. She called a halt to have Hurst double-check her reading.

"I don't know," he said after making his sweep. "It doesn't look like much to me."

Ivins moved close to have a look for himself.

"Your pistol's going to throw off the reading," Nick told him, though she had no idea if it was true or not.

"I'll risk it." He pressed the Glock against the small of her back. "Give me the earphones." He motioned her to make a few sweeps with the magnetometer then yanked the earphones off.

"There's something there. Is it the plane?" he asked.

She shook her head. "The Bloodhounds went crazy when we found the Val. It would do the same for a Junkers."

"What have we found, then?"

"Your guess is as good as mine. We'll mark the spot and move on."

She piled half a dozen small rocks together, and then she and Hurst resumed their sweep. A few feet later, their Bloodhounds recorded a second hit.

"What's going on?" Ivins demanded.

A nightmare if it keeps up, Nick thought, imagining an unending string of holes to be dug. She said, "God knows. Maybe iron-bearing rocks have been washed down from the mountains over the years."

"Shit," Ivins said through clenched teeth as he stamped his feet.

The look of frustration on his face reminded Nick that he had to be as cold as she was, more so even because he wasn't working the Bloodhound. She smiled at him and asked, "What do you want us to do?"

"Keep going."

She marked the second hit and moved on, but the Bloodhounds were silent all the way to the rockfall, which was made up of a mixture of rock chips and boulders, piled twenty feet deep in most places, forty in others. If the Junkers lay at the bottom, reaching it would take all winter.

"Good God," Hurst muttered. "Look at the size of some of these rocks."

Nick scrambled up the icy rockfall with Hurst right behind her. From there, she scanned the entire area one more time. The view convinced her that there was only one possible landing place for miles, and that was the ridge. That Junkers had to be here.

"Nick," Hurst muttered under his breath, "you realize they're going to bury us here, don't you?"

"Yes." Along with sixty million other people around the world, she added to herself.

She switched on her Bloodhound and began edging toward the point where the original landslide had run out of momentum. Hurst followed right behind her, since the top of the rockfall was too narrow and treacherous to go side by side. Ivins covered them from below.

"If luck's with us, the slide pushed the plane ahead of it. If it did, it might not be too deeply buried."

"If we're lucky we won't find it at all."

"I don't think that's going to save us," she whispered.

The rockfall, though sloping away, was still a good ten feet deep when the Bloodhounds sounded their alarm.

"Christ!" Hurst blurted. "Some luck."

Nick beckoned to Ivins. "We've found it! You'd better come and check it for yourself."

"I'll take your word for it. You two start digging while I get the others."

By late afternoon, the four of them—Nick, Hurst, Barlow, and Tyler—hadn't shifted enough rock to make a patio. The larger rocks took the four of them to move. The smaller ones were like sand. Each time a handful was scooped out, another seemed to take its place.

In frustration, Nick gave up on the boulder she and Mike Barlow had been trying to dislodge and squatted down beside it to rest. Before she'd drawn a breath Ivins was beside her, brandishing his nine millimeter. Karen was positioned below and to one side to give her a clear field of fire.

"You're going to have to shoot me," she told him, "because there's no way we're going to dig out your Junkers."

"I have to be certain of its location."

"For Christ's sake. You saw the Bloodhounds. We're either sitting on top of an airplane or a flying saucer. Take your choice."

"The graves could be under here too, so keep moving rock."

"If they are," she said, "they'll just have to stay buried. Besides, look at the sky."

Ivins glanced up for an instant. "So?"

"The storm can't hold off forever."

"I was raised in Minnesota. It looks like this all winter, even when it isn't snowing."

"Storm or no storm," Nick said, "this rockfall isn't going anywhere."

"She's right," Karen called from below. "We'll have to come back in the spring with heavy equipment if we're going to move that much rock. It's either already too late, or it'll keep through the winter."

"Forget it," Ivins said. "They'll never let us back in."

Nick stood up. "Don't you think it's time you showed me the pilot's diary?"

"It didn't give specifics about the graves."

"I'm a specialist when it comes to graves, so get on that satellite phone of yours and call McKenna. He can read his precious diary to me."

"That won't be necessary. I brought a copy along, though I don't see how it'll help."

"If it doesn't," Nick said, "you and E-Group are going to have to get along without the Spanish Lady."

"Mister McKenna doesn't like bad news."

Karen said, "Right now I don't care what he likes. I'm freezing, and it's getting dark. Let's get out of the wind."

"All right," Ivins agreed reluctantly, "but tomorrow morning we start digging again. *Where* is up to Doctor Scott."

40

Nick couldn't stop shaking as she crawled into the lean-to. Even inside, out of the wind, she continued to shake. Without their bodies and lanterns to warm it, the lean-to had grown cold as a tomb. She hugged herself as she waited for Ivins to close their makeshift door behind him.

"Christ!" he sputtered. "It's a deepfreeze in here. We'd better light the rest of the lanterns."

Once that had been done, Nick felt relieved to see that everyone else was shaking as badly as she was, Ivins included.

"We're going to have to risk a fire," Karen said. "There's plenty of kindling in here from when the roof collapsed."

"Not until the handcuffs are on," Ivins told her.

"My fingers are too cold to work."

"Some doctor you are." Ivins flexed the trigger finger on his free hand. "At least one of us is in working order."

"You do the handcuffs, then."

Ivins snorted. "Look at them. They're in no condition to run away."

You're absolutely right, Nick thought as she caught sight of a piece of kindling sharp enough to qualify as a splinter. They'd die of exposure if they ran. It was better to make a fight of it here and now. She tried flexing her fingers, but they were so numb she couldn't feel them.

Her eyes measured the distance to the splinter. She guessed it to be just out of reach. She could lunge for it, of course, but would her fingers have the strength to hold on? And even if they did, would she have time to stab Ivins before he started shooting?

The breath from her sigh hung in the air like a frosty question mark. Sooner or later she'd have to try for the gun, but now was not the time. Her reluctant fingers and Karen's second gun made the risk too great.

"You first, Scott," Ivins said, breaking in on her thoughts. "Hands behind your back."

"And the diary?" Nick said.

"Do as you're told and we'll soon be nice and cozy here."

Cozy seemed an impossible goal, even after Ivins got a fire going. He started small, waiting to see which way the smoke drifted. At first, it hung in the icy air like fog, but gradually rose to form an overcast at the lean-to's apex.

When Ivins added more wood, the rising heat began forcing the smoke out through chinks in the old roof. Within minutes the fog dissipated completely, and Nick felt warm for the first time all day. Watery eyes and a sooty taste in her mouth were a small price to pay for an end to her shakes.

She leaned back against the log wall and closed her eyes. She must have fallen asleep, though she had no sense of time passing, when someone shook her shoulder. She opened her eyes to see Ivins smiling at her.

"Time to rise and shine," he said.

She groaned.

He snorted. "Your morning paper's arrived." He released her bonds.

Nick blinked and looked around the lean-to. Everyone else was sleeping, even Karen. Nick swallowed dryly. Her throat burned.

Ivins waved papers in her face. "Here's the diary you wanted to see." He then kicked Hurst. "Let him read it too."

She rubbed her eyes. Her hands were so swollen from the handcuffs she had trouble holding the paper. As she read each page she handed it to Hurst.

The diary had been kept by a man named Samuel Lovett. At first, it read like a travelogue. In 1919 three men, bonded together by their survival of World War I, pooled their resources to buy a Junkers airplane. They called themselves and their plane the Flying Dutchman. They took off from New Jersey and hopscotched their way across the United States and finally north into Alaska. In those days airports didn't exist, especially in rugged country. To survive, they created their own fuel dumps along the way, sometimes in clearings, sometimes along a dirt road wide and straight enough to serve as a makeshift runway.

One of the three, Jack Thomas, was a mining engineer. It was his opinion that an airplane would give them an advantage the gold rush miners never had, the ability to cover a great deal of ground quickly. Time was critical since they couldn't count on more than a few months of good weather a year where they were going. The only thing limiting their mobility was the availability of suitable landing sites.

Finally, they reached the Hammersmith Mountains. They arrived a month later than they'd planned, but even so they hoped two months of good weather would be enough. Thomas showed them how to pan for gold in the streams coming down from the mountains. Had they been further south where the weather was better, they could have made a living by panning eight or nine months of the year. But this far north, that wasn't an option. Besides, Lovett wrote, they were after the motherlode. Finding it meant back-breaking work. An exploratory trench was dug in the frozen earth, to no avail, and finally, a shaft was sunk into the mountain itself. To accomplish that, timber had to be cut to shore up the tunnel. Even so, the deeper they burrowed into the mountain, the more excited they became. Not only was the digging easier, but there were signs of gold. It was only a matter of time until they struck it rich, Thomas assured them.

By then, provisions were running low. Point Bristol was the nearest place to resupply. At first, one of them was going to stay behind to act as a guard. But the danger of claim-jumpers in such a remote location seemed so unlikely, they decided to risk it.

Besides, as Lovett wrote,

> we are all longing for a hot bath and night in a soft bed. Mike and Jack intend to share theirs with female companions, but I will remain true to Mary.

Nick blinked. The lingering smoke inside the lean-to had tears streaming down her cheeks.

The diary didn't say if they'd found women or not. But the final entry made one thing clear. They'd found the Spanish Lady.

Sighing, Nick reread the last page.

> . . . kept hoping it was just bad booze, but when I heard the death rattle in Jack's throat I knew it was all over. I've heard that sound too many times before. Somehow I managed to get the plane back, though not in one piece, and I buried them. I did the Christian thing, a permanent testament, but there'll be nobody to do the same for me. I hope you get this, Mary, because my last thoughts were of you. Tell Ned Duffy he was right.

Nick looked at Ivins and said, "It doesn't say where Lovett buried them."

"For Christ's sake woman. If it had, we wouldn't need you, would we?"

"We're on permafrost here. Down a few inches the ground will be frozen solid."

"If Lovett could bury them, you can dig them up."

"And if he was sick with the Spanish flu? How much strength would he have had, then?"

Ivins spread his hands and smiled. One of them still held onto the Glock. "That's your worry. It will be light soon. You can start digging then."

But where? She closed eyes against Ivins's maddening smile. Sick or well, Lovett would have had one hell of a time digging graves in the permafrost.

Then it hit her, a line from the diary. *We dug an exploratory trench in the frozen earth.* Lovett had no need to dig graves. One was already there, ready-made, with loose earth just waiting to be tossed onto the bodies.

Not bad, Nick told herself. Elliot would be proud of you. The bodies were here all right. The logic was inescapable. Or at least plausible. But the *where* still eluded her.

And what about Lovett's mention of a permanent testament? What did that mean? A marker maybe. But what kind? A wooden cross would have disintegrated long ago in this climate. Besides, where would he have found the wood anyway? From the timbers in the mine? Surely, they'd be too massive.

She shook her head in frustration. Big or not, there was no sign of any permanent marker.

Probably, Lovett hadn't bothered with such niceties. Why would he? Back in 1919 nobody would have come looking for them, or their markers. Lovett would have known that. He knew he was a dead man. He also would have known the futility of writing to his wife, but he went ahead and did it. That made him a man of faith as far as she was concerned. Such a man might think of prayer as a permanent testament.

"How long have you had the diary?" Nick asked, opening her eyes to a squint.

"Several years at least. I'd have to check with Mister Mc-Kenna."

"The diary belongs to Mary Lovett or her heirs. Did anyone check to see if she was still alive?"

"Come on. She'd be over a hundred by now."

"People do live that long."

"Okay, so we looked. Does that make you happy? We couldn't find her. No Mary Lovett. Not even a death certificate. So many people were dying in those days that their record keeping was overwhelmed. What does it matter? It's not like we were going to pay a finder's fee."

Nick kept swallowing until she had breath enough to say, "I suppose a vaccine against the Spanish Lady would be worth a lot of money, but there hasn't been an incidence of this strain of flu since 1919."

Ivins laughed. "Believe me, there will be again."

"You bastards," Hurst spat, struggling onto his knees. He tried crawling toward Ivins.

Ivins moved so fast his legs blurred as they kicked out. His heels smashed into Hurst's chest, hurling him back against the log wall, where he curled into a ball, gasping for breath.

"Anyone else?" Ivins asked.

Both Barlow and Tyler, awakened by the noise, shook their heads.

Nick said, "I'd be careful if I were you, Mister Ivins, you need us in one piece."

"He's still breathing, isn't he?"

Royce checked Hurst and nodded. "What was all the fuss about?" she asked.

"Mister Hurst, here, was all upset because we weren't going to pay anything to the Lovett family," Ivins replied sarcastically.

The doctor gestured eagerly. "You people don't seem to realize what we're sitting on." She patted the dirt floor beside her. "The Spanish Lady is buried here. Think about that. Think about what she could do if she came back to life today. In 1918, the virus took four months to circle the earth. These days, with jetliners in the air around the clock, she'd spread like wildfire, worldwide in four days. Our scientists at E-Group project sixty million dead, minimum. Panic will be universal. Billions of people will demand inoculations. If they don't get them, our way of life will come to a violent end, and only E-Group will be in a position to stop the chaos."

"But only after you've started it," Nick pointed out.

"By then, nobody will care who or why, they'll just want their shots. Now all you have to do, Doctor Scott, is find where the bodies are buried."

41

Nick blew on her hands. Her fingers felt like sausages, her arms numb after a night in handcuffs. She blew louder to attract Hurst's attention, hoping he understood the silent message she'd been transmitting with her eyes during their meager breakfast. An answering smile of reassurance would have been nice, but he remained stone-faced, hunched in the opposite corner of the room.

She clenched her teeth in frustration. The doctor had taken up a position near the door, too far away to jump without getting shot, but still close enough to be in earshot.

Nick sighed. What did it matter? They were dead anyway, so they might as well die taking a stand. But as she wet her lips to blurt out her plan, Ivins shouted from outside the lean-to.

"Okay, Karen, send them out on all fours. You bring up the rear."

"Give me some credit," Karen shouted back before using her pistol to gesture them on their way.

After the warmth of the lean-to, the outside air started Nick shaking.

"I checked the thermometer, Doctor Scott," Ivins said as soon as she got to her feet. "You'll be happy to know it's ten degrees warmer than yesterday."

"It always warms up just before it snows," Nick said to wipe the grin off his face.

"For your sake, I hope it holds off until you find the bodies. Otherwise, you're going to be pretty damned miserable. Now, where are we going to start?"

"I have no idea," she lied.

Ivins grabbed hold of Hurst and yanked him to his feet. "What about you? You've seen the diary. What do you think?"

Hurst shrugged. "The man didn't say where he buried them. You read that for yourself."

Ivins swung his pistol in Nick's direction. "Well, Doctor Scott?"

"The way I see it, as long as you need us to dig, we stay alive. With any luck, we'll be digging here for years."

Ivins lunged at her, jamming his pistol against her cheek.

"I can't read a dead man's mind," she said, forcing herself to speak calmly.

"Give me your best guess, then."

"I'm an expert. Experts don't make guesses."

"Bitch," he spat and raked the pistol along her cheekbone hard enough to draw blood.

"Easy," Karen said.

"Stay out of it," Ivins shot back.

"Listen to me. I saw her giving Hurst the high sign while you were outside using the phone. I think she knows where to look. Maybe they both do?"

He leaned close to Nick's ear. "Is that right?"

Nick said nothing.

"So be it." He pushed her to one side, raised the pistol, and calmly shot Hurst in the thigh.

Hurst collapsed like a pin-stuck balloon. For an instant his mouth gaped silently, then he screamed, a sound so shrill hairs rose on the back of Nick's neck as she rushed to his aid.

"Oh, Gordon," she said, "I'm so sorry." She had never thought that Ivins would actually fire.

Ivins checked the wound and said, "You're not going to die, not unless I've lost my touch and clipped an artery."

Wide-eyed, Hurst screamed again.

Ivins began circling. "Now, who's next. What about you, Doctor Scott? Would you like to join the ranks of the wounded?"

"All right," she said. "I'll show you as soon as Gordon gets some medical attention."

"Why not. Mister Hurst may not be able to dig, but he'll have other uses."

42

The city room was at about the same strength as it had been for the past month. Newmark had failed to report to work at the beginning of the week, but he hadn't been any help for days anyway. He'd gradually given up any pretense at sobriety and had started openly drinking in front of Green, who'd strangely decided to ignore him. On Wednesday, Bernstein, who'd been gone for two weeks, had shown up, a pale shadow of himself.

One goes, one comes back, Duffy thought. Life goes on, or does it? he wondered. The epidemic was raging. They'd stopped trying to keep up with the death notices. Families had stopped complaining if the death of their nearest and dearest wasn't included in the paper. In some cases whole families seemed to go in a single day. And still there were no headlines. Health bulletins were buried on the back page.

"It's only a matter of time," Green said, holding up the pasteup of the day's paper. The headline screamed: TURKS SURRENDER! WE'VE GOT THE HUN ON THE RUN. He grinned. "Doesn't that have a rhythm you can sing to?"

"You want to sing?" Duffy replied. "How about:

> *"I had a little bird,*
> *Its name was Enza,*
> *I opened the window*
> *And in-flu-enza."*

"That's not in very good taste and doesn't even rhyme very well." Green sniffed. "People don't want to read about the flu. People want to read about kicking the stuffing out of the Hun. You'd better get busy with more dispatches from the front. The great American public is starving for news about the America Expeditionary Forces."

Duffy plowed through the reports. Most dealt with the fall of the Ottoman Empire, but he noticed a small item buried under Other Dispatches. *Pershing requests additional 1,500 Army Nurse Corps.*

Either the fighting was not going as well as the people at home thought or something terrible was happening over there. Duffy's thoughts were interrupted by the copy boy, who had managed to stay healthy so far. "Man to see you, Mister Duffy."

Duffy looked up and spotted Sam Lovett waiting in the reception area. He hurried over.

"Lovett, what brings you here?" he called. His throat felt constricted and his heart thumped in his chest, threatening to tear from its moorings. "What's wrong?"

Lovett reached over and grabbed Duffy's hand. "Not a thing," he answered. "You never called. You've never given us a chance to thank you properly. Now you'll come tonight. We won't take no for an answer."

Duffy reeled. The memory of seeing Mary threatened to tear

him in half. On the one hand he'd tried his best to put her out of his mind, but now that Lovett was standing in front of him he realized that he could hardly restrain himself from rushing to her side to see if she was as beautiful as he remembered.

"There's no need to thank me," he mumbled. "Really there isn't."

"For saving my wife's life? I'll not be content until you break bread with us. Do you still have our address?"

Duffy nodded.

"Seven o'clock, then."

Duffy knew he should plead a prior engagement, but his tongue seemed like lead in his mouth. To see her again, to see that alabaster curve of her neck, those gleaming tendrils of red hair clinging to her cheeks, it was more than he could bear. He remembered his mother, in the heat of the kitchen, her auburn hair clinging to her cheeks as she prepared the evening meal. He blushed. Self-knowledge came in a blinding flash, every bit the equal of the morning's first shot of rye. His mother's wedding picture, lost in a fire years ago, could have been Mary.

Then he pulled himself together and prepared his excuse, but the words that came out of his mouth were, "I'm looking forward to it."

43

Nick led the way. The rest followed. Even Hurst, who'd been bandaged and given a pain-killing shot, managed to limp along, bracing himself on Mike Barlow's strong shoulder. But his face looked dead-white and glistened with sweat despite the cold. Tyler was being used as the doctor's beast of burden, lugging her aluminum equipment cases and a folded canvas tarp.

Nick stopped beside the rock markers where the Bloodhounds had registered their initial hits.

"You said these were mineral deposits," Ivins commented.

"I hadn't read your diary, then."

"So?"

"Lovett wrote that he'd marked the graves. A pilot's marker, he called them."

"So?"

"I'm guessing he used what he had available, pieces of his Junkers. I'm also guessing that since he was sick he didn't have the strength to dig graves in this kind of soil. That leaves us with the exploratory trench he mentions in the diary."

"Not bad." Ivins nodded at the doctor. "How do you want to do this?"

"You supervise the digging but don't get too close to them while they work. The rest of you"—she made it a point to glare at Nick—"be careful with your shovels. If you slice open a body you expose the virus."

Nick shuddered at the thought. Don't panic. Think. But her mind felt as cold and unresponsive as her half-frozen feet.

Karen pointed her pistol at Tyler. "Over here." She paced well away from the rock markers. "Spread the tarp and set out my gear."

Once that was done, she knelt on the tarp, snapped open one of the cases, and quickly erected a foot-high tripod with a thermometer attached.

"Twenty-eight degrees," she read.

"Like I said, it's warming up," Ivins announced.

"I'll keep an eye on it. We're safe as long as it doesn't thaw. Now, put them to work."

"You heard her," Ivins said, gesturing with his pistol as he backed up a few paces.

Nick looked at Barlow. "Tell me you've dug up bodies before."

He shook his head. "I can't say I've had much practice digging bodies up."

"We'll have to go slow, then. Remember, no holes, no punctures. Just strip away the soil little by little."

She laid out a six-foot square around one of the rock markers.

"Jesus," Barlow muttered. "That's a lot of dirt."

"I don't care," Hurst said. "I'm going to freeze to death if I don't do something."

"You're in no condition to dig," Nick told him.

"Watch."

They each took a corner of a six-foot square—Hurst, Tyler, Barlow, and Nick herself—and slowly worked toward the center. Within a few inches the ground was frozen solid, and they exchanged their shovels for picks. But the picks, designed to be swung overhead for the best leverage, had to be used like surgical instruments, chipping into the ground a handful at a time. The work was not only backbreaking but terrifying each time one of the sharp points dug into the tundra.

But working was better than resting. When you rested, your sweat froze.

As the day progressed, blood began soaking through Hurst's bandage. By noon, his blood was leaking freely. Despite that, color had returned to his face. Or had infection set in and with it fever? Either way, fever or blood loss, Nick figured Hurst couldn't keep up the pace much longer.

Making matters worse, Ivins refused them a lunch break, or even time out to change Hurst's bandage. But he did allow them to munch on energy bars as they worked.

Their rate of progress, Nick estimated, was two inches an hour, though their pace seemed to be slowing. Certainly Hurst's was.

"Time?" Nick shouted at Ivins.

The man stared at her like she'd lost her reason, then shrugged and said, "Three o'clock."

Seven hours at two inches an hour, she calculated, put them at a depth of one foot, two inches. The question was, how deep was the trench Lovett had used for a grave? An exploratory trench, he'd called it in his diary. Just what did that mean? And why dig it here?

She took a quick look around. Nothing obvious occurred to her, so she went back to considering depth. Anything was better than thinking about what they were after, or what it would mean to find it. Three feet would be deep enough for a grave in this climate. Maybe even two feet, she amended, though that was probably wishful thinking on account of her blistered hands.

She glanced at the dark, leaden sky. How much daylight

left? Probably no more than two hours. Four more inches at best, more likely three. That meant they had one more day of digging ahead of them at least. One more day of life.

Hurst, who'd been prying at the frozen earth with a pick, suddenly keeled over on his side. As he did so, the toe of his boot dislodged a fist-size nugget.

"Get him out of there and keep working," Ivins shouted. He was pacing nearby, stamping his feet and flailing his arms to keep warm.

Taking comfort from the thought that Ivins looked worse than she felt, Nick grabbed one of Hurst's arms, Barlow the other. Together they dragged him out of their shallow pit. They propped him against a boulder that provided some shelter from the wind.

Tyler stared at them as if in a daze.

Nick slipped back into their hole and examined the nugget. It was gold all right. Using her fingers, she scooped the tundra Hurst had loosened before his collapse. There were more nuggets underneath.

She grabbed a handful, sat back on her haunches, and laughed.

Ivins came closer, but not too close. "What the hell's wrong with you?"

I have nothing to lose, she thought, and threw the nuggets at him.

He lurched to one side to keep from being hit.

"We're rich!" Nick shouted.

The others stopped work to gape at her. Even Hurst managed to raise his head to stare.

"We've struck gold," she clarified.

Ivins dropped to one knee to retrieve one of the nuggets Nick had thrown at him. Karen joined him to take a look.

At the other end of the hole, Barlow began rooting in the soil. He, too, came up with a handful of nuggets, which he held out toward Ivins as if offering a bribe.

If only it was that easy, Nick thought, and started digging with the point of her pick. The chunk of soil that came free was flecked with gold. There'd been bags of it once, she suspected. Bags probably long since disintegrated, though the gold they contained would still be here, concentrated in one area. Or maybe there were bags intact, deeper down. This was no exploratory trench. It was a cache, a hiding place. And the only grave site available. Lovett's marker, his permanent testament, was a fortune in gold.

Another probe of her pick unearthed more nuggets, which she casually tossed out of the hole and onto Ivins's feet. Gold had dulled his caution and he was perched on the lip, staring down, open-mouthed.

Nick grinned up at him and went back to digging by hand.

"This is nothing," Ivins said.

"Are you crazy?" Tyler told him. "There's a fortune here."

"You're talking millions, I'm talking billions. Stop digging."

Nick ignored him.

"You heard me," he said. "You've wasted the whole day, for Christ's sake."

"Think about it," she said. "You can see how hard it is to dig, and there's four of us. So what chance would a man alone have, unless he already had a hole dug to use as a hiding place."

"You're saying the bodies are in there, too?"

"If they're not," Nick told him, still prying at the frozen earth with the tip of her pick, "I have no idea where to look."

"You're forgetting the rockfall."

"For that, you'll need the Corps of Engineers."

She set the pick aside and tugged loose a clump of nuggets. Protruding from the hole they left behind was the toe of a man's boot.

Part of her, the archaeologist, felt triumphant; the rest of her lurched backward to escape the contaminated body.

"What the hell!" Ivins muttered.

Nick pointed. Barlow and Tyler scrambled out of the hole. Hurst opened his eyes, blinked blindly, and closed them again. Nick felt certain he'd seen nothing but his own feverish vision.

"We've found a body," Ivins shouted at Karen. "A toe anyway. A boot."

"How many times have I told you, I need the lungs," the doctor replied.

Ivins pointed his pistol at Nick. "You heard the doctor. And since you're the expert, Nick, you uncover the body."

Nick stared down at her glove, the one that had touched the boot, and held her breath against the virus that could be swarming there.

"Expert or not," Ivins went on, "you're expendable now that we have a body. Uncover the rest of it."

"Tell her not to worry," Karen shouted. "The temperature's been dropping steadily for the last two hours. It's twenty degrees now. At that temperature you'd have to chew on the corpse to infect yourself."

Sure, Nick thought, if it was so damned safe why did the doctor have a contamination suit spread out on the tarp?

Do you want to end up like Hurst here?" Ivins nudged Hurst's wounded thigh, now coated with icy blood. Hurst didn't so much as groan.

Ivins kicked the thigh hard enough to crack the ice.

"All right, goddammit," Nick said, and went back to work, using the point of her pick like a dental probe to work loose the nugget-filled soil surrounding the body. Her slow progress had Ivins pacing, but he didn't complain. No doubt he realized hers was the safest way. A puncture wound, no matter what the temperature, would spread body matter just waiting for a thaw.

After an hour, she'd stripped away enough of the frozen soil to expose a man's chest. By then the light was fading fast and the doctor, who now wore a contamination suit, called a halt. She waved Nick away from the grave.

Nick joined Tyler and Barlow, who looked none too happy to have her so close, but Ivins wanted them bunched together. Hurst was left where he lay.

Karen switched on a powerful, battery-powered lantern and circled the grave, examining the body from every angle.

"Doctor Scott," the doctor said finally, "did you nick the body at all?"

"No."

"All right, we're home free for the moment. I'll extract my tissue samples in the morning and test them. With any luck we won't need to dig up the second body."

"Why not take the samples now?" Ivins said. "The sooner we finish, the sooner we get out of this place."

"It's too risky in this light. I want to see what I'm doing. I'm dealing with the Spanish Lady, not some two-bit amoeba."

"We've got kerosene lanterns," he reminded her.

"That's a risk I'm not willing to take. Now let's get out of the cold and have something to eat."

"What about her?" Ivins said, pointing at Nick. "I don't want her sharing space with me."

"Chances are it's perfectly safe," Karen replied.

"Well, I'm not risking it."

"Put in her in one of the tents, then. She and Hurst. Don't worry, Doctor Scott. We'll give you a sleeping bag. You'll survive. You may even survive your date with the Spanish Lady."

"What do you mean?" Nick asked.

"Back in 1918, they tried to figure out how long it took for the flu to incubate. They tried infecting all kinds of animals. They found that the only two animals that seemed susceptible were pigs and humans. I'll need a test subject to determine that the virus is still alive."

"See any pigs around?" Ivins chimed in.

44

Nick lay side by side with Hurst. He'd been too weak to move when they dragged him away from the grave and zipped him into a sleeping bag. Since then Nick had been coaxing him to eat one of the energy bars the doctor had provided.

Nick's ankles had been tied together, this time with the real thing, steel shackles. But they hadn't bothered to restrain Hurst. He lay on his back without moving, an untasted energy bar clasped in his hand.

The night wind howled, flapping the sides of the tent and sending a shiver up Nick's spine. She unwrapped another energy bar and chewed methodically, hardly tasting it. She had to take in calories; she had to keep up her strength.

By God, she wasn't going to go meekly. She'd pick her time and fight back.

Her shaking subsided. She wasn't cold at all, she realized. The insulated sleeping bag was doing its job, as was her parka, which lay on top like a comforter.

She sat up with a start. Thank God they hadn't tied her hands. She slipped an arm out from inside the sleeping bag and felt the pockets of her parka. Her flashlight was still there.

Praying the cold hadn't killed the batteries, she switched it on. Its bright beam she took as an omen, the first step in fighting back. Now, if only Hurst was up to taking that next step.

She turned the light on him, and caught her breath at the sight of his ghastly, sick complexion.

"Gordon," she whispered, though why she bothered keeping her voice down she didn't know. The wind was in full cry. "Gordon," she repeated.

When he didn't answer, she shook him gently.

"No," he groaned, turning his head away from the light in his face, "no more food."

She shifted the light away from his eyes. "Gordon, I need your help."

He opened his eyes to narrow slits. "Enough with the pep talk. I'm in no shape to help anyone, myself included."

"We can make them pay."

Wincing, he raised his head far enough to prop a hand under it. "I'm sorry, Nick."

"I don't want your apology. I want your help."

"It's your Val I'm sorry about. I was going to steal your thunder. The only trouble was that the joke was on me, too."

"What are you saying?"

"You heard Ivins say that they paid a hundred thousand for me. Guess what. Alcott only offered me fifty thousand dollars to join the expedition. He pocketed the rest. In addition, he was going to cut you out."

"Why?"

"He told me you were hired over his objection."

The image of her father pulling strings flashed through her mind. She shook it off and said, "Gordon, we'll never get another chance like this."

Hurst unzipped his bag halfway and sat up. "Jesus!" he gasped, grimacing in pain. He reached a hand inside his sleeping bag; it came out soaked in blood.

"I'm dead already. What do you want me to do?"

"They've left two things unprotected, the communications satellite and the extra food, which is stored in the tent next to us. Since all I can do is crawl, you'll have to climb onto the roof and sabotage the satellite dish. While you do that, I'll see what I can do about the food."

"We'll all go hungry," he said.

"That's the point."

"Jesus, to think I felt sorry for you." He wiggled his way out of the sleeping bag. The effort started his wound bleeding profusely.

He looked at her and said, "We could have been good together."

She kissed him on the forehead.

He touched her on the arm, an act of farewell, and left the tent.

45

The day was dark, darker than the day before, and the bear sensed that a great storm was on its way, an early beginning to winter this year and a longer hibernation. To survive, more food would be needed. But foraging had grown sparse. The berries were long gone, and small animals harder and harder to find.

She tested the air. Men were still nearby. They would have food, though going near them again would be risky. Still, her cubs would need to feed once more before they slept for the winter.

She called to her cubs, but they ignored her summons. She growled. Still they didn't come. Instead, they moved away from her, sniffing the air, a sure sign they were tracking food, probably the man-smell she too had detected.

She hurried after them and caught the new scent. Blood. A man's blood, growing stronger with each step. The smell overrode her usual caution. She charged into the lead, with the cubs following behind.

As the blood scent grew stronger so did the man smell. More than one man, her nose told her. That meant more danger. But it also meant more food. Not just the usual food, but the bodies of men. She had developed a taste for it.

A nearly silent growl rumbled in her throat, a sound only her cubs were close enough to hear.

As one, the three bears slowed, proceeding carefully now, though their mouths watered in anticipation.

46

The icy ten-foot crawl to the supply tent left Nick shaking so badly her fingers couldn't manage the zipper on the entrance. Blowing on them didn't help. In frustration, she sucked them warm. That and a quick look with her flashlight did the trick and she managed to tug open the zipper.

Inside, the tent was crammed with sealed plastic containers. Lugging them over the mountain from their original base camp must have taken a lot of work. They represented more than one of what Nick had thought to be romantic assignations.

She opened the nearest container and found it filled with energy bars and freeze-dried high-calorie survival food. She crammed a handful of bars into her pocket and kept searching. On her fourth try, she found what she needed, plastic jugs of kerosene.

She unscrewed the safety cap and doused everything inside the tent. Then she opened a second jug and slipped outside to wet down the tent itself.

That done, she squatted down, doing her best to stay out of the wind, and waited for Hurst. Minutes passed. How long could it take to rip out a few wires? she asked herself. Forever if you were as weak as he was, she answered. Or never if he'd collapsed somewhere.

She drew a breath of icy air, steeling herself. She'd have to go after the satellite dish herself, ankle shackles or not.

So be it.

She ripped a piece of lining from her jacket to make a wick and stuffed it into the last jug. She shook the jug to make certain that the cloth was fully saturated and struck a match. She breathed a sigh of relief as the wick caught. It burned indolently compared to gasoline.

Mentally crossing her fingers, Nick rolled the jug through the open flap and into the tent. In seconds, flames began to spread.

She turned around and started crawling after Hurst.

She heard a sound so terrible she froze in place. It rose to a high-pitched shriek before being cut off abruptly. Only then did Nick hear the growls.

Oh my God, she thought. That was a human being. "Gordon," she called out, trying to stand only to lose her balance because of the shackles. Frantically, she began crawling toward the sound.

Someone yelled. Ivins, she thought.

Beyond the flames, a beam of light appeared.

"Bears!" Ivins shouted.

The light came bobbing toward her.

"We've got to help Gordon," she called.

A gun fired so close she felt its concussion.

The muzzle-flash lit Ivins's face as he came out of the darkness, a flashlight in one hand, his pistol raised in the other. He fired again, and for an instant Nick thought he was shooting at her. Then he was beside her, his legs spread in a shooter's stance, his flashlight probing the night, his Glock at the ready.

"Who screamed?" he asked.

"I think it was Gordon Hurst. We've got to try to help him."

"We left him in the tent with you."

"He must have wandered out in a daze," she lied. "I was asleep."

"Bullshit!" Ivins snapped. "Haven't you got eyes? He set the fire, the bastard. He got off lucky with the bears. I'd have—"

Someone else screamed, higher pitched this time. Probably the doctor, Nick thought, though terror could turn anyone into a soprano. Shots thundered from the other side of the cabin.

The sound started Ivins firing blindly into the darkness. The moment he ran out of ammunition, he dropped to one knee to slam in a fresh clip.

"Fucking bears. They ought to be extinct."

Nick rattled her shackles. "Get me out of these."

Ivins lurched to his feet and shouted, "Karen!"

"I need your help," the doctor answered, her voice quavering.

"Fuck," Ivins muttered. "What else can go wrong?" He started to leave.

"My shackles," Nick pleaded.

He looked down. His smile seemed to flicker in the firelight. "Why not? I don't think you're going anywhere with those bastards on the prowl." He tossed her the keys.

She scrabbled to unlock the shackles. By the time she was free, he was out of sight and the flames from the tent were dying out. She switched on her flashlight and searched the darkness for bears. But there was nothing to see but a blood trail.

God almighty, she breathed. Gordon's blood must have attracted the bears. Part of Nick felt sick, knowing she'd as good as killed him. The man had been wounded, how could she have expected him to cope with the satellite dish? She should have gone herself.

Get hold of yourself, she thought. The blame was Ivins's, not hers. He'd been responsible from the moment he shot Hurst. But the kiss to his feverish forehead haunted her.

She peered into the darkness, gripping the flashlight so hard her entire arm shook. Would its batteries last long enough to show her the way over the mountains in the dark? The thought of negotiating those crevasses without a light held her fast.

"Goddammit, Karen," Ivins called out from the other side of the cabin, "where are you?"

"Over here."

"For Christ's sake, where's here?"

"I see your light," the doctor answered. Her voice sounded shakier than ever. "Keep coming."

Nick pivoted slowly in place, holding her flashlight at arm's length. Every moment, she expected to see feral eyes peering back at her. But the light swept full circle without catching any sign of life.

"Nick!" Ivins shouted. "Get over here, now!"

If you want to survive, she told herself, now is the time to start running.

"Nick, did you hear me?" Ivins called.

She drew a deep breath but didn't move. Tyler and Barlow were probably still in their plastic handcuffs inside the cabin. She already had Gordon on her conscience.

"Coming," she answered through clenched teeth.

The doctor's parka had been shredded from her left shoulder all the way to her wrist. If it hadn't been for the garment's heavy padding, the bear's claws would have ripped open her arm all the way to the bone. As it was, there were three deep gashes running the length of her forearm.

"They've got to be sutured," Karen winced, "and I can't do it all by myself."

They crawled inside the cabin and the doctor gingerly gave herself a local pain killer.

"You swab, I'll sew," she instructed Nick.

Barlow and Tyler were freed so that they could hold the lanterns, while Ivins watched from the doorway, his nine-millimeter at the ready. Beside him stood an assault rifle. Every so often he'd mutter, "Fucking bears," like a mantra.

Once the wounds were closed, Karen painted her arm with

Betadine and then, with Nick's help, wrapped the arm with bandages.

Finally, Karen nodded at Nick and said, "For what it's worth, thank you."

Nick didn't bother to reply.

"Don't get sentimental, Doc," Ivins said. "Keep your mind on why we're here."

"I damn near wasn't here," Karen answered. "If she'd gone after my right arm, I wouldn't have been able to get off a shot."

"I hope you hit her."

"I don't think so, though I must have scared her off. The other one, too." She shook her head slowly, as if afraid the movement might be painful. "We shouldn't have separated out there."

Ivins shrugged.

"One minute I'm out there alone trying to see what the shouting is about," the doctor continued, "and in the next two bears come out of nowhere."

"That wasn't shouting you heard," Nick said. "It was Hurst screaming."

"My God," Tyler said. "Is he dead?"

"He'd better be," Ivins answered. "You saw what the bastard did to our supply tent? If I'd gotten a hold of him, he'd still be screaming."

Tyler began to cry.

"Shut up, I've got to get some rest," Karen said. "Tie them back up."

Ivins checked his watch. "Why bother? It'll be light in an hour or so. Then we'll get your samples and our job's done."

Karen nodded at the others. "Theirs isn't."

Ivins smiled. "Hurst got off lucky. He met a bear. The rest of you are going to meet the Spanish Lady. Now get yourself some shuteye, Doc. I'll keep watch."

He exchanged his Glock for the assault rifle. "If one of those bears pokes his nose in here, I'll machine-gun the bastard."

47

Ned Duffy sat in the newsroom staring at the copy he'd just pulled from his typewriter. He clenched his fists to keep from tearing it up.

"For Christ's sake, Duffy," his city editor shouted, "how long are you going to sit on that? We've got a deadline coming up and I've got a hole on page two the size of my shoe."

"It's crap!" Duffy shouted back.

"Of course it's crap. That's why I gave it to you to write."

Green, the city editor, had been assigning similar stories for weeks now. Upbeat features, he called them, vignettes to make the *World's* readers appreciate their lives and stop thinking about their troubles.

The one Duffy had just written told

the story of a veteran returning from the war minus a leg, and how he'd overcome his adversity.

"It's a lie," Duffy added.

"Not when you interviewed him it wasn't."

"He died yesterday."

"We don't have to report that," Green said. "Our readers want happy endings."

"He died of the flu."

"Says who?"

"His doctor."

Green left his desk to shake a finger in Duffy's face. "You know the orders. The flu's under control. The epidemic is over. We've printed that, so it must be true." He snatched up the pages and retreated toward his desk.

"Jesus, Duffy," Green muttered the moment he sat down. "Your lead stinks. What's happened to you? There was a time you could wring tears from a stone. Hell, that subway piece of yours made me weep like a baby." He sniffled to prove his point. "But this . . ." Green waved the pages. "If it wasn't for page two, I'd dump this here and now. I'd fire you, too, if I wasn't so short of people."

"Because of the flu," Duffy reminded him.

"You hear me?" Green shouted. "I ought to fire you here and now."

Duffy opened his mouth. The words, "I quit," were on their way out when his phone rang.

"Praise the Lord," Green said. "Maybe we've got something to report."

"Duffy," he said into the phone.

"Ned, it's Sam Lovett."

Duffy's hands started shaking. Lovett had never telephoned him at the *World* before. Maybe something was wrong with Mary. God, please don't let her be sick with the flu.

"What's wrong?" Duffy asked, his voice as shaky as his fingers.

"Not a thing. We want you to join us for supper, that's all. Mary's cooking your favorite."

Duffy sighed with relief, then caught himself. Why dinner tonight, Friday? Sunday was only two days away, their once-a-month Sunday that had become the most important thing in Duffy's life. Though for Mary and Sam, he suspected, those Sundays were an act of charity, when they took pity on a lonely bachelor.

"But what about Sunday?" Duffy said.

"Don't worry. We haven't forgotten. But tonight's special. We have a surprise, two of them really."

Mary greeted him with a hug as always. And it left him breathless just as it always did and feeling a bit guilty. When he stepped back from the embrace, he saw that her eyes were red as if she'd been crying.

"Don't look so worried, Ned," Lovett said, seeing Duffy's concern. "Mary's a little upset is all."

"What kind of surprise is this?" Duffy asked.

"You'd better sit down," Lovett said.

"Don't frighten the man," Mary said. "Just pour him a drink and tell him."

Duffy blinked in astonishment. The Lovetts never served liquor. Mary didn't believe in it.

"Now I am frightened," he said, accepting a glass of red wine. Mary, he noticed, didn't take one for herself.

Lovett touched glasses with him. "We used to make toasts like this in France, before we took off on our flights. Against the cold, we told ourselves, but we were just plain scared."

"I thought you liked flying," Duffy said.

"Not when they're shooting at you."

Duffy, conscious of Mary watching him, sipped his wine. Lovett took his in a gulp, set down the glass, and said, "Well, here goes. Ned, we want you to be our baby's godfather."

Duffy's mouth dropped open.

"Don't look so panicked," Lovett told him. "It won't hurt a bit. Besides, we owe you everything. If you hadn't gone into that tunnel, Mary would have been lost. So we won't take no for an answer. Isn't that right, Mary?"

Duffy turned to see tears spilling from her eyes.

"If it's boy," she said, taking his hand, "we want to name him after you, Ned."

"I . . ."

"You're a good man, Ned," she went on. "It's a name to be proud of."

The look on her face, in her eyes, made him want to cry. He wanted to tell her he wasn't the man she thought he was. He was a drunk, a reporter who never let truth get in the way of a good story, a man who preyed on the misfortunes of others.

And yet she was staring at him the way no woman had since his mother.

"May we take that as a yes?" Lovett said.

Duffy managed a nod.

"Good man. Now drink up and I'll pour us another. This is a celebration, after all."

"Tell him the rest," Mary said.

"There's something else I'd like to ask of you," Lovett said. "I want you to look after Mary while I'm gone."

"Gone? Where?"

"Let me show you something."

"He's been waiting all day for this," Mary added, her voice strained.

Lovett took a brochure from his pocket. It showed a silver airplane with a single engine.

"I've bought it," Lovett explained. "Well, a third of it. I've gone in with two friends of mine from the air corps. Funny thing is, the plane's German, just like the ones we were shooting down in the war. We've named her the Flying Dutchman."

"It looks expensive," Duffy said.

"It took most everything we had, all three of us going in together. That's why I need you to look after Mary. She's got enough to tide her through until I get back, but in her condition, I'd feel better if she had a friend to call on."

"I still don't understand," Duffy said. "Where are you going?"

"To Alaska to get rich, so I can buy Mary everything she's ever wanted."

"I've got everything here," she said.

"She's right," Duffy told him. "Besides, now's not the time to be traveling, not with the flu spreading. Look what's happening in San Francisco. Everyone there's been ordered to wear masks."

"It's too cold in Alaska for the flu. Besides, one of my partners flew for a mining company before the war. He knows the best places for prospecting. We've got to go now to prepare for the spring."

Duffy looked at the man and shook his head. Once he might have been glad to see him leave, so that he could have a chance with Mary. But not now. Now, Duffy realized that he wasn't good enough for a woman like Mary, and that his friends at the *World* weren't friends at all, not compared to a man like Lovett.

"That mining company is probably there already," Duffy pointed out.

"Not where we're going."

48

Nick awoke instantly, angry with herself for falling asleep. Ivins was stamping his feet.

"You heard me," he said. "Everybody up."

Why? she thought, hearing the echo of Ivins's words from last night. If she was going to meet the Spanish Lady, why move at all?

Karen groaned and sat up. Her face looked paste-white, her eyes dull and bloodshot. Sweat beaded her forehead.

"Come on, Doc," Ivins said, prodding her with his toe. "This is your day to shine." He snorted. "Shine might not be the right word, since it's starting to snow."

Only then did Nick notice the flakes on Ivins's parka. She bit her lip in frustration. He'd left them unguarded to go outside and check the weather. Had she been awake, she might have been able to do something. The others must have been asleep, as well.

"I tried to report the good news to McKenna, that we'll have our samples before the end of the day, but the phone's out."

Nick coughed to keep from smiling. Gordon had managed to get to the satellite dish before the bears got to him.

"How are we going to call in the chopper, then?" Karen asked.

"We'll have to hike back to the cars and drive out of here."

"I need another shot," Karen said and quickly injected herself. Within seconds, her eyes began to glitter and her forehead flushed.

"Do you need help getting dressed?" Ivins asked her.

"I'll manage," the doctor said and donned one of her disposable contamination suits.

When the doctor was ready, Ivins crawled backward out of the cabin ahead of Nick, his rifle never more than a few feet from her face. The moment they were on their feet, he jammed the barrel against her spine, and shouted, "Send out the others."

Barlow and Tyler came next, each pushing one of the doctor's medical cases in front of them. Karen Royce brought up the rear.

"It looks like Christmas," Ivins said, gesturing at the landscape with his assault rifle.

A thin dusting of snow covered everything. More snow was falling.

"Son of a bitch," Ivins blurted. "Look." He pointed at the cabin's roof, where the satellite dish had been ripped from its moorings.

Thank you, Gordon, Nick said to herself.

"Bastard bears," Ivins shouted.

He swung around, his rifle at the ready, as if expecting to see them sneaking up on him. "One shot at them. That's all I ask."

"Forget the damned bears," Karen said. "I've got work to do."

"Better you than me," he replied and gestured everyone toward the grave they'd opened the day before.

The snow failed to hide the carnage at the grave. One body had been torn free of the tundra, partially exposing the second body beneath it. From what Nick could see without a close examination, the bears had mauled the bodies rather than fed on them. The thought crossed her mind that long-frozen flesh hadn't competed with Gordon's warm body.

"Sweet Jesus," Karen murmured as she dropped to her knees beside the grave. "The bears are contaminated."

"Can they carry the virus?" Nick asked.

"I can't say for sure, but they've been at the lungs. Pieces of it could stick to their claws and even their teeth." She rubbed her wounded arm. "I may be infected."

"You disinfected the wound," Ivins pointed out.

"I can't take the chance. We've got to start for Anchorage immediately so I can get proper treatment."

Ivins shook his head slowly. "You knew the risk."

"If I have the flu, I could give it to everyone else once it incubates."

"How long does it take to incubate?" Ivins asked.

"It's hard to say. They didn't have the technology in 1918 to pin it down. Based on other strains, two to three days, probably."

"There you go, then. I figure we can drive to Anchorage in a day, so that gives us a day to play with. Besides, you brought along antibiotics."

"None of which work against the Spanish Lady, you idiot. How many times have I told you? Antibiotics don't work against a virus. Don't you ever listen to what I have to say?"

"Just get your samples, Doc. And now that we have both bodies, get samples from each."

She glared at him.

"Do you want to go back to McKenna empty-handed?"

She rocked on her heels. "I'll need the other body out of the grave, so I'll have room to work."

"You heard the doctor," Ivins said. "Start digging."

The work was nastier than the day before. Not only was it snowing, but the pieces of the upper body had to be pried free in order to get at the corpse deeper in the grave. With each piece came an imaginary army of virus, crawling over Nick like microscopic insects. Her skin itched. Her face itched. Her nose itched. More than anything she wanted to scratch. But to touch her face with her gloved hand was too great a risk.

Hours went by. The second body was deeper into the permafrost and, as a result, harder to free. The soil around it, even the gold, was solid ice. Each time Nick chipped at it, she held her breath, lest she penetrate the flesh.

Finally, Ivins got impatient. "For Christ's sake, Doc. Isn't that deep enough?"

Judging by the look on Karen's face, she would have preferred to have the body completely free of the grave so she wouldn't have to set foot in it.

"It's noon already," Ivins said. "We'll be driving in the dark as it is, unless of course you want to wait a while before starting back to Anchorage."

"You're a bastard, you know that," Karen told him.

"Sure. Me and the bears."

The doctor moved forward slowly in her cumbersome suit. Nick's view of the corpse was obscured by the bulk of the contamination suit. Suddenly there was a sharp crack that echoed up the mountain side. Ivins whirled around, his arms outstretched in a shooter's stance, looking for the source of the sound.

"I just cracked the breastbone," the doctor's muffled voice floated out of the grave. "The lungs look in good condition. I just need to peel back the ribs."

There were two sickening snaps and half an hour later, Karen climbed out of the shallow grave gingerly holding a small metal flask. "Let's hope the virus survived. If it did, this theromoflask should preserve it." She held up the receptacle before her. It reflected dully in the weak sunlight.

"Strange to think that such a small container could hold

such vast potential." She nodded at Nick and the others. "Too bad we don't have time to test it."

Ivins grinned crookedly. "Not to worry, Doc. You're our test subject now. Step over here with me, Doc. The rest of you line up next to the body."

Tyler gave a low moan.

I've waited too long, Nick thought. Standing there, looking down, she knew she was staring at her own grave.

49

Nick had no choice. She and the others were about to be slaughtered like cattle. She had to try, as futile as it might be.

Ivins was closest to her. She'd leave Karen to Barlow. She didn't think that Tyler was of much use.

But before she could launch herself at him, the doctor rammed her pistol against Ivins's head.

"Drop the rifle," she ordered.

"What the hell are you doing?" he asked in disbelief.

"There's been a change of plan."

Ivins started to turn toward the doctor as if trying to bring his rifle to bear. Before the muzzle had completed the arc, Barlow lunged at him, grabbed the rifle, and twisted it so violently bones cracked in Ivins's fingers. He opened his mouth to scream just as Barlow rammed the rifle against his chest and fired. The concussion flung Ivins's body backward into the open grave, where it lay twitching meaninglessly.

Barlow retrieved the dead man's pistol and then turned toward the doctor without taking his eyes from Nick and Tyler. "Karen, you can leave the tidying up to me. Pack your gear. We're getting out of here pronto."

Karen glared at Ivins's body. "The bastard didn't care if I'd caught the virus or not."

"The fool didn't recognize me, even though we'd been in the same meeting. I guess clothes really do make the man." Barlow's tone was mocking.

He adjusted a lever on the rifle. "I've switched to full automatic. One squeeze of the trigger and you both splatter."

He stepped back another pace before gesturing at the open grave. "Now, clean up that mess. I want that hole covered up and everything in it."

"I'm a personal friend of Mister McKenna," Tyler wailed. "I've filmed documentaries and commercials for him all over the world."

"McKenna ain't here, in case you hadn't noticed. But when I see him, I'll give him your regards. I work for him, too. Actually, I just resigned."

"Who are you?" Nick asked. "And what happened to Mike Barlow?" Nick had a sinking feeling that she already knew.

"The Spanish lady killed him, I'm afraid, with me standing proxy for her. As for me personally, Barlow's as good a name as any." He smiled. "The new Mike Barlow, Karen, and a friend of ours in Washington are going to hold an auction once we've got ourselves a vaccine. The highest bidder wins." He winked at Tyler. "Who knows? Maybe our Mister McKenna will be lucky, after all. Now police up those bodies. And stack them in carefully. I don't want anything showing aboveground."

Nick swallowed repeatedly to keep from being sick. Even so, her mouth tasted of bile as they wrestled with Ivins, whose life's blood was already frozen to his parka. As careful as she and Tyler were, the dead man barely fit into the shallow grave.

"Tamp them down," Barlow ordered.

When Nick looked at him, dumbfounded, he waved his rifle impatiently. "Jump up and down on them, for God's sake."

Nick shook her head.

"If I shoot you now, you don't have a chance. But you never know with guinea pigs. They might survive."

Nick didn't move. Either way, she figured, she was dead already, she and Tyler both. There was no time for testing, not with the doctor already exposed and in a panic to reach Anchorage.

"You don't need us," she said, wishing he'd drop his guard for even a moment and give her an opening. "You've already got your guinea pig, the doctor."

Barlow chuckled. "Karen wouldn't like the sound of that." He turned the rifle on Tyler. "What about you? Are you a hero, too?"

Tyler jumped into the grave and went to work.

"That's the way," Barlow urged, "pack them down good."

Nick couldn't bear to look. She tried to block out the sounds that Tyler's boots made punctuated by his sobs. She winced with every snap of bone. Instead, she kept her eyes on Barlow, wondering how close she'd get before he killed her.

He smiled back at her. "I can read your mind, lady."

Nick took a step toward him.

"Too late. Our filmmaker's done his job. Check it out. The man's a human compactor."

In spite of herself, Nick looked at the mess in the grave.

"You see," Barlow said. "There's room for one more."

Tyler had one foot out of the grave when Barlow shot him through the head, timing the act so perfectly that Tyler toppled into the opening he'd just created.

Nick couldn't breathe. Her knees trembled as she waited for the next shot.

Barlow snorted. "Relax. Like I said, there's only room for one. Now let's go back to the cabin and grab ourselves a couple of gas cans, so we can have ourselves a nice cremation."

"Then what?" she managed in a fear-strangled voice.

"Like you said, Karen's the guinea pig, but it's a long hike back over the mountain to the cars. If she gets sick, I'll need you to tote her gear." He looked her up and down and smiled suggestively. "And maybe keep me warm."

She forced herself to breathe deeply. Barlow had just made a mistake. He'd kept her alive because he considered a woman less of a threat than a man.

She returned to the cabin, taking stock along the way. She had energy bars in her pocket. The rest of the stores had gone up in flames, thanks to her. Just how well stocked that left Barlow and the doctor she didn't know. Maybe it didn't matter. Maybe Barlow would drop his guard just long enough for her to douse him with the gasoline meant for the corpses.

She ground her teeth. The matches she'd need to set him ablaze were in her backpack, and that was still inside the cabin.

She retrieved the gallon cans and started back, with Barlow following close behind her, but not close enough to swing a can at his head.

Calm down, she told herself. Like the man said, it was a long haul over the Hammersmiths. She glanced their way, but they were hidden by the falling snow.

By the time Nick reached the grave, her arms ached, more from tension than from the weight of the one-gallon cans.

"Douse them good," Barlow said. "Every drop. We don't want to leave any meat for those bears, do we?"

As she poured, Nick kept reminding herself that Tyler was past caring, as were the long-dead pilots. Ivins, she hoped, would burn all the way to hell.

Once she emptied both cans, Barlow said, "Will you do the honors, or should I?"

Nick patted her pocket theatrically, reassuring herself in the process that the energy bars were still in place. "Sorry, no matches. I guess we'll have to leave them for the bears."

"You shouldn't underestimate me." His hand snaked beneath his parka and came up with Ivins's Glock, which he cocked before dropping the assault rifle on top of Tyler's body. Only then did Barlow dig into another pocket for a disposable lighter. It lit instantly, producing a long flame.

"Stand back," he said.

Nick turned to see the doctor running toward them.

"We have a mourner," Nick said sarcastically.

"Stop!" the doctor shouted.

Out of the corner of her eye, Nick saw the flaming lighter arcing through the air. Intense fire erupted from the grave.

The doctor arrived out of breath. "You idiot," she wheezed. "Ivins had the car keys in his pocket."

"Put him out, then." Barlow gestured at Nick to comply.

Halfheartedly, Nick grabbed a shovel and scooped snow onto the flames. When that had no effect, Karen pitched in. But by the time they'd smothered the fire and waited for the bodies to cool, there was nothing left of the keys but misshapen metal.

Nick smiled. She had a chance now, with a little luck. And with a little more luck, she'd teach Barlow never to underestimate a woman. Practically her mother's words.

Nick laughed out loud as one of Elaine's favorite mantras came back to her. *Men always underestimate us. Remember that. A woman doesn't have to be physically strong to get her way, only devious.*

50

Nick fell to her knees to catch her breath. The forced march over the mountains had left her sweating despite the freezing cold. This was the result of being used as a beast of burden, lugging two backpacks and Karen's sample cases. The man she still thought of as Barlow and the doctor had carried only their weapons.

He nudged Nick with his toe. "Do you know anything about cars?"

"No," she lied.

"Funny, I seem to remember something about you and cars. You were arrested for stealing one, once."

"So I took a joyride. That doesn't make me a professional car thief."

He turned his gaze on Karen, who glared back and said, "What now, genius?"

"We look for spare keys."

"And if there aren't any?"

He shrugged. "Then, we walk back the way we came. I figure it's a hundred miles to the ranger station. It's flat country mostly, so we ought to be able to make three miles an hour, easy. That's twenty-five miles a day if we walk for eight hours. More if we push it. We'll be home free in three days, maybe four."

"I told you before, the flu can incubate in two days. If I've got it, I could be dead in three, especially exposed to temperatures like this."

"Then you'd better help look for the keys, hadn't you?"

"And her?" Karen said, waving her pistol in Nick's direction.

"Cuff her. If we're walking, we don't want to lose our baggage handler." Barlow laughed. "Who knows? She might have other uses."

Once Nick's hands were tied, Barlow started with the Ford that still had its tires intact, breaking a side window to get in. Karen broke into the next in line.

Watching them work, Nick felt certain she could hot-wire the car, no matter how fancy its electronics. And once its engine was running there'd be warmth from the heater, and she could stop shaking. No, better to stay cold, because once they didn't need her, she'd be too dead to shake.

She stared down the narrow road that had brought them to the refuge, and winced at the thought of a hundred-mile trek in this kind of weather. Thank God it had at least stopped snowing for the moment.

"Nothing, for Christ's sake," Barlow shouted when they'd run out of Fords. "What kind of people travel around with only one set of keys?"

"People who don't expect you to set fire to them," the doctor snapped at him. "Your stupidity has killed us."

"You, maybe."

"You have no idea how infectious the Spanish flu can be. If I have it, you could be infected already, or soon will be." She nodded at Nick. "Her, too."

Barlow chewed his lip for a moment. "I have an idea. Keep Nick covered for a moment."

The instant the doctor turned, Barlow smashed his fist across her forearm. Her pistol went flying.

Karen sagged to her knees, moaning and cradling her arm. But by then, Barlow had backed well away from her.

"Thanks for the warning, Karen," he said. "From now on you keep your distance. Otherwise, I kill you here and now. Do you understand?"

"You bastard."

"You too, girlie," Barlow turned to Nick. "You both keep your distance."

"How far?" Nick asked, smiling.

"What about it, Karen, how far can those germs of yours fly?"

"Fuck you."

Barlow laughed. "I'll let you know when you get too close. Now start walking, the both of you. And don't get any ideas. I'll still be close enough to shoot you."

5₁

Ned Duffy stood beside Mary, watching her husband and the two other pilots inspect their airplane. Lovett had assured him that the craft, a German Junkers, was the best plane in the world for their purposes. Looking at it though, with its corrugated metal fuselage, it reminded him of the siding on the hangar.

Mary gripped his hand. Her touch made his heart ache. Lovett was a fool for leaving such a woman to go prospecting for gold, and in Alaska for God's sake. Just to get there, they'd have to fly across the entire country before heading north. The thought of it started Duffy's head shaking.

"What's wrong?" Mary asked quietly.

"I was just thinking."

"I know. But Sam's mind is made up."

Duffy said nothing. He'd heard all Lovett's arguments. *Mary deserved better than he could give her, working as a salesman. A gold mine would change all that.*

"The war changed him," Mary said.

Lovett should have been happy just to be alive and with a woman like Mary, Duffy thought, but kept it to himself.

Out on the runway—that's what Lovett called it, though it wasn't much more than a dirt road—they were topping off the tanks with gasoline.

Lovett waved. He, like his two companions, wore a leather coat and leather aviator's helmet, with goggles attached.

Mary waved back and tried to smile bravely, though Duffy could see her lips trembling.

"Sam told me the summer is very short where they're going. If they're lucky and strike gold right away, he told me they'd be back in six months. Do you think it's true?"

"Your husband's a lucky man."

She squeezed his hand. "You always say that."

"He survived the war, didn't he? And he's got you."

"They may have to stay over another year if they don't find gold right away. It would be too hard to fly back and forth, he says."

"I'm sure it won't come to that."

She stared up at Duffy with tears in her eyes. "He wouldn't be here to see his baby born."

Duffy opened his mouth to say, your husband's a fool, but stifled the impulse.

"Don't look like that," Mary said. "He's a good man."

"Ask him not to go. Beg him if you have to."

"If I did, he might stay behind."

"That's the point," he said.

She shook her head. "He'd regret it the rest of his life. I don't want that on my conscience."

"His place is here with you."

"Promise me, Ned, you won't tell him what I said about him being here when the baby's born. I'd never forgive you."

"In that case, I won't."

"Swear it."

"I swear."

"Thank you, Ned. Here he comes. Remember, not a word."

A moment later, Lovett snapped to attention in front of them and saluted. "We're ready to go."

Duffy nodded. "I'll leave you two alone to say good-bye."

"Don't go far, Ned," Lovett said, "there's something I want to say."

"I'll take a closer look at your airplane, if you don't mind."

"Help yourself."

As Duffy walked away, he could hear Mary sobbing quietly. Lovett's partners, Duffy couldn't remember their names, showed him around the airplane, explaining its finer points. But he didn't hear a word. All he could think about was Mary and her baby.

He nodded at something one of the pilots said, then glanced back at Mary to see her and Lovett embracing. When they broke apart the look on her face was radiant, but the moment Lovett headed toward Duffy, her radiance gave way to anguish.

Lovett grabbed his hand. "Ned, I owe you everything for saving Mary. So you're in this, too. We'll all be rich together. Now take care of her for me, won't you?"

"Of course."

"Good man."

"The Alaskan gold rush has been over for years," Duffy reminded him.

Lovett grinned sheepishly. "It's a big country. That's why this is the chance of a lifetime. Hellfire, it would have passed me by if I didn't know you were here to look after her."

Duffy swallowed hard and longed for a drink, though he'd given it up weeks ago at Mary's urging.

"Besides," Lovett added, "I know how you feel about her. I know you'll look after her if something happens to me."

"I—"

Lovett clapped him on the back. "Don't worry. Nothing will."

"Good God, man, haven't you been reading the papers?"

"You told me not to trust them."

"There's an outbreak of flu in Alaska."

"I survived Germans shooting at me, didn't I? I'm indestructible."

"You're a fool."

"Maybe you're right, Ned Duffy, but tell me that again when I get back."

52

Nick led the way, carrying both backpacks and the doctor's sample cases. The doctor walked close behind her, still nursing her arm. Behind them both came Barlow, shouting, "Pick up the pace. Mush."

Nick grimaced against the ache in her shoulders. Originally, she'd guessed the aluminum cases to weigh no more than ten pounds apiece, fully loaded. But that had been on the other side of Hammersmiths, miles ago. Since then, their weight had doubled, and redoubled, or so it seemed, until now they felt like lead weights. She couldn't possibly pick up the pace. Her backpack was a stone waiting to crush her the moment she relaxed her guard.

Think about something else, she told herself. Focus on the road ahead, anything. Just keep going, one foot after the other. In desperation, she counted paces to herself, like a soldier marching. But her aching muscles weren't fooled. A hundred miles like this and she'd be dead. So why not stop right now and get it over with? Let him shoot her.

She was about to do just that when Karen stopped walking and said, "Hold up, Nick. Let me take one of those cases."

Nick dropped them in the snow and bent at the waist breathing so hard her frosty breath billowed around her.

"Goddamn it!" Barlow yelled. "Keep moving."

"She's slowing us up," Karen replied. "We're going to have to take turns carrying the cases."

"Not me," Barlow said, keeping his distance. "You two figure it out, but don't take all day. And I want you walking side by side from now on."

He gestured at the women to move closer together, obviously to narrow his field of fire.

"Bastard!" Karen spat as she grabbed one of the cases with her good hand.

Winded, Nick could only mutely nod her appreciation.

"Don't thank me," Karen told her. "The faster we walk, the better my chances."

Nick said nothing. There was no need. Karen's eyes said what they both knew, that there was no way they could reach the ranger station within the flu's two-day incubation period, not even if they doubled their pace.

"For Christ's sake!" Barlow bellowed. "Move it!"

They hadn't gone more than a hundred yards when it started snowing again. At first, only a few lazy flakes fell, but within moments they were walking in a swirling, white blizzard. Quickly the road turned into a white stripe in an even whiter landscape.

Nick had to walk with her head down to keep from straying off the track. As the snow deepened, it clung to her boots. Soon her feet felt leaden. Her toes itched with the cold.

When Karen stumbled, Nick grabbed her without thinking.

"Don't worry," the doctor said, turning away from her to

speak. The Spanish Lady was virulent as hell, but chances are in this deep freeze you'd have to kiss me to catch it."

"You can't be certain you've been infected."

"Let's hope she has," Barlow joined in.

Nick glanced over her shoulder to see that he'd moved closer now that the snowfall was limiting visibility.

"Our virus has to be tested. Isn't that right, Karen?"

The doctor said nothing.

Barlow snorted. "Think about it. You can't cause a worldwide panic if your virus isn't a killer. And don't think for a minute that Karen here won't test the stuff on you if she survives."

He laughed. "You two can be the start of our epidemic."

Karen stumbled again. This time Nick let her fall in the deepening snow.

"Don't just lie there," Barlow shouted at the doctor. "I've got a schedule to keep."

Karen scrabbled to her feet and began brushing the snow from her clothes.

"What's the matter with you?" Barlow snapped. "I hope you're not sick already."

Karen shook her head, but Nick saw the fear in her eyes.

"It's too soon to incubate," Karen said. "Two days, remember."

Barlow held up one finger. "That's today." He added a second finger. "Tomorrow's something to look forward to, then, isn't it? Now move."

The doctor glared at him for a moment, then started forward again.

"You, too," Barlow said, pointing his Glock at Nick. "Right beside her."

Nick struggled to catch up. As she did, she realized the doctor's stumble had taken them slightly off course. They were now off the road and veering farther from it all the time. There appeared to be a cleared path branching off from the road and plunging into the forest. She couldn't tell if it was natural or man-made.

Nick risked a quick look over her shoulder. Barlow was five paces back, watching them, not the road.

"There's a rock, watch your step," Nick said, taking the doctor's arm as if to steady it, and then applying just enough pressure to keep them bearing to the right.

"Thank you," Karen said.

The doctor, Nick realized, was walking with her eyes narrowed to slits as protection against the wind-driven snow. She applied more pressure to Karen's arm.

With each step a voice screamed inside Nick's head. *Stop! Without the road you can't find your way back. Without the road, you die.*

Her teeth chattered.

Survive! her brain screamed, but somehow she kept up the gentle pressure on the doctor's arm.

Out of the corner of her eye she saw the white ribbon, all that remained of the roadbed, disappear into the nothingness of falling snow.

Nick released the doctor's arm to switch the sample case into her other hand. Even without her nudging, the doctor continued to swing to the right.

So be it, Nick thought, wondering how long before they were all dead of exposure. Several days, she decided. Sooner if the weather turned colder. She prayed the Spanish Lady would die along with them.

For a while, she watched for landmarks that might lead her back to safety if ever she escaped Barlow. But the snow was erasing everything but the trees.

Soon she knew they were truly lost. Since the road itself didn't run straight, but curved its way through the refuge, it could be anywhere, to their left or right, or even running parallel to their present position.

She raised her head to peer at the darkening sky. If the stars came out, she could navigate by them, something Elliot had taught her. The only trouble was you had to know where you were to start with. Otherwise, directions were meaningless, especially in the wilderness.

Funny, she thought, Elliot had always said an airplane would get her killed.

Karen came to a halt. The trees were crowding in, and it had become apparent, even to someone as exhausted as she was, that the road had disappeared.

Barlow looked up. "Bitches!" he screamed. "You've wandered off the road."

Karen peered down at her feet as if astonished to see featureless snow instead of the roadbed.

"Where are we?" Barlow shouted.

They turned to face him. Karen shook her head, looking bewildered.

Nick said, "How should I know?"

He lunged at her, his pistol raised to strike, but at the last minute caught himself, and pivoted away without making contact. "Move! Back the way we came. We've got to retrace our steps before the snow covers them."

"It's late," Nick pointed out. "It'll be dark soon."

"Move," he commanded.

The light was gone in less than an hour, and the snow was coming down harder than ever. Their footprints, barely discernable, would be erased long before morning.

Finally, Barlow had no choice but to call a halt and take shelter beneath the boughs of a pine tree. At the base of its trunk, the fallen pine needles were relatively dry. Nick settled her back against the rough bark. Karen did the same on the other side of the tree. Barlow sat as far from them as the spread of the overhanging branches allowed.

"Throw me one of the backpacks," he said.

Nick was too tired to throw it. The best she could do was shove it toward him.

"Survival manuals say we should huddle together for warmth," Nick told him.

"Not me," he answered. "You two women get as cozy as you want."

Karen leaned partially around the tree to whisper, "Keep your distance from me, Nick. I'm sick."

"So soon?"

"I'll know by morning. How many energy bars do we have?"

Nick reached into the pack. "One carton. About two days' worth, I think."

"We'd better eat at least two tonight. We've got to keep warm."

Oddly enough, Nick wasn't hungry, but she knew the doctor was right. Calories meant warmth. She slipped off her gloves long enough to unwrap an energy bar, then chewed slowly to make each mouthful last. The three bars in the pocket of her parka, she'd keep to herself as an emergency ration.

Barlow, she knew, had another carton in his backpack that he had picked up from the base camp. That meant twice as much food for him.

Once she'd finished her second bar, Nick wiggled into her sleeping bag, where she lay shaking and waiting for her body heat to build up. She remembered reading a survival manual that said freezing was an easy way to die. Like hell. That had probably been written by someone sitting in front of a warm fire.

Finally, after what seemed like hours, her shaking subsided and she felt warm enough to slip off her parka and use it for a pillow. She closed her eyes and tried to sleep, but her body betrayed her. Her stomach started growling with hunger.

Think about something else, she told herself, but her mouth watered at the thought of just one more energy bar. Think, for God's sake. Think of a plan. Maybe, when Barlow fell asleep, she could sneak away and find the road back to the cars. You're fooling yourself. There was no road anymore, just snow.

The Fords had four-wheel drive; they could make it through the snow. But she had to find them first. If she didn't, she'd die alone.

To hell with that. She wanted to see Barlow dead, and with him the Spanish Lady. The only way to do that was to outlast the bastard.

53

Death was reaching for her. At the sight of it, Nick came awake instantly. Her dream gave way to reality as fingers shook her.

She lurched upright in the darkness, struggling to free herself from the prison of her sleeping bag.

"Shush. It's me, Karen," the doctor whispered. "I'm running a fever. The Spanish Lady has me."

Nick resisted the temptation to reach out to her.

"In a hospital I'd have a chance, but here in this cold"—the doctor's breath rattled—"I won't make it through tomorrow."

"I'm sorry."

"I thought I knew what I wanted, but instead I got what I deserved."

"Nobody deserves this," Nick answered.

"Erickson was easy," the doctor continued. "He was an old man. I persuaded myself that I was really doing him a favor, but the others . . ." She made an effort to pull herself together. "It will be light in a couple of hours. Get out of here. Make a run for it. Otherwise, you'll end up like me."

"What about Barlow?" Nick asked.

The doctor's quiet chuckle brought the hairs up on Nick's neck. "There was a time when he found me very attractive. At least he pretended to. Every man's fantasy, he told me. Let's just say I'll kiss him good-bye for you."

"He won't let you get that close."

"Don't you hear him snoring?"

Until that moment, Nick hadn't noticed.

"I'll give you a few minutes," Karen whispered. "Now leave. Like I said, you've got a chance, I haven't. The virus got directly in my bloodstream from the bear's claws."

The finality in her voice gave Nick no option. She rolled up her sleeping bag, stuffed it into her backpack, and started crawling away. After a few feet, she rose and walked forward cautiously, hands stretched out in front of her in case she ran into something in the dark.

The sound of shots started her running.

By dawn, Nick thought that she must have walked miles, though she had no idea in which direction. Her state of exhaustion said that it didn't matter. All she wanted to do was lie down and go to sleep.

Do that and you won't be getting up, she thought to herself.

"So sue me," she told her nagging conscience, but kept walking while chewing dispiritedly on one of her three remaining energy bars. One down, two to go. After that . . . After that didn't bear thinking about.

Her world had become a white blur. There were no distinguishing landmarks, except for a couple of spindly trees. She would have welcomed anything.

She stomped her feet. They still ached, a good sign. She kicked at the snow, yearning for a sign of the roadbed. But it was hopeless. She knew that. She could be standing on the road itself and wouldn't know it. And even if she were, she wouldn't know which direction to turn, not without the stars to guide on, or a sight of the Hammersmiths.

The thought of the surviving Ford tantalized her. She could see it in her mind's eye. It was no more than a day's journey on foot, even in her condition.

She stopped abruptly to check her tracks. As far as she could tell, she was walking in a relatively straight line. But one of her legs would be imperceptibly shorter than the other. Everyone's legs were uneven. That imperfection would inevitably lead her in a circle, right back to where she started. If that happened she wouldn't have the strength to try again.

"Doctor Scott," a voice said, startling her so badly her bladder threatened to give way.

Nick whirled to see Gus coming her way. She waved him off. "I could be infected."

He stopped short and questioned her comment with a tilt of his head. As quickly as she could, she told him about the Spanish Lady. As she spoke, she could hear the panic rising in her voice.

"It comes down to this," she concluded finally, "the Spanish Lady got the doctor in two days. If I make it through today, I ought to be all right."

"If you have a sickness, we will share it," Gus said, putting his arm around her.

Nick tried to push him away, but was too weak. She acknowledged to herself that his presence was a comfort. "One is not alone," she said to him.

"One is not alone," he answered. "Now, I'll take you back to the ranger station."

"It's too far," she said. "I haven't the strength."

"You must try."

She shook her head.

"I could construct a sled. My people no longer do this. Instead they ride around in snowmobiles, but I think I could manage."

"There are no dogs."

"I will be the dog."

She put her arm on his shoulder. She felt his muscles jerk and saw a spasm of pain cross his face. "You've been hurt," she cried.

"The bear," he answered. "But you see that I am not dead. Although it prevented me from reaching you sooner, it turned out that it was, after all, only a bear."

"Could you lead me back to camp?" Nick asked.

"It is in the opposite direction from help," Gus observed.

"But it's closer to where we are now, isn't it?"

"It is useless to go in that direction."

"Just tell me one thing," Nick persisted. "Can you get me back to the cars?"

"Why?"

"Because you're hurt and I'm exhausted. They're a lot closer than the ranger station."

"They are no use to anyone. There is no way to start them, unless you have the keys."

"Just get me there, and we'll ride out of here in style."

54

Ned Duffy was certain that he had a hangover. The headache thundered inside his brain like a loose cannon caroming along the sides of his head. His mouth was dry and he staggered into the tiny bathroom of his bed-sitter and filled his tooth glass with water. The mirror above the sink showed him a haggard face with bloodshot eyes. It took him a minute to realize that he hadn't had anything to drink for months. Not since Mary had given birth to little Sam.

He groaned and staggered back to the bed, falling heavily on it. He supposed he'd have to call in sick. Now that the newsroom was nearly back up to full strength he wondered how Green would take it.

He pulled himself off the bed and

managed to slip on a pair of pants and a shirt. He staggered down the hallway to the communal phone, fumbling with coins until he found the right one.

"City Desk," he said to the exchange.

Green came on the line.

"It's Duffy," he managed to croak. "Can't make it in."

There was silence on the end of the line and for a moment Duffy thought that he hadn't managed to speak loudly enough. He was gathering the energy to speak again, when Green replied.

"You don't sound too good."

"Feel rotten," Duffy gasped. "I'll be in tomorrow."

"Sure," Green said. "See you tomorrow." There was a pause, then Green continued, "Duffy, take care."

Duffy nodded then realized that Green couldn't see him. What the hell, he lurched back toward his room, not noticing that he had left the receiver hanging. His knees gave way halfway there.

The tunnel was hot, there was no air. It was stifling and he couldn't breathe. He clawed at his celluloid collar to remove the tightness at his throat. Everywhere shadows floated around him like disembodied souls. He could hear the cries of people trapped in the train wreck. He wanted to turn back, but it was so dark he had lost his sense of direction.

Suddenly ahead of him he saw a dark form, so deeply black that it shone like polished jet. He felt himself moving forward. As he came closer he could make out the figure of a woman dressed in black. She was the most beautiful woman that he had ever seen. Lust grew in him with a heat that threatened to consume him.

She reached out a hand to take his, but his own felt like lead. Somehow he knew that to touch her was to touch a fire that no man could withstand. His hand moved forward of its own accord.

The tunnel started to leak and rivulets of water coursed down his head. A hand grasped his, but it was cool and lifesaving. He opened his eyes and saw the most beautiful woman he had ever seen.

"Mary," he sighed.

"Welcome back to the living, Ned Duffy." Tears were streaming down her cheeks.

"How long have you been here?"

"It's been three days. That's how long you've been out of your head."

"How did you know that I was sick?"

"I'd come to tell you that I'd got bad news. I got a letter from a supply company complaining that Sam had never come to pick up an order of goods he had placed. It took them two months to track me down. You know that he hadn't written in a while. I put it down to the isolation and the work, but he would have needed those supplies."

"Don't be afraid, Mary." Duffy tried to rise, but found that he didn't have the strength to lift his head. "When I get over this we'll track him down. I'm a reporter, remember. That's what we do, track things down."

She shook her head. "We both know he's gone. I think we knew the day we decided to name the boy Sam instead of Ned."

"Mary, I . . ."

"Rest easy." Mary smiled. "You've been more than good to me, Ned Duffy. Whatever the future holds, I can tell you this, with you by my side I'll never be afraid."

55

It was harder than Nick remembered. Her fingers were stiff with cold and the ignition system for the Ford was one that she'd never seen before. In addition, her thumb was bleeding from the edge of Gus's hunting knife, the only sharp instrument available to strip the wires. Her confidence began to ooze away.

Gus might have had a chance without me, she thought. He could have made it to the Ranger Station on his own. Now we're both stuck here. He's used all his strength to get me to the cars and I don't think I can walk one more step.

It had been a longer trip than she'd imagined, and the effort convinced her that she'd had no chance to make it to the ranger station. When they'd finally reached the abandoned camp she hardly recognized it. If it hadn't been for the cars she would have kept on walking. Everything was covered by snow and all the tents looked like they'd been flattened.

"There is still a store of food. I covered it when I went in search of you," Gus had said. "I'll get it while you work your magic."

And now Gus hovered next to her, anxiously. She was ready to scream. If it hadn't been for his obvious pain and general debilitation she would have yelled at him to go away. She tried to think back to the casual lesson that her childhood friend had given her. "The wire from the ignition to the starter wire on the left, cross over tight," she mumbled to herself. She closed her eyes and felt Billy Meeks guiding her from the past. One more twist should do it. The edge of the wire pierced her already damaged thumb, but her cry of pain was drowned out by the sound of the motor roaring to life.

They were on the road some time, Nick struggling to keep the car on track and Gus scanning the landscape for landmarks, when a shrill persistent noise broke Nick's concentration. Damn, she thought. All they needed was engine trouble.

"There seems to be a ringing coming from under your seat," Gus pointed out.

She stopped the car and searched under the seat. The noise was being made by a cell phone that must have been forgotten during the bear attack.

"Hello?" she answered.

At first, there seemed to be nothing but static and strange electronic sounds, then she heard a distant voice.

"Royce? This is McKenna. Can you hear me? Why the hell haven't I gotten a report? I've had to retask the satellite to get through. I can barely hear you."

Before Nick could answer, the voice continued. "Get off the phone and put Ivins on."

"I can't do that," Nick said.

"What did you say? What do you mean you can't do that? Can you hear me?"

"Ivins is dead," Nick said simply.

"Dead?" McKenna shouted. "And the sample? Don't tell me you didn't get it, Royce."

"Oh, Doctor Royce got it all right, but then it turned around and got her."

There was a pause. "Who is this?" McKenna demanded. "Who am I speaking to?"

"Your worst nightmare," Nick replied and broke the connection.